THE LOVE INTEREST

VICTORIA WALTERS

Boldwood

First published in Great Britain in 2024 by Boldwood Books Ltd.

Copyright © Victoria Walters, 2024

Cover Design by Alexandra Allden

Cover Photography: Shutterstock

Every effort has been made to obtain the necessary permissions with reference to copyright material, both illustrative and quoted. We apologise for any omissions in this respect and will be pleased to make the appropriate acknowledgements in any future edition.

A CIP catalogue record for this book is available from the British Library.

Paperback ISBN 978-1-83518-951-1

Large Print ISBN 978-1-83518-947-4

Hardback ISBN 978-1-83518-946-7

Ebook ISBN 978-1-83518-944-3

Kindle ISBN 978-1-83518-945-0

Audio CD ISBN 978-1-83518-952-8

MP3 CD ISBN 978-1-83518-949-8

Digital audio download ISBN 978-1-83518-943-6

Boldwood Books Ltd
23 Bowerdean Street
London SW6 3TN
www.boldwoodbooks.com

To my agent Hannah Ferguson – thank you for supporting me and my books for ten years!

love interest

noun

1. [countable, usually singular] a character in a film or story who has a romantic role, often as the main character's partner.

1

What makes a great love interest?

- Attractive but flawed
- A fully realised character with their own agency
- Chemistry and conflict with the protagonist

I looked up from the textbook I was reading – *How to Write Romantic Fiction* – to check the university library was still empty. I had just opened up the doors and from the past three months working here, I'd gathered that the first hour was usually quiet as students were either rushing to an early lecture or were still in bed recovering from the night before. So, I was using this time to read some of the books as I shelved them from the returns trolley. And this one, used on the Creative Writing degree course, had caught my eye immediately.

I had always wanted to write my own romance novel. But I was stuck with how to create a love interest for it. The leading lady I could come up with easily but the man she fell in love with – a blank.

After I closed the romantic fiction textbook and shelved it, I walked towards the classics section, my eyes moving naturally to some of my all-time favourite love stories. What I needed was to create someone as perfect as Mr Darcy. I sighed out loud. Who wasn't looking for their own Mr Darcy? You had to admire Jane Austen. Not only had she created a character that women were still swooning over in a completely different century to the one she had written him in, but she'd done so never having found a real-life love interest herself.

We had that in common. Maybe that was why I was finding it hard to come up with the male lead in my story. I had no romantic hero of my own to base him on.

I picked up a copy of *Pride and Prejudice* and slid it back into its rightful place. Ever since I'd read it at the age of twelve, I had devoured romantic stories. I knew what kind of man I fell in love with on the page, so why was it so hard to write one myself?

'Morning, Liv!' came a cheerful voice in a hushed whisper. I peered around the stack to see Stevie walking towards me, brandishing two takeaway coffees in her hand. I had recently joined as an assistant librarian and Stevie was my supervisor, having worked in the library for two years.

'I've never seen a more beautiful sight,' I said, walking over to take the cup she offered me with a grateful smile. 'You're a star.'

'That, I know,' she said with a grin. 'I love your outfit today, very librarian chic,' she added.

'Well, thank you.' I did a pretend curtsey. I always tried to dress up for every occasion. And work was no exception. Today, I wore a pencil skirt with a blouse tucked in, court shoes and black-rimmed glasses. Completing the look was a slick of bright red lipstick and gold hoop earrings visible on one side as I'd tucked my dark shoulder-length hair behind my ear. 'And I love your headband,' I said to her. She always wore one to push back her blonde hair and today, it was a pretty pearl one.

'I just got it from Amazon,' Stevie said as she walked over to the desk near the doors, took off her coat and hung it next to mine on the hook.

I took a sip from the takeaway cup and let out a moan. 'You always find the best coffee,' I told her.

Stevie and I had bonded immediately on my first day thanks to us both hating our real names (Stephanie and Olivia), having an addiction to coffee and being loud and proud bookworms.

'A coffee place has just opened down my road and, based on this, I think I'll be a regular. Ooh, I need to charge my Kindle,' she said, pulling it out of her bag. 'I always feel like I'm committing a librarian sin using it but you know what my flat is like.'

I nodded. I'd been round there a few times and the phrase 'no room to swing a cat' must have been patented after seeing where she lived. It was cute and cosy though, and I knew she loved being able to live on her own. 'It doesn't matter what you use to read books, it's still reading. Although it is sad you can't even have a bookcase.'

Stevie sat down in one of the swivel chairs behind the front desk. 'At least I get to live out my library fantasy here.'

'Ever since I saw *Beauty and the Beast*, I've dreamed of having my own library but I think this will be the closest I'll ever get living in London.' I looked around and smiled. This was a gorgeous library. Housed in the main building of one of London's oldest and most prestigious universities, it was huge with floor-to-ceiling windows that offered a view of the city, which other people had to pay thirty quid for at the top of The Shard.

I'd worked here for three months and it felt like home already. I had been stuck, knowing what I wanted to do with my life yet being too scared to actually go for it, so when my brother had suggested I move in with him rent-free so I could pursue my dream, I'd bitten the bullet and moved from our hometown in Hampshire. Dan was an influencer, creating online content and earning money from working with brands on TikTok and Instagram, and was encouraging of me trying to write a book. So I could contribute some money though, I'd looked for a part-time job and I had found this assistant librarian position at the university for three days a week. I'd helped out in the library at my own university and had worked in several bookshops since leaving so it had been a great find.

Being surrounded by books all day was quite simply my idea of heaven. Now all I needed to do was make the dream of writing my own come true.

'Shall I carry on shelving?' I asked Stevie when we'd finished our coffees.

'Yes, please. I better go through the emails,' Stevie said. 'Which means navigating our clunky intranet and dealing with students begging to keep their overdue books even longer.' She gave a long-suffering sigh.

'Ugh, students.' We shared an eye roll. 'Good luck,' I added, leaving her to it. I still found the intranet tricky to use so I didn't envy her task.

As I shelved books, I thought about the one I'd looked at about writing romantic fiction. What I needed to do was write a man that had readers swooning like I swooned over Mr Darcy and, let's face it, countless men in the pages of my favourite books.

But what kind of man made me swoon?

'Definitely tall, dark and handsome...' I whispered to myself as I put the books away.

The sound of a conversation nearby broke through my musings. I tutted. It amazed me that, considering how long libraries had been around, people still struggled to be quiet in them.

Holding a copy of *Jane Eyre* to my chest, I rounded a bookstack.

'Can you please lower your voices?' I hissed, expecting to see a pair of gossiping students. When I realised it was two grown men I had admonished in my best 'stern librarian' voice (yes, I had practised it at home), I stopped in surprise.

'I'm so sorry, Liv,' one of them said, still talking loudly.

My cheeks turned a little pink when I realised I had told off the assistant to my boss – the vice chancellor at the university.

'I didn't realise it was... sorry, carry on,' I replied hastily.

'You had every right to tell me off. I have a loud voice and I forgot we're in a library,' Jasper said, looking at me with a warm smile. 'I'm glad to see you are keeping everyone in order.'

'Olivia is good at keeping order,' a deep voice with an Irish accent said from beside him.

I had been so flustered, I hadn't paid much attention to the man with Jasper but as he spoke, I turned and looked up at him – even in my heels, he was very tall – and then, if it was possible, my blush deepened. I'd recognise that irritating smirk anywhere.

I couldn't believe it. Aiden bloody Rivers was standing in my library. How? Why?

'Hello, Olivia,' he said, his Irish accent more pronounced than ever as he said my name.

'Oh, do you two know each other?' Jasper asked, surprised, glancing back and forth between us.

My eyes narrowed. Unfortunately, we did, but I forced myself to be civil in front of Jasper.

'Aiden,' I said tightly.

'We're old family friends,' Aiden said in that easy way of his.

'I had no idea you were coming in today,' I said through gritted teeth. How dare he show up in my workplace? I hadn't seen him since my brother's birthday.

'Well, you've always raved about the place so when Jasper called me, I knew I had to come and look around for myself,' Aiden said, his smirk widening as he looked at me.

I took in his green eyes, the way his mouth curved up at the corner, the way his almost-black hair waved slightly around his temples and ears, and the outline of his muscular arms underneath his smart jacket. I rarely saw Aiden wear anything but a T-shirt and ripped jeans and I had to admit a suit looked good on him. Very good even. It was a fault with the universe that the perpetual thorn in my side was really rather nice to look at.

'And I know you love surprises,' Aiden said with a smile that to Jasper would seem friendly but that I knew meant he was enjoying my discomfort.

'Oh, do you?' Jasper asked me. 'I'll have to remember that. And it's great to hear you've been enjoying working here as much as we've loved you joining the team.'

Was it my imagination or were Jasper's cheeks turning as pink as my own? I smiled back at him, flattered by what he had said but annoyed with what Aiden had just told him. 'Well...' I started, not sure what to say without calling Aiden a liar. I hadn't seen Aiden since May so I definitely hadn't raved about the university. And I didn't enjoy surprises either – they made me nervous. I couldn't plan an outfit if I didn't know what was happening. 'Why did you say you were here again?' I asked the still smirking Aiden, clutching my book even tighter to my chest in case I felt the urge to lob it at him.

'I didn't,' he replied.

'Oh, I'm just showing Professor Rivers around, aren't I?' Jasper said cheerfully. 'Giving him the tour, introducing him to key staff members...' He trailed off and looked like he wanted to say more but couldn't. 'Well, I suppose we'd better carry on,' he said, turning to Aiden.

I frowned, confused why Aiden would even want a tour here,

but it was too awkward to demand an explanation in front of Jasper, which I felt sure Aiden knew by the smug look on his face.

'Lead the way,' Aiden agreed.

Jasper glanced back at me. 'I'm sorry again for disturbing the peace, Liv. Maybe I'll see you in the staff lounge later?' he asked, running a hand through his shaggy fair hair.

'Oh, yes, maybe,' I said, making myself turn from Aiden to look at Jasper, whose eyes lit up. He gave me a goofy wave and set off for the double doors.

Aiden paused and stared into my eyes for a moment. I returned his stare defiantly, even as I could feel my pulse quickening. I wondered what he was thinking. Then he raised an eyebrow. 'I know those glasses are fake,' he said.

'What's going on? What are you up to?' I hissed, my efforts to keep calm disintegrating now Jasper had left us alone.

Aiden was a professor in Film Studies at Bath University and was usually miles away from me. It was disconcerting to have him here on my turf.

'That's for me to know and you to find out. See you later, Olivia,' he said, dropping me a wink before sauntering away after Jasper.

'It's Liv,' I hissed, although I knew it was pointless. He delighted in calling me by my full name. I mimed throwing the book at his retreating head then stalked back to the front desk, my blood heated as it always was after an encounter with Aiden.

'Okay,' Stevie said, her blue eyes twinkling as she stared at me across the desk. 'Who was *that*?'

2

Sinking into the office chair next to Stevie behind the front desk, I reached for my coffee and took a sip.

'Oh, I finished it,' I said, staring at it accusingly.

'I have a bit left; you look like you need it more than me,' Stevie said, swapping my takeaway cup for hers. 'Drink, then tell me who that fittie was with Mr Elbow Patches.'

'He wore elbow patches one time...' I trailed off and drained the rest of her coffee. Poor Jasper. I had to agree with Stevie though, he did dress more like he was fifty than thirty. I took a breath. 'That was Aiden Rivers. Mr brother's best friend,' I explained, still unable to believe he'd just been in my library.

'Really? Where have you been hiding him?' She looked at me keenly. 'Are you okay? You look shell-shocked.'

'I didn't even know he knew what a library was,' I said. 'He should be in Bath at his university, not here in mine.'

'I mean, there are quite a few people here, I wouldn't say it's *your* university...' She trailed off at my withering look. 'You're right. He should have asked permission.'

I nodded even though I knew she was being sarcastic. 'Except he never asks permission, not when his mission in life is to wind me up. It's been the same since we were teenagers.' Ten years of knowing Aiden and he still got under my skin. I pulled out my phone. 'I wonder if Dan knows Aiden is in London. I usually only see him at Christmas and on Dan's birthdays. I try to avoid him as much as I possibly can.'

'Why? He looked like someone right out of a romance novel to me. Tall, dark, handsome...'

My fingers froze on my phone screen. Aiden? A romantic novel hero? I loved Stevie but she really had no idea. Shaking my head, I messaged my brother.

Aiden just suddenly showed up in my library! WTH?!

I looked back at Stevie. 'Trust me, he's no romantic hero, even if in some lights he looks a bit like Mr Darcy. And has a sexy accent.'

Stevie stilled from her typing and gaped at me. 'What kind of sexy accent?'

'He's Irish.'

She groaned. 'And next you'll tell me he has a gorgeous girlfriend.'

'Actually, he's recently single.' Dan had told me that Aiden and his girlfriend, Zara, broke up over the summer but I had no idea what had happened between them. They had been together for two years, which she deserved a medal for.

'Well, that's good news,' she said brightly then paused as she saw my face. 'Nope, definitely not good news. Um... what's wrong with him? Why don't you like him if he looks like Mr Darcy and has a sexy accent?'

'God, don't ever tell him that, he has a big enough ego as it is. No, Aiden may have the looks but not the personality. He's...' I tried to find the right word. 'Irritating. He loves to push my buttons. I almost threw my book at him just then.'

Stevie laughed. 'Well, I'm glad you didn't ruin a copy of *Jane Eyre* on his behalf. What a shame he's annoying when he looks like that. Not that he's *my* type.' She emphasised the word and I knew she was trying to say she thought he was my type.

'Why can't Mr Darcy be real?' I asked for what felt like the millionth time. Stevie was as single as I was so I knew she got it.

She snorted. 'Men like that don't exist in real life.'

'I want someone romantic. Maybe if I could find one, I could write my novel.'

'I keep telling you, all you need is a fantasy man. Just write the man of your dreams. Someone who would never disappoint you.'

'I think you're right. I just need to write about the kind of man I would want to sweep me off my feet.'

'Yes, because it'll never happen in real life. You'll never find a real-life male muse, trust me.'

I tried not to let it, but my mind wandered to Aiden again. I was so confused as to why he was touring the university with Jasper. And suspicious too. Because when it came to Aiden, it was always best to be on my guard. If he had a chance to annoy me, he always took it.

The last time I saw him, on Dan's birthday, he announced he was buying everyone a shot of tequila except 'Olivia because she can't handle her drink. Remember your twenty-first, Dan, when I had to carry her home? Or that Christmas when she was singing carols so loudly, and badly, someone opened their window to tell us they had called the police?'

Then, when Aiden overheard me telling Dan I thought a guy in the bar was fit, he told me he was 'clearly out of my league'. And to cap off the night, he watched as another man asked for my number and after I recited it, merrily informed him that 'I'd given him a fake one but not to worry as he had dodged a bullet.'

Dan had taken my glass of wine out of my hands to stop me from pouring it all over Aiden.

I huffed. 'You're right, men in real life are like Aiden, not Mr Darcy.'

'So, why was Aiden here anyway?' Stevie asked.

'I have no idea. Jasper said he was showing him around. Aiden claimed I'd raved about the university to him, which is a lie. I haven't seen him since before I moved here. He's a professor at Bath so maybe he wanted to see how things are done here?'

My phone buzzed and I checked my brother's reply.

That's weird. I'll message him. I'm making your favourite for dinner so don't be late! Xx

I smiled. That had cheered me up. I needed to stop thinking about Aiden and why he had suddenly appeared like that in my library. I blamed it on the surprise element. I usually made sure I was prepared to see him when I knew our paths would cross, so that was why I was so flustered. I tried not to think about what new ways he might be coming up with to torture me.

'I better finish that trolley,' I said, standing up reluctantly.

'Okay, I'll finish replying to these emails and then we can sort through the new books we got in. Don't forget to catch up on the book we're reading – I'm two chapters ahead and we need to finish and discuss on Friday.'

'I will.'

* * *

The day passed quickly once the library got busy and I barely had time to chat any more with Stevie as we both were helping students and professors and keeping everything as tidy as we could. As it became time to start asking students to leave for the day, I went back to the shelves I had restocked earlier. I decided I would check out the *How to Write Romantic Fiction* textbook and make some notes from it.

I was supposed to be here in London to finally start writing my novel but I had struggled since I'd arrived. I needed to just start it, and Stevie was right: I'd never find the right man to base my male character on. I needed to imagine my dream man and use him instead. I could see what he looked like. Tall, dark and handsome – 'my type' as Stevie had said – dressed in a suit with a voice that could make a woman melt. And I wanted him to be muscly, the kind of man who took care of himself. Personality-wise, I wanted intelligent, funny, kind, loyal – someone you could count on. And he definitely needed to be romantic.

'I think you could write a really great love story,' Stevie said as I stowed the textbook in my bag and she pulled her coat on.

'I hope so; it's something I've always wanted to do. What are your plans tonight?'

We walked over to the doors together. 'I'm going to finish that series I've been watching, eat a big bowl of pasta then have a long soak in the bath. How about you?'

'Dan is making risotto then I'm going to make notes on this book. I feel inspired today,' I said, stepping to the side of the doors as Stevie locked up the library for the night.

'I'm glad you took the job here, Liv. It's so much more fun now.'

'Me too.' I felt like I'd made a friend for life. We walked out of the university building and down the stone steps. 'I'll see you Friday for my next shift?'

Stevie gave me a quick hug. 'Keep me posted on the book!'

She waved and set off in the direction of her flat, whereas I turned towards the park which I needed to walk through to get to my brother's flat in Islington.

It was a warm evening for September so I stowed my cardigan in my bag and walked just in my blouse and pencil skirt, wishing I hadn't worn quite such high heels. But I needed all the extra height I could get. I loved seeing all the trees just starting to turn while the late sunshine beat down on them. I was enjoying living in London – there was so much to see and do, and it was fun living with my brother for the first time since we both had left home for university. I breathed in the air that promised autumn was on the way and felt good about making a start on my own romance novel.

I passed Angel Tube station, turned into our road and walked up to Dan's flat. It was on the first floor of a converted Victorian townhouse and I could hear voices inside as I let myself in. I guessed Dan's boyfriend Theo was over for dinner.

Opening up the door, I called out, 'Honey, I'm home,' – our usual greeting now I'd moved in.

'Honey, we're in here,' a voice called back, which stopped me in my tracks.

There was no mistaking that Irish accent.

3

Aiden was here? I was seeing him twice in one day? What had I done to deserve this?

I wondered if I could turn around and make a run for it.

'Hurry up, Liv, it's almost ready!' Dan called.

It hit me then. The delicious smell of my favourite dinner. My stomach rumbled on cue. I'd have to put up with Aiden for this meal.

With a heavy sigh, I paused by the large mirror in the small hallway and checked that my red lipstick wasn't smeared all over my face and my hair wasn't looking too crazy after my long walk home. After I hung up my bag on the hooks in the hall, I took out the *How to Write Romantic Fiction* textbook and carried it with me, taking a deep breath as I walked in.

I loved this flat. The tall ceilings, the light that streamed inside in the mornings, the Scandi vibe décor my brother had cultivated, and the fact that his job as a social media influencer meant it was always full of freebies I could try.

'How was work today?' Daniel was cooking in the kitchen. He

gave me a warm smile. Dan was a couple of inches taller than me with the same dark hair, although his was cut to frame his face and large hazel-coloured eyes.

'It was fine,' I replied, my eyes darting towards Aiden sat on one of the bar stools behind the kitchen counter involuntarily.

'Olivia told the assistant to her boss to be quiet today when he was showing me round. It was hilarious,' he said with a grin.

I rolled my eyes. 'I didn't see it was him; students are so noisy sometimes. Anyway, Jasper was lovely about it.'

'He didn't stop talking about you after that,' Aiden said, looking aggrieved. 'It was boring.'

'What did he say?' I asked, before I remembered who I was dealing with.

Aiden smirked. 'I couldn't possibly betray any confidences.' He patted the bar stool beside him. 'Come and sit down, Olivia. Dan is cooking some hideous vegetarian dish for us.'

'Oh no, that means you'll have to actually eat a vegetable,' I said, pretending to look horrified. 'Will you be okay or do you need to Deliveroo a burger?'

'Don't put that idea in his head,' Daniel warned me then turned to Aiden. 'And you won't even know this is vegetarian, it's that good.'

Daniel and Aiden were two years older than me and had been best friends since they'd met working part-time at a cinema. They'd bonded over their mutual love of films and been close ever since. I knew Aiden was fiercely loyal to Dan and was a good friend to him. But to me, he'd been nothing but irritating for the ten years we'd known him. I made sure to give back as much as I could. The result was an ongoing battle that neither of us was willing to accept defeat in. To Dan's constant exasperation.

I climbed up on the stool, putting the textbook on the counter in front of me. I wondered what Jasper had said about me, but there was no way I was going to beg for Aiden to tell me. He would enjoy it far too much. I tried to push him out of my head. 'It smells great,' I said to Dan. 'No Theo tonight?'

'He's taking a class,' Dan explained. His boyfriend was a talented artist and taught night classes at a local college. 'When you said Aiden was in London, I invited him for dinner. You know I always make too much.'

Now I regretted telling Dan I'd seen Aiden today. I resisted the urge to give my brother a dirty look.

'So, what did you think of the university?' Dan asked Aiden, oblivious to my annoyance.

Aiden swivelled on the stool, moving his legs out so one brushed against mine.

'Can you stop man-spreading please?' I complained, crossing my legs the other way.

'I can't help it if I need the extra space.' He waggled his eyebrows at me.

'You wish,' I snorted, making sure I didn't drop my gaze downwards at all.

Dan cleared his throat, drawing our attention back to him. 'The university?' he repeated.

'The film department facilities are so great. They have this new camera that...'

I tuned out Aiden's enthusiastic speech about cameras and other high-tech equipment the university had and opened up my textbook.

'It sounds great,' Dan said after Aiden had droned on for God only knew how long about the film equipment. 'When will you know if they'll make a formal offer?'

'Friday, Jasper said.' Aiden leaned over towards me then. 'What are you reading, Olivia? Is it smut?'

'None of your business,' I retorted, trying to shield the cover, but Aiden read the title out loud. I sighed. 'I'm just doing research for my book.'

'That's great,' Dan said enthusiastically. 'I keep telling you those short stories you write are amazing – you will be brilliant at writing a novel. You just need to start.'

While I studied English Lit at university, I had written during any spare minute I had from my course and entered a couple of my short stories into competitions. I had even won first place in one and had another published in a women's magazine. But I really wanted to write a novel. 'I'm trying to think about what makes a good love interest in a book so I can come up with one. Why do we all love Mr Darcy so much, for example?' I said, letting out the same dreamy sigh I always did when thinking about the man.

'I don't see what all the fuss is about – he barely speaks,' Aiden commented.

'Some women find that preferable to men who talk too much,' I replied, giving him a pointed look. 'And anyway, how would you know? You've never read *Pride and Prejudice*.'

'Actually, I read it a couple of years ago. After you got drunk at Dan's birthday party and talked for an hour about what a great book it is.'

'Firstly, I did not talk about it for an hour—'

'You did, I timed you. It's a shame you don't drink that much now, you always did embarrassing things after you'd had a few too many.'

Which was exactly why I had stopped drinking too much in Aiden's presence – he never let me forget anything embarrassing I had ever done. Case in point right now. 'Secondly,' I continued, 'it is a great book and just because you can't appreciate it—'

'It was okay,' he interrupted. 'But the film is better.'

'You would say that,' I said with a dismissive wave of my hand. 'Usually, the film is never better but the nineties BBC series is pretty perfect, I have to admit.'

'God, one glimpse of a wet white shirt and you're salivating,' Aiden said, looking at me aghast.

'I'm not!' I protested.

'That scene *is* a classic though,' Dan remarked.

'Exactly,' I said, beaming at him. 'Anyway, let me read this chapter. Annoy Dan instead, please.'

'But it's much more fun to annoy you,' Aiden said, leaning over and trying to turn the pages of the book. 'So, does this deal with steamy scenes?'

I moved the textbook out of reach. 'I don't know. But I'm writing a love story. If there is any sex, it will be there to further the story, not for...' I trailed off, feeling like I'd just walked right into a trap.

Aiden's smirk was more pronounced than ever. 'Titillation?'

'God, gross.' I grabbed the book back from him and turned to my brother. 'This is why I don't tell men I'm writing romance.' He raised an eyebrow. 'Straight men,' I corrected. 'They just don't get it.'

'I get it,' Aiden insisted. 'I love a good romcom, I teach a whole class on them. But I also know they are all fantasy, just like your romance books. Men and women like that don't exist. And if you get too obsessed with them, you'll never find anyone in real life. You'll always be looking for perfection. And then it's too hard for anyone to ever please you.'

'Reading romance doesn't make you hard to please. It gives you standards. Why shouldn't we wait for someone special and not settle down with just anyone? Why shouldn't we want someone to treat us well and be romantic?' I said, my voice rising with indignation.

'The problem is your standards mean you end up reading a book alone in your room every night.'

'How do you know I'm doing it alone?' I fired back.

'Am I wrong?' Aiden's lips curved into a grin. 'You're always telling me you prefer men in books.'

'Oh definitely, when men in real life are like you.'

'You couldn't handle a real man,' he said gruffly.

'Show me a real man first,' I retorted.

'On that note,' Dan said loudly, 'dinner is served.'

He gave me a look. I knew it well. It was his 'stop arguing with Aiden please' look. I gave him one back to convey that Aiden had started it. Dan rolled his eyes and resumed his task, dishing up the mushroom risotto onto three plates. Then he whipped out his phone and took both a photo and video of the finished result.

'Does a tree fall in the forest if no one takes a picture of it?' Aiden quipped as he tucked into the food.

'Got to keep my followers happy,' Dan replied, not rising to the bait. It didn't matter to him if people didn't take his job seriously; he loved it and he made good money at it too.

'Let me get one of you with it,' I said, holding my hand out.

He gave me the phone and I took some shots of him in the kitchen. Dan was used to people thinking what he did wasn't really a job but since moving in, I'd come to realise how creative he was.

'Actually, this is pretty good,' Aiden said, gesturing to the risotto.

'Maybe you'll give up meat then,' Dan suggested as he came around the kitchen counter and sat on the third bar stool.

'Let's not get crazy,' Aiden replied.

I took a bite. 'Ooh, so good,' I moaned.

'Get a room, Olivia,' Aiden commented.

I waved my fork in the air. 'I happily would with this risotto.'

'Reason 150 why you're single.'

'Takes one to know one,' I said cheerfully back. He glared at me but had no comeback.

Finally, Aiden was single too so he couldn't use my lack of a boyfriend as fodder for teasing me any more. I was dying to know what had happened between him and Zara, his girlfriend of two years, but didn't want to give him the satisfaction of asking. Also, Dan would want to know why I wanted to know, so I couldn't ask him either.

'Hang on,' I said, frowning and thinking back to their earlier conversation that I'd only been half listening to thanks to Aiden's very boring talk of film cameras and equipment. But suddenly, one part of their chat came back to me. 'What were you both talking about before? Something about a formal offer on Friday?'

Aiden looked across at me with a smug look on his face. 'That's why I was being shown around today. The university are considering me for the Head of Film Studies position.'

Struggling to swallow my last mouthful, I grabbed a glass of water and took a long gulp, feeling both Aiden's and Daniel's eyes on me. I coughed dramatically.

'Are you okay?' Aiden reached out to thump me on the back twice. Hard.

'Ow!' I waved him off. 'It was a job interview?'

'Yes, you have heard of those, right? And the job is a step up, a promotion, more money, freedom to set the course, and it's a prestigious university. It would be a good move for me.'

'I really hope you get it, mate,' Daniel said, oblivious to the horror that was washing over me.

'I'm hopeful, as they approached me,' Aiden replied. 'Olivia, close your mouth, you look like a fish.'

I clamped my mouth shut, all appetite fading away despite the deliciousness of Dan's meal. Aiden might be moving to London? And working at the same university as me? The man who drove me crazy. Who I usually only had to see twice a year. Now I might have to see him every day!

It would be okay, I told myself. It was a huge city after all, with so many people, so many places to hide. Surely I would be able to avoid him easily.

Right?

4

After dinner, as I washed up dishes in the kitchen, Dan suggested we all watch a romcom that had just been released on Netflix, but Aiden shook his head.

'I'd better get the last train back,' he said.

'Stay here and get the first one in the morning,' Dan countered as he opened the fridge and pulled out a bottle of beer, waving it in Aiden's direction.

I kept my back to them, hoping Aiden would say no.

'Oh, go on then, how I can refuse beer and a romcom?'

'And popcorn,' Dan added, going to the cupboard to pull it out. He looked at me. 'You'll watch it with us, right?'

'I probably should make some more notes on this textbook. I can't keep it for very long.' I hesitated. I really wanted to see the movie but Aiden had annoyed me enough for one day.

'You can do some work afterwards, it's not a long film. And it'll be research for your book too, won't it? I'll make the popcorn sweet and salty...' Dan gave me a pleading look.

I could never refuse my brother.

'Okay, but I get the armchair,' I said, walking into the lounge area.

As Dan made the popcorn, I curled up in the armchair and Aiden sat on the sofa, grabbing the remote to turn on the TV. It was dark outside now so I switched on the fairy lights strung over the fake olive tree behind me in the corner and when Dan came in, he lit one of his fancy scented candles. I tried not to think about how this could have been a romantic night in if there were different people here.

'Here we are.' Dan handed me a bowl of popcorn and took another bowl to the sofa for him and Aiden. 'We haven't watched a film together since Christmas.'

'I've only seen Olivia once since then,' Aiden said, glancing over at me.

'Some people are best seen in small doses,' I replied.

'Don't be so hard on yourself,' Aiden said, smirking. 'Ready to start then?'

Before I could respond, he started the movie. I folded my arms across my chest and tried to tune him out as I got into the story about two friends who realised they were actually in love with one another.

'That was cute,' I said when the credits rolled against a romantic song I needed to add immediately to my Spotify Current Faves playlist.

'I wish they'd make it less obvious how it's all going to end though,' Aiden said. 'Also, I don't buy that you can be friends for that long without realising you fancy each other.'

'Relationships can develop though. First impressions aren't always right,' I argued, thinking back to my first impression of Aiden when we'd met as teenagers. It was very different to how I thought about him now.

'There has to be a spark if you are going to become a couple though,' Aiden said, looking over at me. 'Even the hate-to-love stories you like so much have a spark right from the start.'

I had no idea how he knew I loved an enemy-to-lovers story. But then again, I did tend to wax lyrical about books, given even the slightest ammunition.

'Well, yes, even if they are arguing from the start, you know they find each other attractive,' I mused.

'Another unrealistic part of these movies,' Dan joined in. 'They are both always fanciable – that doesn't happen much in real life.'

'Says the man who's met the love of his life,' I replied. I knew Dan was smitten with Theo. I tried not to feel jealous.

'Relationships are much harder work than Hollywood ever shows,' Dan said, getting up and heading into the kitchen with our empty popcorn bowls.

I took a sip of my Coke and wondered what he meant by that. Theo hadn't been over in a couple of days but they always seemed solid to me.

'Tell me about it,' Aiden agreed then yawned. 'I'm shattered. I think I need to head to bed if I'm ever going to get the early train back to Bath.'

'I'll help you with the sofa bed in my office,' Dan said.

'I really think you should give your male character an accent,' Aiden said to me as he stood up. 'The ladies love my voice. They think it's sexy.'

I tried not to remember what Stevie had said about his accent.

'First impressions might make them think that yours is sexy, I grant you,' I said, 'but once they start talking to you, they'll realise the voice doesn't fit the man.'

'I think the lady does protest too much,' he said with a grin. 'Sweet dreams, Olivia.'

I gave him the finger behind his retreating back.

I was grabbing a glass of water in the kitchen a few minutes later when Dan returned.

'Are you seeing Theo this weekend?' I asked as casually as I could.

Dan drained the rest of his beer. 'Yeah, we thought we'd go to that new exhibition at the Tate. Do you want to come?'

'Maybe you should go without me. I don't want to be a third wheel for a date.'

'As if either of us ever thinks of you as that,' he replied. 'And they have that great bookshop next door, and don't forget the cupcakes in the café,' he said, waggling his eyebrows.

I laughed. 'Okay, you know my weaknesses. As long as you guys don't mind.' I watched him drop his beer bottle into the bin. 'Everything is okay with you two, right?'

Dan hesitated for a moment. 'Sure. Of course.' He shrugged. 'Right, I'll see you in the morning.'

'Goodnight,' I said, wondering if he was being completely honest with me. I went to my room, pausing just before I entered to glance at the closed door of Dan's office/spare bedroom. Aiden's mention of first impressions replayed in my brain. We'd met at a party and I had thought he was the most gorgeous man I'd ever met and although I disputed it now, I had thought his accent was sexy that night.

Shaking my head, I hurried into my bedroom and closed the door. I blamed that on the fact that teenage me had had very little experience with men.

Ten years later, I knew much better.

* * *

I dreamt that I stood by a lake half-blinded by the sun, watching as a man climbed slowly out of the water, his hair dark and tousled.

He was wearing a white shirt and it was soaking wet, rendered almost completely see-through.

'Mr Darcy,' I mumbled, looking at the defined muscles on his chest under the clinging cotton. I walked towards him as if I was floating. I reached out and touched his chest, looking up at his handsome face. His lips curved into a smirk and his eyes were a sparkling green.

'Olivia,' he said in a gruff voice as his arms came around my waist. My hands moved up his chest to his solid shoulders and then into his hair. 'You are the most beautiful woman I have ever met,' he said before pulling me close and pressing his mouth against mine.

A moan escaped me as our lips met. He tasted like coffee and he smelt like a musky aftershave I faintly recognised. When his tongue explored mine, I pressed in closer to him and he held me tightly. I could feel the muscles in his chest against me. His shirt was making me wet but I didn't care. I broke the kiss to lift my arms up and he eagerly pulled off the pretty floral sundress I was wearing. I watched as it floated to the ground and he pulled us down onto the grass so we were kneeling face to face.

'Do you know how much I want you?' he half-growled as his mouth moved to kiss my lacy bra. He reached for one of the straps and pulled it down from my shoulder slowly before kissing me across my collarbone and then lower until his mouth found my exposed nipple.

'Mr Darcy,' I breathed, my hands finding that delicious chest of his again. 'We really shouldn't be doing this out here.' I tilted my neck to the side as his tongue played with my nipple.

He stilled. I opened my eyes to find him looking at me.

'Don't stop,' I said, disregarding my previous statement. My body craved his. I leaned towards him again, willing him to carry on. But he remained still.

'I'm not Mr Darcy,' he said breathlessly.

I shook my head. 'Of course you are, you came out of the lake in the white shirt. I...' My words died on my lips as the sun slipped behind a cloud and I was no longer dazzled by it. Then I could see that I was looking into a very familiar face.

'Olivia,' he said, his Irish accent purring my name.

'Aiden,' I said, reaching up to touch his lips.

'Are you disappointed?'

Hesitating, I brushed my finger across his smirk.

'No. Don't stop,' I pleaded desperately. Our lips met frantically and I pulled him down on top of me. 'Don't stop.'

He undid my bra and tossed it onto the grass. His mouth found me again and then his hand slid down my chest and my stomach, making me arch my back in pleasure.

Aiden leaned over me, putting his mouth close to my ear. 'I won't stop until you're screaming my name,' he whispered.

I woke up with a start.

I opened my eyes, confused, blinking as sun pooled on my face. I groaned and rolled over to look at the clock. It was early, the sun rising out of my bedroom window, streaming in through a gap in my curtains. I dug my face into my pillow as my dream came back to me. God. That had been hot. I squeezed my thighs together as frustration rolled over me. It had felt so real and intense and... I bolted upright.

It had been about Aiden.

My cheeks flushed as I remembered pleading with him not to stop. Surely it had been an innocent mistake of my subconscious? I had watched the *Pride and Prejudice* lake scene before bed as research for my book. And clearly, I'd mixed up Mr Darcy with the man who had invaded my workplace and flat yesterday. My mind had just got jumbled up. It didn't mean anything, I told myself firmly.

But I touched my lips. The feeling of Aiden's mouth against mine wouldn't go away.

I needed a distraction, and fast. I jumped out of my bed. My restlessness needed to be channelled into something productive.

I decided to do some morning yoga. My mum had had us doing it since we were kids, along with meditation and any wellness practice she could think of. But yoga had stayed with me. It really did refresh my mind and body, and honestly, I needed that this morning. Anything to shake off the weird feeling I had – like an itch deep inside that I couldn't quite scratch.

Pulling off my nightdress and trying desperately not to remember Aiden taking off my dress in my dream, I quickly exchanged it for my yoga leggings and crop top. I teased my hair into a bun on top of my head and placed my yoga mat under the window so I could enjoy the morning light. Then I grabbed my laptop and found one of my favourite yoga routines on YouTube.

I took a long inhale and exhale before I pressed play. The stretches would be perfect to help clear my mind of everything and everyone else, and just focus on my breath.

And it worked.

Until...

My eyes flashed open as I moved into a headstand. I could hear Harry Styles blasting through my peaceful moment. For a second, I was confused. I mean, Dan loved Harry (didn't we all?) but he, like me, preferred a quiet morning.

Then I remembered it wasn't just us in the flat.

I descended from my headstand and stopped the video with a sigh. I couldn't focus on my breathing when all I could hear was music. Any lingering thoughts of my sexy dream about Aiden were rapidly replaced by irritation that he'd ruined my calming morning.

This was a feeling towards Aiden I was used to. And this was definitely more preferable than what I'd felt when I woke up. I clung eagerly to my anger.

'So bloody thoughtless,' I grumbled as I slid my feet into my slippers and stalked out of my bedroom.

'Okay, so I know you have no care for other people but even you must realise that 7 a.m. is not the time to play music at that volume?' I shouted as I stepped into the kitchen.

But when I got to the doorway, I stopped in my tracks and took in the scene. Aiden was making coffee, bopping along to the music. And, Jesus Christ, he was shirtless.

I couldn't help it. I stared.

Aiden was a gym fiend. I knew he went pretty much every day, and his body was evidence of that. I took in his defined muscles. His chest was lean and still slightly tanned from the summer and as my eyes drifted up, I saw his dark hair was wet and tousled from the shower. I bit my lip. Inadvertently, Aiden was reminding me of my wet shirt dream.

I won't stop until you're screaming my name.

Oh God. I fought hard to keep hold of my irritation with him because I was in danger of slipping back into a very different kind of frustration. And that was frankly mortifying to admit, even to myself.

Aiden saw me then and turned around.

'What?' he called over the music.

I shook my head to clear it of any thoughts of wet shirts and lakes and how good Aiden looked right now and reminded myself that he'd ruined my yoga routine and was a chronic pain in my bum. I opened my mouth to tell him just that but then I saw him take in my yoga outfit, which didn't leave a lot to the imagination, I supposed. It felt like his eyes were grazing over my head to my feet in a way that seemed very unlike how he usually looked at me. It rendered me unsure what to say. But then it felt like I must have imagined it because he abruptly went back to pouring out his coffee.

I reached over and turned the speaker down to a soft background level.

'That's better,' I said with relief. 'I know you wish you were Harry Styles but that volume is not acceptable at this time in the morning. I was trying to do a relaxing yoga routine,' I complained.

'I think my abs are better than Harry's,' Aiden remarked, flexing an arm before settling on a bar stool with his coffee.

'I don't want to look at your abs, thank you very much. Can't you cover up? You're like a peacock showing off!'

Aiden looked across at me, that irritating smirk of his back. 'Ah, so you think I have good abs, Olivia?'

Exasperated, I made myself look firmly away from his bare chest. I would not give him the satisfaction of looking at it again.

'I'm worried I'll be put off my breakfast actually,' I huffed and then, to move the conversation away from his bare chest, which he was making no effort to cover up, I added, 'And can you try to actually call me by my name for once?'

He grinned. 'Woke up on the wrong side of bed this morning, did you?'

'I was fine until I saw you,' I replied, my cheeks flushing despite my best efforts as I remembered how I'd woken up. 'Is there enough coffee for me?'

He shrugged. 'Sorry. You'll have to make your own.'

'For goodness' sake,' I snapped, feeling rather hot and bothered, and I wasn't sure it was all in a bad way.

'Maybe you need a "no talking before coffee" rule in the mornings?' Aiden suggested.

'I wasn't at all grumpy until you blasted Harry Styles and probably woke up the whole building.'

Dan shuffled in then in his silk pyjamas. 'He is preferable to an alarm clock though,' he said.

Aiden grinned and I flashed him a glare.

Seeing my face, Dan said, 'Sit down, Liv, I'll get us both a cup of coffee. And how about a bagel? I bought some yesterday from the bakery you like.'

'Okay,' I said, slightly mollified, and I crawled up onto a stool, making sure to keep one in between me and Aiden as a buffer.

'I love that new workout set,' Dan said as he made coffee and toasted a bagel for us.

'It was one of your freebies,' I told him. 'I might get Mum one for Christmas; she'd love it.'

'Speaking of the woman who birthed us, she said she'd call us later from the silent retreat – they are having a "phones allowed hour" apparently.'

We smiled at one another. Our mum loved a wellness retreat – she was a personal trainer at a gym near our family home in Hampshire and was health and fitness personified. After our dad had left when we were little, she had given up her job in an office and transformed her life.

'Ooh, delicious,' I cooed as Dan handed me a mug and plate with my bagel slathered in peanut butter – my favourite. I saw him give Aiden a look as he sipped his coffee and realised that Aiden was being quiet for him. 'Why are you both being weird?'

'We're not,' Dan assured me.

I looked over my mug at my brother. I wasn't sure I believed him.

'Oh, look at the time, I'd better run,' Aiden said. 'I can't miss my train and be late for work.'

He hurried into the spare room and emerged five minutes later dressed in what he'd worn yesterday. It really was unfair how quickly men could get ready. His phone buzzed in his hand.

'Oh,' he said in surprise. He looked up at Dan. 'It's Zara.' He pressed a button on his phone. 'I guess I'll call her back when I'm on the train.'

'Are you okay?' Dan asked.

Aiden's eyes flicked to me then back to Dan. 'Sure. I'll talk to you later. Thanks for... everything.' He lifted a hand to wave and headed for the door before pausing to look back. 'Oh, Olivia, you have peanut butter on your top,' he said, and with a grin, he left the flat.

I let out a breath now that he had gone and then looked down and realised Aiden had been right – I'd dropped a big bit of food on myself. 'Fabulous,' I muttered, grabbing a napkin to dab at it. I looked at Dan and casually added, 'Aiden didn't seem happy to hear from Zara.'

Dan looked confused. 'Oh, well, I doubt he is after she cheated on him, right?'

'Huh? She cheated on him?' I finally knew why they'd broken up. 'I would have guessed the other way around.'

'Why do you always think the worst of Aiden? I don't get you two and how much you argue. You're both such great people,' he said, shaking his head.

'Well, he's always picking fights with me,' I said, though I knew I sounded childish.

Dan raised an eyebrow. 'I'd say it's fifty-fifty. But never mind, I know it's all just in fun. You both enjoy teasing each other.'

I stared at my brother. Did I enjoy it? I opened my mouth but no words came out. Thankfully, Dan carried on talking, oblivious to how much he had confused me.

'Anyway, Aiden was pretty shocked when he found out and ended things. I mean, the trust was gone. And I think it showed him that she wasn't the one, you know? I never thought she was good enough for him to be honest, but there we go.'

Now I felt even more confused, trying to take in the fact that Aiden hadn't been the bad guy in their relationship like I had assumed.

'Another bagel?' Dan asked.

'No thanks, I'm going to have a shower,' I said, climbing off the stool. I went into the bathroom, hoping a long steamy shower would cure my grumpiness. I turned on the shower and stepped under the water and shrieked.

'What's wrong?' Dan called out.

'Aiden used all the bloody hot water,' I called back, shivering.

I jumped out of the shower, then decided it was probably for the best and stepped back in, under the cold water, letting it wash away thoughts of Aiden's bare chest once and for all.

5

I tried to distract myself from worrying about Aiden's job interview on my day off. I made notes from the romance novel textbook as I had to bring that back to the library, and I finished the novel that Stevie and I were buddy reading.

But Friday came around too soon, and then I couldn't stop thinking about when Aiden would find out if he was going to be offered a job at my university. It was busy in the library as a new course had started and everyone needed to collect their books for it, but my mind was only half on the job if I was honest. I was really hoping that Aiden wouldn't be offered the department head job, or if he was, that he would think twice before accepting because it would mean working in the same place as me. I was certain that he couldn't want that either.

As lunchtime approached, we finally got a chance to breathe in the library as the students scattered to fuel up for their afternoon lectures.

'What a morning,' Stevie said as I joined her at the desk. 'Oh, hi, Priya.'

One of the university's lecturers, Priya, came over. 'Can I order ten of these textbooks for the new module I'm running next month? I'm ordering them before the new Head of Film Studies is appointed so they can't change what I'm planning,' she said, her eyes twinkling.

I pounced on the mention of Film Studies. 'Do you know what's happening with that?' I asked, hoping I sounded casual when in fact my heart was thumping at the thought of Aiden being given the position.

'No one tells me anything,' Priya said. She eyed Stevie. 'You know what it's like. The chancellor and vice chancellor make all the decisions then leave poor Jasper to tell everyone else.'

'It's like when the old assistant left,' Stevie said to me. 'I was told someone would be recruited but I had no say in the process. Luckily, they picked you,' she added with a smile.

I smiled back but I was disappointed they didn't have a clue who would get the Head of Film Studies role.

'I've logged that book on the system,' Stevie said to Priya. 'It should be in by next week. I'll email you so you can let your students know when it arrives.'

'Thanks, Stevie.'

Stevie turned to me when Priya had gone. 'You'd better head for lunch before we get another rush.'

'Okay,' I said, pulling out the romance fiction textbook from my bag. 'I need to return this soon, so I'll finish making notes on my break.'

'Good plan,' Stevie said. She peered at the doors. 'Speaking of Jasper...'

Jasper walked up to the desk. 'Good afternoon,' he greeted us cheerfully. He glanced at me shrugging my jacket on. 'Are you going to the cafeteria? I was heading that way too.'

'I am, I'll come with you,' I said eagerly, thinking that I could ask him about the vacancy now I knew he was the one with the insider knowledge. I turned to Stevie. 'Want me to get you anything?'

'No thanks, I have leftovers,' she replied as I went around the desk to join Jasper. 'No need to hurry back, I don't need much of a break,' she added, flashing me what could only be described as a suggestive smile. She was convinced Jasper had a soft spot for me. I shook my head at her as I followed him out.

'That looks interesting,' Jasper said, nodding at the book in my hands as we walked down the stone steps and across the courtyard towards the cafeteria.

'I've always wanted to write my own book and I'm determined to finally start one.'

'I think it's admirable. I have zero imagination, so I admire anyone creative. Facts and figures, that's my forte.'

'Well, I admire anyone logical because I definitely am not,' I replied with a laugh.

We walked into the cafeteria, which was busy as it served both students and staff. It was a huge, long room with different sections like a food court at a shopping centre.

'I was so surprised to see Aiden here the other day,' I said, broaching the subject most on my mind today.

'We've had a vacancy for someone to head up our film department for far too long and Professor Rivers is very highly regarded so it was a relief to everyone that he agreed to come and have a chat with us.'

I tried to hide my surprise. Aiden was rarely serious around me; I couldn't quite picture him standing in front of a lecture room full of students and teaching them.

'He's always been such a film buff. I remember when he first watched *Pulp Fiction*, I couldn't get him to stop raving about it,' I said, shaking my head. Aiden was the same way with films as I was with books.

Jasper chuckled. 'I do love passionate staff.' He looked directly at me. 'Our library is lucky to have you. I know how much you impressed everyone in your interview.'

'Even if I still don't fully understand the intranet,' I said with a shake of my head. I'd worked in bookshops before and I had helped out when I was at university in the library there, but this one had been a steep learning curve. Luckily, Stevie was so enthusiastic and helpful that I'd soon found my feet. 'Oh, veggie lasagne, I have to get that,' I said, looking at the specials board.

'Are you vegetarian?'

'Since I was twelve. My mum started to get into health and fitness then and said we should give it a go. We never went back.' I loaded a plate onto my tray with a side salad and a water. 'So, did you think Aiden was a good fit for the job?'

'We're making a final decision today. Don't be nervous, he made a very good impression.'

'He did?' I knew my voice sounded high pitched.

'And we should thank you. I got the impression he wouldn't have considered the move if you weren't here,' Jasper added, moving away to put some food on his tray.

I gaped at his back. Aiden surely should have been put off by the fact I worked here too, not encouraged by it. He'd probably just felt the need to be polite about me during his interview, I decided.

Jasper returned and we stood awkwardly for a moment with our trays.

'Right, I think I'll take this outside,' I said with a nervous laugh when he didn't say anything. 'I need to finish this book as it needs to be returned. And I can't give myself a fine.'

'Oh, yes, right, good idea. Um...'

I paused. 'Yes?'

He shook his head. 'Never mind. Have a good rest of your day.'

He waved as I walked away and I wondered what he'd been

about to say. Jasper had been friendly since I started here, and elbow patches aside, he was nice looking. And clearly intelligent and kind. A few times, I had wondered if he was trying to flirt with me but I got the impression that didn't come naturally. I wasn't sure whether to encourage him or not. I hadn't been on a date since I moved to London, but was I excited by the idea of one with Jasper? I didn't know. My dating history had been a series of damp squibs so far, and it felt like finding my own love interest might prove impossible.

I tried to ignore Aiden's voice echo in my head.

The problem is your standards mean you end up reading a book alone in your room every night.

Leaving the cafeteria, I found a free bench in the courtyard to enjoy the September sunshine. Opening up the textbook to the last section on romantic tropes, I ran my finger down the list.

Friends to lovers
Grumpy sunshine
Love triangles
Student–teacher
Enemies to lovers

My finger hovered over enemies to lovers. It was my favourite trope. I wondered if that was what my book should include. I loved the part in *Pride and Prejudice* where Mr Darcy makes a really bad impression on Elizabeth. She declares she will never dance with the man and when they do end up dancing together, sparks fly. What if I could create chemistry like that? After all, I did know a lot about conflict.

Unwittingly, Aiden came into my head again. I had been unsure I could write a romance when I lacked it in my own life but I did know what it was like to have an annoying person around, someone that would make a good enemy for my leading lady.

Picking up a pen, I jotted down some ideas in my notebook. I needed to get the combination right of my characters being attracted to one another but having a reason that they disliked each other. They needed a misunderstanding, or they needed to be rivals in something – their first encounter is irritating to them both but also something they can't stop thinking about.

A light breeze fluttered around me as I frantically wrote ideas down before my lunch break was over. I knew what setting I wanted to use immediately. The seaside. Perfect for a budding romance. And I knew I wanted to start my story with my leading lady meeting her love interest for the first time. The meet-cute.

Or in this case, the meet-hate.

I jotted down notes for a potential opening scene. A moment where my leading lady met her love interest. For now, I called her Lily and thought she could be sunbathing, minding her own business, when suddenly a volleyball is thrown right onto her towel. She could then look up and see her potential love interest – I'd call him Adam for now – asking for the ball back, not apologising for the disruption. Annoyed, she could throw the ball in the opposite direction. As he stomps off to get the ball, Lily could hate herself for noticing his muscly arms, his bare chest and tanned legs underneath his shorts.

I thought back to when I first met my own nemesis. How I had, unfortunately, noticed his good looks like my character would do. Like Aiden had said, first impressions could be very wrong. I winced to think about how I had lusted after Aiden the night we'd first met. I had only been a teenager, but still, I should have known better.

That whole night had been humiliating for me. An embarrassing moment I wished I could forget.

What was it about embarrassing moments though?

They liked to pop up when you least expected it to remind you what a fool you'd made of yourself. I then thought back to my Aiden-was-Mr-Darcy dream and felt my skin flush. Even my subconscious liked to embarrass me it seemed. Thank God Aiden would never know about that. He did, however, know about the night we met. And that was why I preferred to spend as little time as possible in his company. But now with the looming prospect of him getting a job offer here, that might become impossible.

My phone vibrated on the table, interrupting my tortured thoughts. It was a voice note from Dan asking me to please buy milk on my way home. I checked the time. Crap! I hadn't realised my break was over. I grabbed my things and threw my lunch container in the bin then dashed back to relieve Stevie.

I was glad I'd never told anyone about what had happened with Aiden as it had been mortifying, but at least it would help me when it came to writing my own enemies-to-lovers story because I had the enemy part all right. I'd have to cross the lovers bridge when I came to it. That would not be a 'write what you know' situation but I'd read enough romances, I hoped, to help make it work. I decided as I walked back into work that I'd give Adam the same Irish accent as my real-life nemesis. It would help make it even easier for me to put myself in my leading lady's shoes.

I smiled, knowing that I was going to have fun pouring my hate for Aiden onto the page.

6

I had spent the rest of the day on tenterhooks. When I finished work, I hurried back to the flat to find Dan had already left for a date night with Theo so I'd have to wait for him to get home to know if there had been any news from Aiden about the university job.

Thankfully, Stevie came over after dinner and was in the mood for drinking wine.

I poured us each a glass and carried them over to Stevie who was on the sofa, her legs curled up beside her.

She waved her Kindle in her hand when I appeared. 'I think he might be my perfect man,' Stevie declared, referencing the leading man in the book we had both just finished reading. 'I like how bossy he is.'

'I don't think I could deal with a bossy man,' I said as I handed her one of the glasses then sat down beside her.

'That's because you are the bossy one.'

'Hey!' I cried while Stevie sniggered. 'Well, I just think it's nice when a man checks in with what you want and doesn't just make demands.'

'But I love an alpha male, I can't help it,' Stevie said wistfully.

'I don't think you would in real life,' I said, gesturing so passionately, my wine spilled a bit. 'Oops! Good job it missed the carpet. Dan is still annoyed from when I dropped nail polish my first week here.'

'This is why I like living alone.'

'You wouldn't want a bossy man moving in then,' I pointed out.

She sighed. 'I suppose not. And it's pretty unlikely after I've sworn off dating since the summer.'

I nodded. I knew Stevie had deleted her dating apps after deciding she couldn't take any more bad dates. 'It's been that long for me too. Aiden has been the only straight man to enter this flat since I moved in.'

Stevie raised an eyebrow. 'And he might be spending a lot more time here.'

'I really hope not,' I said. 'I haven't heard that he's been offered the job so...' I held up my fingers and crossed them. Surely the university would have told Aiden by now? I started to relax a little bit.

'Is he really that bad? You've never once fancied him in the whole time he's been Dan's best mate?'

I was glad I'd drunk enough wine that Stevie would assume my pink cheeks were due to that and not from being embarrassed about the fact I had indeed once fancied him. I shook my head vehemently. 'He is too irritating for me to even notice his looks.' I hid my face behind my glass and took a sip of wine. It wasn't a lie exactly, though the sight of his bare chest in the kitchen the other morning floated back into my mind.

'Shame,' Stevie said. 'I could have lived vicariously through you. Ah well, we shall both just enjoy our girls' nights instead.' She clinked her wine glass against mine. 'And fictional men at least never let us down. Not like the ones in real life.' She shuddered. 'I keep flashing back to my last date who complained about everything in the restaurant, and we ended up being asked to leave.'

I groaned. 'That was the date from hell. Second only to my worst date ever when he turned out to have been one of my secondary school teachers.'

'You definitely win there.' She gulped some wine. 'But what about Jasper? He took you out to lunch. And he does seem like one of the nice ones.'

'He just came to the cafeteria with me. We went our separate ways once we'd bought our food,' I said.

'He is always coming into the library now. He never used to, so I'm sure it's to see you. His face lights up when you talk to him. So sweet.'

I smiled. 'I mean, that is cute, and you're right, Jasper does seem nice...' I trailed off, wondering if calling him 'nice' was actually a compliment. 'I don't know,' I said. I wasn't sure that I was attracted to him. I thought about what Aiden had said to me. 'You don't think that we've set the bar too high, do you? That because of our love of romance novels we're too hard to please?'

'I think we expect the bare minimum and that's a stretch for most of the men out there today. Nope. We don't need to settle. I know what real love is like and that's what we deserve.' Stevie looked wistful. I knew she had had a serious relationship in the past, something I'd never had, but she didn't love talking about it. All I knew was he'd broken her heart. She brightened up. 'Maybe great guys are about to come into our lives. Or we've already met them and are yet to realise.'

'I think we'd realise,' I said and then downed the rest of my wine. 'It's the ones that make you think they are the men of your dreams but instead turn out to be a nightmare that are the problem.'

'Amen to that,' Stevie said, clinking her glass against mine.

'Okay, let's move back to fictional men. Our favourite kind. Tell me about the ideas you've had for your book; you said you've come up with the beginning?'

'Yes, I came up with what I want to be the opening scene where the two main characters meet each other and instantly take a dislike to one another although they both acknowledge the other one is hot.'

'I love it when you know as a reader two people are perfect together and you can't wait to find out when they realise it themselves,' Stevie said, clapping her hands. 'I only have one question – can I read it?'

'You'd really want to?' I asked.

'Too bloody right! I read one of your short stories and thought you were a brilliant writer. I'd love to read the first three chapters when you've written them. Pretty please?'

I laughed. 'Okay. Actually, feedback would be useful as I have no idea if I can really do this.'

'Of course you can!' Stevie said firmly. Then she sighed. 'You really are giving me food for thought with your book. It's inspiring you trying to make your dream of becoming an author come true. It makes me think about the dream I've always had of working in publishing.'

'Did you ever apply for any jobs?'

Stevie nodded. 'I tried before I got my first library job but I didn't get anywhere. Maybe because I wasn't exactly sure which role I'd want. I just want to work with books. And I love that I get to do that in the library, but, you know...' She shrugged.

'Well, I think you'd be brilliant working for a publishing company. You are so knowledgeable. I think you should reconsider trying again,' I encouraged. 'I'm not the only one who can go after my dreams.'

'You make it sound easy.'

I snorted. 'I wish. But if you don't try, you'll never know.'

'I'll think about it,' she promised.

The flat door opened then and Dan called out hello as he walked in, followed by Theo.

'Hi, you two, was your meal good?' I called back. 'We're putting the world to rights over wine.' I gestured to our glasses. I looked at Dan as he walked in, trying to gauge whether he'd heard anything from Aiden.

'It was, I'm so full,' Dan said. 'How are you, Stevie?'

'Just peachy,' she replied cheerfully.

Dan grinned. 'Glad to hear it.'

'Any news to tell us?' I asked Dan, desperate to know if I was in the clear or not.

'No, only Theo telling me all about what's happening at the Tate tomorrow,' he replied.

'I can't wait to see the exhibition,' Theo said eagerly. 'It's meant to be beautiful.'

Theo was a little older than my brother, with curly dark hair and a beard that he kept trimmed to perfection. He glanced at Dan. 'But I don't mind if you'd rather I go alone; I know you're not into modern art.'

'I'm happy to come,' Dan said. 'I just get annoyed because I think your work is better than most of what's in there.'

'Well, I think you might be biased but I appreciate it,' Theo replied.

Theo sold his paintings on Instagram, which was how they'd met – Dan had become a customer and asked him out to dinner. Two of Theo's colourful acrylic paintings of the seaside hung in the living room. He really was talented.

'Plus, I can do a TikTok vlog,' Dan added.

Theo sighed. I always got the impression he didn't fully 'get' Dan's job of showing his life online. Theo sold his work but that was it. He didn't post anything about his personal life. 'Are you still coming, Liv?'

'Yes because Dan said there would be books and cake.'

Theo chuckled. 'Want to join us, Stevie?'

'I wish I could, but I have the Saturday shift. I said to Liv, I'm putting Toby and Jamal on the next few weekend shifts.'

'I can do the next one,' I offered.

'But then we won't be working together.'

'Veto that then,' I said. 'Your plan was better.'

'My Uber is here,' Stevie said as she checked her phone. 'I'd better head off and get some sleep. I have to open up the library in the morning.' She gathered her things and I walked her to the door. 'Enjoy the Tate and don't forget to send me the first three chapters when they're written.'

'And I'm the bossy one?' I asked as we hugged goodbye. 'I will. Hope work isn't too bad tomorrow. I'll see you on Monday.'

I watched as the Uber car pulled up and she climbed in, waving before she closed the door.

'You did say you'd take a week off soon,' Theo was reminding Dan as I returned to the kitchen. I hung back slightly, noting the tense tone in his words. 'We need the break.'

'I'll try, I told you,' Dan snapped back.

I felt awkward, like I was walking into an argument, which was really strange as I'd never seen them argue before. I cleared my throat so they knew I was back.

'Who fancies ice cream?' Dan asked. 'We didn't get dessert out.'

'Sure,' Theo said, turning away so I couldn't see his expression.

'Liv?' Dan asked, smiling at me.

I still felt awkward, but I knew it would be weirder if I said no. I'd never usually turn down ice cream. 'Cookie dough?'

'You even have to ask?' Dan said.

I went to sit by Theo on the stools and he smiled at me, but there was still a tension in the room that worried me. 'So, Dan said you're going to submit some pieces to that new gallery?'

Theo nodded. 'I'm going to give it a try. I'm probably not right for them but I have that series I did of London that could work.'

'I love those pieces,' I said enthusiastically. 'They'd be crazy not to take them,' I added as Dan passed us each a bowl. Then his phone rang and he mouthed, 'Aiden.' I watched as he walked into the living room to speak to him privately. My pulse picked up.

'And I heard you've started writing a book?' Theo asked.

I turned back from watching Dan. I couldn't hear what he was saying to Aiden and that was incredibly frustrating. My foot tapped against the stool as I tried to focus on what Theo had said. 'It's very early days,' I said. 'But it feels good to have started something.'

'Good. I think it'll be great. You love romance novels.'

'I'm just worried that doesn't mean I can write a good one myself though.'

Dan came back over to us. I held my breath.

'Well, they offered him the job. I knew they would! And Aiden has accepted – Head of the Film Studies department. He's going to be working at your university, Liv,' he said happily. 'And that means Aiden is coming to live in London!'

It felt like my ears were ringing. I stared at my brother as the news sank in.

'Oh, that's great,' Theo said.

Dan looked at me. 'He didn't ask but I offered to let him stay here for a bit. They want him to start next week and it'll take a while for him to find a flat. You know what it's like here. That's okay with you, isn't it?'

I spluttered. That explained why he and Aiden had been shifty before Aiden had left the other day. They'd planned this! Not only would I now have to see Aiden, I'd have to live with him too? I shook my head. 'Dan, is that such a good idea?' I asked. He had no clue about what had happened when I'd first met Aiden but he knew what happened when we were around one another. 'You know how much we argue and that's only hanging out, like, twice a year!'

'Oh.' Dan's smile faltered. 'But that's all in good fun. You just like to tease each other, right? And it won't be for long. Just until he can find somewhere. We are the only people he'll know here.' He gave me a pleading look.

What could I say? It was Dan's flat and I wasn't paying any rent – he wouldn't let me – so I couldn't exactly kick up a fuss about him helping out his best friend for a while. I cursed myself for not telling Dan about why seeing Aiden was so mortifying for me but I had never been able to bring myself to admit what happened. And it was the only thing I was grateful to Aiden for – he hadn't said anything either. I swallowed hard. 'Um, well, I guess so,' I found myself saying.

'And don't worry, I'll make sure he doesn't blast Harry Styles or take all the hot water again.'

They were the least of my problems. I would now have to see Aiden every day!

So much for this being a big enough city that I could avoid Aiden. Not only was he now going to work in the same place as me, but he'd also be living with me too. I'd never be able to escape him.

I picked up my spoon and took the biggest bite of ice cream I could manage. And then, as if the news I had just heard wasn't bad enough, I got brain freeze.

7

The sun was shining the following morning, which helped to brighten my mood. I stood in front of my full-length mirror to straighten the bow on my blouse. I was wearing a black pleated skirt with it and a headband as I was going for a Blair-Waldorf-at-a-New-York-City-gallery look. I picked up my bag and hurried into the kitchen. 'Sorry, sorry, sorry,' I said as Dan had already complained four times that I was making us late.

He grinned. 'It's fine. I told you half an hour earlier than we needed to leave so we're right on time.'

I hated it when he did that.

Rolling my eyes, I walked out the door ignoring him. Dan had to hurry to catch up as I flounced along our road towards the Tube.

'I just didn't want Theo to get annoyed waiting for us there,' he said, wrapping an arm through mine and giving me what I call his 'puppy eyes'. 'You know how he feels about lateness.'

'That's because he doesn't have to do hair, makeup and pick an outfit. He just combs his hair and throws on a shirt,' I replied. 'I'd be on time too if I could just roll out of bed and go out.'

Dan chuckled. 'But look – it was worth the effort because you look gorgeous.'

I gave him a withering look. 'No need to take the piss.'

'I wouldn't lie about style. We have to take a photo for the 'gram at the Tate; they'll go nuts for this look.'

'Okay, and one of us together,' I said, giving his linen suit an approving look. 'And I know how you can make it up to me,' I said, pointing to the Starbucks we were walking past.

'Only because I'm desperate for coffee too,' he said, shaking his head.

I laughed and we went inside and both got iced lattes as the sunny morning demanded it. We carried on walking to the Tube and made our way to the Tate.

Theo was waiting outside when we arrived. We threw our take-away cups into the bin as we approached. I hadn't slept well worrying about Aiden moving in so I had drained every last drop of my coffee and was already wondering how soon I could get another one. Theo was wearing jeans and a shirt, about which I gave Dan a pointed look as we greeted him.

'Right on time,' Theo said with surprise as he kissed Dan then gave me a hug.

'Don't,' Dan warned him. 'She'll make another speech about it. Come on, let's go in and look at this exhibition.'

Sighing, I followed them into the shady coolness of the Tate Modern. I didn't know much about art, but I liked how Theo always pointed out pieces and explained why he liked them. The exhibition he particularly wanted to see was a display of sculptures by a new London artist.

'Look at this one, it really shows the city perfectly,' he said as we stood by two silver rings entwined on a stand. Dan glanced at me and I had to hide a smile. Dan was like me. Not great at all this but he did it for Theo, which was sweet.

'This will be good for Instagram,' he said as we turned to see a wall of blue paintings. 'Stand over there, Liv.'

'Seriously?' Theo asked as I walked over and posed for Dan. We ignored his barb as he began to take photos and then we swapped places, me taking some of him. We then turned hopefully to Theo.

'Would you take a picture in front of your favourite books?' he asked me, but then gave in and took Dan's phone so he could get a couple of us together.

'Books are my favourite backdrop,' I said, grinning at him. 'I'm sorry we're not art connoisseurs but you know we love your art.'

Theo smiled. 'How can I criticise your taste then? Come on, let's go to the café; you two have had enough sculptures for one day I think.'

As we walked through the gallery towards their restaurant, we noticed a small group of people looking at something with rapt attention. Theo immediately walked over and we followed, although when we got closer, I could see that it wasn't a piece of art that had caught people's interest at all, but a couple. The man was kneeling on the ground and she gasped as he held out a ring box.

'It's a proposal,' I cried, standing on tiptoes to watch eagerly. This was more enjoyable than looking at art. I watched, my heart melting as the man asked her to marry him, wondering if this place had been where they had met or been on their first date. Or maybe she just loved it here. Or one of them was an artist like Theo. I longed to know their full story. (Yes – a romance reader who loves proposals. I was definitely a cliché!)

'Oh, that's so sweet,' I said as the woman said 'yes', and the man jumped up to hug her while everyone started to clap. 'God, I hope I get that one day,' I added wistfully. 'Wouldn't it be so romantic...' I began, but I realised that Dan was looking at his phone and Theo had already turned and was walking away. I wondered why they were acting so weird. 'Dan, are you okay?'

'Let's get lunch,' he replied, putting his phone in his pocket and following Theo who was walking very quickly.

I grabbed my brother's arm. 'You're not telling me something.'

He glanced at Theo's back and sighed. 'If I tell you, don't say anything right now. We'll talk later, okay?'

I nodded, wondering what the hell was going on.

'Theo proposed to me and I said no,' he said before setting off towards the café again.

I stood still, watching my brother's retreating back, stunned. Theo had proposed? And Dan hadn't told me?

Hang on.

'He said no?' I said aloud to myself, earning a few confused glances in my direction from people around me.

'What am I always telling you, Olivia?' a voice called out. 'You shouldn't talk to yourself.'

Startled, I turned to see Aiden walking towards me, hands in his pockets. He had on his usual jeans and T-shirt combo, and that irritating smirk on his face.

I glanced up at the ceiling.

'Anything else you want to throw at me today, universe?' I asked in despair.

'Hello to you too,' Aiden said when he reached me. 'Anything in particular you're having an existential crisis about?'

'Want a list?' I asked. I wouldn't even know where to start.

'Melodramatic as usual.' Aiden tutted. 'Maybe the universe isn't the problem.'

'Hmm, maybe you are,' I snapped. I couldn't believe I was seeing Aiden again; I thought I'd have some space before he invaded it once again. 'What are you even doing here anyway? Do you even know what art is?'

'I brought some things to the flat and Dan said to meet you guys for lunch before I head back to pack up the second lot. Then I'll be moving in tomorrow.' His smirk deepened. 'Roomie.'

'Tell me a one-word horror story,' I said.

Aiden sighed. 'You're not even going to say congratulations, Olivia?'

My eyes narrowed. He had to know I wasn't excited about the idea of us living and working together. I knew he couldn't be happy about it either but I supposed his new job softened that blow. I had no such reward for having to put up with him. Aiden watched me as I hesitated. If it was anyone else, of course I'd congratulate them. This was a big deal for him, I knew that, but I was sure he wouldn't be happy if the shoe was on the other foot. I held Aiden's gaze as he watched me, waiting for me to say something. What was it about this man that made it so hard for me to think straight?

'Aiden! You're here! What are you both doing?' Dan called out then, beckoning us to where he and Theo were at the entrance to the café.

I exhaled in relief and turned around. 'We're coming,' I called back eagerly, setting off towards them. Aiden moved past me; his legs really were infuriatingly long.

Watching his back, I really hoped he'd find his own place soon because I had no idea how I was going to manage living in the same flat as him. I was sure he would want to move out quickly too; I knew he didn't like being around me either.

I followed the others into the café and my attention was caught by something other than Aiden. I paused and looked at the stunning view from the windows across London. The sun was streaming in through the glass, pooling in circles on people's faces as they all squinted but smiled at it. I smiled myself as I took in the scene. This was what I loved about the city. It still surprised me.

When I turned around to find the others, Aiden was behind me, giving me a funny look.

'What?' I asked, touching my face in case I had something on it.

'Uh, nothing,' he said, clearing his throat and walking quickly over to Dan and Theo as they hunted for food.

That was odd. But then again, when were my interactions with Aiden not odd? I eyed Dan and Theo. With Aiden's sudden appearance, Dan's news had slipped from my focus. But now what he had told me flooded back. Theo had proposed. And Dan had said no. I was flummoxed. And desperate to know the full story.

Why would Dan say no when I knew he loved Theo? No wonder I thought things hadn't been quite as they usually were between them.

It was worrying. They seemed like the perfect couple. If they were in trouble, there was no hope for me that I could ever make a relationship work.

I wandered over and picked up a tray, looking at the food on offer.

'We're going to a bookshop afterwards,' Dan was saying to Aiden as I joined them. 'If you want to come.'

'I'm not sure I have the stamina for that,' Aiden said. 'Olivia in a bookshop sounds mildly terrifying. Will you get her out again before dinner?'

He reached for the last chocolate muffin on the stand in front of us but I leaned over and took it before he could touch it.

'Oh, sorry, I didn't realise you wanted it too,' I said, smiling sweetly as I walked off with my tray to the coffee station. I could feel his eyes burning into my back but I refused to turn around. I inhaled and exhaled a calming breath and reminded myself that I would soon be surrounded by books that I could buy, and that made me a feel a lot better about everything.

8

Annoyingly, Aiden did come to the bookshop with us as he wanted to stretch his legs more before driving back to Bath, but no one could spoil looking at books for me. We left the Tate and walked into the small shop. I was excited to visit a new bookshop. I'd had a weekend soon after moving here where I'd tried to go to as many as I could. There were so many that you could turn a corner and suddenly find a new one to explore. I'd never get tired of it.

I left Aiden and Dan near the entrance and smiled at Theo as he walked straight to the art section. I went as I always did to look at the new books first and then deeper into the shop because there was always one to discover that you didn't know about. My phone rang as I traced my fingertips along the spines of the books on the shelves in front of me.

'Hi, Mum,' I answered in a hushed voice, used to being in the library.

'I'm out of the silent retreat. I pulled over just outside the gates to ring you,' she said happily.

'It didn't make you want to give up your phone for good then?' I teased.

Maybe I should have gone with her; a week of silent reading sounded pretty good to me. Then again, there would have been so many wellness activities, I wouldn't have got the chance.

'God, no. I'm dying for conversation! I might go to the local pub and just sit and listen to people. Where are you anyway?'

'A bookshop. I went with Dan and Theo to the Tate so this is my reward.'

'Olivia, look!'

I gritted my teeth as Aiden waved a book from the other side of the shop at me.

'Who's that?' Mum asked instantly.

'Aiden,' I said with a sigh. 'He came to bring some of his things to the flat and he'll be back tomorrow with more and to...' I gulped. 'Move in.'

'I'm so jealous,' Mum said. 'You'll all have so much fun together! It reminds me of the good times I had before I met your *father*,' she said, the bitter emphasis on the word still there all these years later, after he'd disappeared out of our lives. 'I lived with a group of girls...'

'Who are you talking to?' Aiden asked as he came closer.

'My mum.'

'Let me say hi,' Mum said eagerly and so loudly that Aiden heard. He held out his hand. Reluctantly, I handed my phone over and turned back to the books as Aiden said hello and talked about how excited he was for his new job.

'It should be fine, depending on how moody Olivia is in the mornings. No, you're right, I'll make sure there's plenty of coffee and not speak to her—'

I cut Aiden abruptly off, wrestling my phone back off him.

'I have to go, Mum,' I said as he leaned against the bookshelf, watching me in amusement.

'Doesn't he have such a lovely voice on the phone?'

I really hoped he hadn't heard that; he was already smug enough about his accent.

'I wouldn't know; luckily he never phones me,' I said, giving him a withering look.

'I can rectify that,' he hissed. He held out the book he'd been pointing to. I shook my head but he brandished it again.

Rolling my eyes, I snatched the book from him but didn't look at it, hoping he would now go away.

'Well, have a lovely time. Send me a picture of what books you buy,' Mum continued cheerfully. 'Oh, and I might come down soon and see you all. I miss you.'

I told her we missed her too and after a drawn-out goodbye, she hung up.

I finally looked down at the book Aiden had passed me and was confronted with a huge picture of Mr Darcy. No, it was Colin Firth as Mr Darcy in the BBC adaptation. I blushed instantly and kept my eyes on the book, not daring to lift them to meet Aiden's in case he guessed anything close to what I'd dreamt about the other night.

'It's a book that goes behind the scenes of how they filmed the series,' Aiden said. 'I thought maybe there was a photo of the lake scene so you could stick it on your wall and scare all your future boyfriends away with it.'

With that, he sauntered off, chuckling to himself.

I turned around and quickly flicked through the book just in case. There was actually a picture of the lake scene in the book. I looked at it with a smile, but this quickly faded when I remembered my dream, Aiden coming out of that very lake with a clinging wet white shirt.

I slammed the book shut. I did not need to confuse my brain between Aiden and Mr Darcy any further, thank you very much. I walked to where Aiden had picked it up and put it back, then a romance book I hadn't read caught my eye. After I'd bought the book, I found the others outside the shop waiting for me.

'Research for your own novel?' Dan asked when he saw the new book in my hands.

'You've actually started writing it then?' Aiden asked.

'Just planning so far,' I said cautiously, unsure if I should even admit that to him.

'Are you going to let us read it when you're finished?'

'As if I would let you read anything I write. You would only take the piss,' I replied.

'I'm used to critiquing my students' work. I could help,' he said with a shrug. Thankfully, he then checked the time. 'Right, I better head off now. I'll be back tomorrow with the rest of my things. Don't miss me too much tonight, guys.'

'We never miss you,' I called to his retreating back. He turned around and mimed stabbing himself in the heart with a knife before carrying on walking away. I bit my lip to stop myself from laughing, which was highly annoying – I really did not want to find Aiden amusing.

Theo chuckled beside me. 'You two. It's going to be hilarious having you around each other all the time.'

'That's one word for it,' I replied dryly.

* * *

Back at the flat, we had dinner but then Theo said he'd head home to his place as we had Aiden moving in the following morning. Dan saw him out and re-joined me as I cleared up the kitchen. I leaned on the counter as he sat on one of the bar stools and finally met my gaze after avoiding it all evening.

'I know, I should have told you,' he said with a heavy sigh.

I nodded. 'When do we keep secrets as big as that?'

But then Aiden and that night when we were teenagers flashed in my mind. I understood better than anyone how you might want to keep something secret. I moved on swiftly. 'Anyway, it doesn't matter. What happened? I mean, why did you say no? Start from the beginning.'

Dan took a breath as he began the story. 'It was Theo's birthday – you know I took him to that fancy new restaurant near London Bridge and then we went up to the top of The Shard? We had champagne and looked at the view of London with all the lights... It was really romantic. Theo just suddenly turned to me and asked me to marry him. I think he had been planning to ask me but maybe not that night? I was so stunned and there were people everywhere, and he must have understood he'd surprised me too much as he said we could talk back at his.'

'Wow,' I said as I wiped the kitchen counter. 'So, what did you say when you went to his flat?'

'I kind of wondered if he wouldn't mention it. Stupid, I know, but up until then, we'd just carried on with the evening like it hadn't happened. But in his flat, he went and got a ring. He'd actually bought me a ring!'

Dan put his head in his hands.

I stopped cleaning and came around the counter to sit next to him. I reached out and touched his arm. He raised his head.

'He asked you again?' I prompted him gently.

'Yes. And there was no misunderstanding then. We were on our own, it was quiet, he had a ring... He was serious. I told him that I loved him but I had honestly never seen myself getting married. He knows about our father walking out on us and that it has always made me, well, averse to the idea.'

I had sometimes wondered if my love of all things romantic was part of a desperate need to believe in love because I'd seen what happened when it fell apart. Our father had left Mum and she'd been heartbroken. And so had we. Dad had supposedly fallen in love with another woman and that meant he'd abandoned his family. Our relationship with him had never really recovered.

'But you love Theo and you guys are happy?'

'Yes, but I'm scared, Liv. Of that kind of commitment. What if Theo leaves me? What if I can't commit and I leave him?' He waited a moment before asking the question I could see was tormenting him. 'What if I'm like our father?'

'You're not,' I said instantly. 'You're always there for anyone who needs you. And you have a huge heart,' I said, trying to reassure him. 'What did Theo say?'

'He was gutted. He asked me if it was a no then and I told him I was sorry – but he was so crushed. So I said I would think about it. I asked for time. But it's like there's a huge elephant in the room between us now. I think he feels like, if I don't say yes, it means I can't love him as much as he loves me, and I worry he'll leave me if I can't do it.'

'Wow,' I said. 'That is tough. I'm sorry, Dan. But I really think you can work it out. You love him. You can make this work.'

'How? It's not like I have any relationship to look to for guidance. I don't know how to make it work. I mean, you know how I feel, don't you? You've never had a long-term relationship.'

I stared at him. Was that really the reason I hadn't ever had something serious with someone? I swallowed. This felt like some deep therapy I wasn't prepared for.

'I think it's more I've never felt that kind of connection to someone that would make me want, or try, a long-term relationship. Because I've seen what can happen when it goes wrong, I want... no, I *need* to be 100 per cent sure of someone to give him my heart,' I said. 'I wouldn't want anything less than the kind of love I read about. I haven't found it yet. But I thought you had.'

Dan looked at me. 'And that's the problem.'

'What do you mean?'

'I never thought I would, and now I have, it's terrifying, Liv.'

I understood. I'd always hoped when I met the right person it would all just fall into place. It would be easy to take that leap. But now I could see it was far from easy. 'You'll work it out, if Theo is the one,' I said.

'I hope so,' Dan replied.

9

I woke up early for a Sunday morning, aware that the peacefulness of the flat was about to be disturbed for God only knew how long. I did a relaxing yoga video, which helped calm my mind a little bit, then I jumped in the shower and put on my usual Sunday-at-home uniform of leggings and a long shirt, pulling my hair into a messy bun.

I had turned over in my mind so many times what Dan had told me last night. I wished I could help him and Theo because I really did think they were perfect for one another but I wasn't sure what I could do. I definitely was not a relationship expert myself.

I walked into the kitchen for a much-needed coffee and bagel, and then settled down with the new novel I'd started reading last night, hoping that a fictional love story would take my mind off everything happening in real life.

The quietness of my morning evaporated when there was a knock at the door announcing Aiden's arrival.

Dan went to answer the door and I leaned back on the bar stool to look at what was happening in the hallway.

'What's in here?' Dan said as Aiden passed him a bag to bring inside. 'It weighs a ton.'

'My movie equipment,' Aiden said. 'I won't set up the projector while I'm here though.' He spotted me then. 'Oh no, don't worry, Olivia, you relax, we don't need any help,' he called out.

I gritted my teeth. 'I wouldn't want to get in the way,' I called back. 'Or accidentally open a box with your pants in.'

'Trust you to be thinking about my underwear,' he returned cheerfully as he headed out for another box. I hid my heated cheeks behind my hands.

'Come on, Liv. He's parked on double yellow lines,' Dan said as he carried a box through to his work room, which Aiden would now be having.

With an irritated sigh, I climbed off the stool and headed to the hall. I put my trainers on and walked outside to Aiden's car.

'I can't believe this still runs,' I commented as I eyed his Mini. He had got it when he went to university and I always found it hilarious that someone of his height and build could even fit in the thing.

'Hey, don't diss Molly, we've been through a lot together,' he said, giving the boot a pat. He passed me a box. 'This one isn't too heavy.'

'I'm not weak,' I told him.

He rolled his eyes. 'If I gave you a heavy one, I'd never hear the end of it and then you complain when I give you a light one.' He picked up a lamp and walked off.

I shook my head, even though, to be honest, he was right. I glanced into the boot before I followed him in, my eyes falling on a box of books at the back. A title caught my eye and I leaned in. Most were film theory or autobiographies from people in the film industry, which I would have expected, but squeezed in alongside them was a copy of *Pride and Prejudice*. I knew he said he'd read it but I hadn't exactly been sure whether to believe him.

At that moment, I saw Dan coming out so I hurried off with the box. I wasn't sure why, but seeing my favourite book in his car, with all of his things, made me smile.

It took half an hour to get all of Aiden's things into the flat and then, while Dan made a cup of tea for everyone, he moved his car to a place that allowed parking.

My phone beeped with a message from Stevie.

The library is so dull without you! Looking forward to a catch up tomorrow. What are your plans today? Xx

I realised I hadn't told her about Aiden, so I typed a message back as I walked into the living room.

The universe definitely hates me! The university offered Aiden the job so not only is he going to be working there, he's moving in until he can find a flat! I'm going to need all the coffee and chats tomorrow. The only way to salvage this situation is to hide in my room and do some writing xx

Stevie replied immediately.

I'm sorry, Liv. On the plus side, it'll be great research for your enemies-to-lovers story though. You can argue with him then put it all in your book haha!! See you tomorrow xx

I sent an upside-down smiley face emoji – it felt appropriate.

'Who are you texting?' Aiden asked as he came into the room and paused a couple of feet in front of me.

'Nosy much? Stevie. She works at the library with me. I guess you'll meet her when you start at the uni. We will need a list of books you want students to use on your course.' I was suddenly filled with alarm as I realised I would actually need to interact with him at work as well as at home now.

'I will make sure to come and see you both then,' he replied, looking amused at the idea.

'I can't imagine you at work,' I blurted out without thinking. It was disconcerting to think of him roaming the university corridors in his suit. Even more so to imagine him teaching students.

Aiden cocked an eyebrow. I wish I knew how to do that. He made it look cool. I looked like I had a nervous twitch when I tried it.

'Dare I ask why?'

He stepped closer and I could smell his aftershave. It was as familiar as my own perfume; he'd worn it for years, and if I smelled it I was always reminded of him, worse luck.

'Um...' I said, trying to focus on his question and not the smell of him. 'You're just never serious. With me,' I said truthfully.

He looked slightly surprised by this, as if he'd expected a joke or an insult. He leaned in closer to me. Unwittingly, my breath hitched at his closeness.

'I can be serious when I want to be, Olivia,' he said, drawing out my name again, practically purring the words.

I lifted my eyes and met his. They were dark. I wondered if mine were too.

I shook my head to clear the fog that Aiden seemed to always create in my brain.

'Well, I look forward to witnessing that,' I said, backing up and trying to speak normally, but I wouldn't have been surprised if I sounded as unsteady as I felt. He grinned. I could tell he knew he'd disconcerted me.

'Who wants a cup of tea?' Dan called from the kitchen, oblivious to our conversation.

'I'm going to do some writing actually,' I said, needing a break from Aiden already. 'I'll see you guys for dinner; we always have a takeaway on a Sunday night,' I babbled before ducking past Aiden and rushing into my room.

I needed some time away from him. For someone I usually avoided and only saw twice a year, this was *a lot*. From the look on Aiden's face, he knew I was freaking out – and knowing him, he was thoroughly enjoying it.

At least I could be productive as I hid in my room for the rest of the day. I decided I would start writing my book properly. I really wanted to write the first three chapters so I could send them to Stevie. And although I was nervous about showing my first attempt at a novel to her, I knew I needed to get over it if I wanted to have something published one day. So I opened my notebook with my ideas in and pulled my laptop onto the bed with me to make a start.

As I had my notes ready, I quickly wrote the opening to the story. After my characters Lily and Adam had their meet-hate, I carried on writing about how they felt about it. I soon got lost in my novel.

Lily is furious with the man on the beach and how rude he was to her but she's also angry with herself for finding him attractive. Adam is also pissed off. He'd had a terrible day: he'd agreed to a volleyball game with his cousins and he felt like he couldn't back out. After the day from hell, all he'd wanted to do was drown his sorrows with some beer, so he wasn't at all pleased about having to play with his cousins. Adam had just wanted to get the game over with but he now realises that he took it all out on Lily.

Both of them assume they won't see one another again until the next day when Lily goes to the beach café for breakfast and Adam is behind the counter.

Adam owns the café and when Lily walks in, he notices her blue eyes, her curves in her denim shorts and the way her hair blows in the sea breeze. She is even more beautiful than he remembers and he feels a need to make up for the bad first impression he made.

'What can I get you? It's on the house after yesterday,' he offers, throwing on his most charming smile, a delicious Irish lilt to his voice.

Lily folds her arms over her chest, annoyed with him still but not about to turn down free food either.

'Fine. I'll take one of everything on the menu,' she says, challenging him with a raised eyebrow.

Adam stares at her. Is she kidding? But he can see she isn't.

'I suppose you think I deserve that. Fine then, coming right up,' he replies, not about to let her see she's impressed him. He's used to women being all over him, but this woman is glaring at him, and he really wishes he could make her smile.

I finished the third chapter with Lily sitting down at a table and Adam coming over with a selection of food and drinks for her.

Lily feels like this man is trouble but his food is delicious and the café is lovely. Lily needs a summer job and this place could be perfect. So, swallowing her pride, Lily asks Adam if he needs any more staff.

I leaned back on my pillows and smiled. I liked that my characters were now about to be thrown together for the summer. Forced proximity could only lead to fun and games.

Before I could chicken out, I attached the chapters to an email and sent it to Stevie, asking her to give me her honest opinion.

10

On Monday morning, I made sure I was first in the bathroom, not wanting to lose out on hot water again. I had butterflies in my stomach, and I wasn't quite sure why. Maybe it was because it felt like two worlds were colliding today. My university work-life and Aiden. I tried not to catastrophise about it but I had no idea how it was going to work. And on top of that, I was still worried about Dan and Theo.

I was dressed and drinking coffee when Aiden came into the kitchen.

'Morning,' he said when he saw me.

I peered over my coffee cup at him. It was still surprising to see him in a suit and I couldn't stop myself from taking in the details as he walked over to pour himself a coffee. The way his shirt draped over his shoulders, the hint of muscles as he moved to pick up a coffee cup and his sleeves ruched up. I decided that looking at Aiden was definitely preferable to listening to him.

'Have I got something on my face?' he asked, catching my gaze.

'Um...' Flustered at being caught looking at him again, I stood up quickly. 'No, but this isn't straight.'

Aiden frowned, not understanding me. My feet seemed to move by themselves as I walked around the kitchen counter to where he was leaning and stepped close to him. I could feel the tension in his body as he watched me with suspicion in his eyes. I smiled, enjoying his discomfort. It was usually the other way around.

I reached up as I held his gaze. 'This is wonky,' I said softly as I straightened his tie. I watched him swallow hard.

'Uh, right, can't have that,' he said after a moment. 'Got to make the best impression on my first day, right?'

Suddenly, I didn't feel quite so smug. I stepped back quickly. 'Right.'

Aiden looked back at me as if he wasn't quite sure what had happened. I felt the same.

'I feel like I'm sending you both off to school,' Dan said cheerfully as he breezed into the kitchen. His words snapped me out of my weird trance. I spun around and grabbed my coffee cup and shakily drained it in one go. 'Should we take a photo to document it like parents who take a picture of their kids on the front step in their uniform?'

'Hard pass,' I replied, forcing a smile. 'I'll just grab my things.'

I rushed out, keeping my eyes firmly away from Aiden. That was the closest I'd got to him for years and I felt almost light-headed. Note to self – don't do that again. It had felt...

I searched for the right word as I grabbed my bag and slipped on my cropped blazer.

...Dangerous.

It had felt dangerous.

When I walked back out, Aiden was hovering while Dan poured out cereal for himself.

'Um, did you want a lift in with me?' he asked me, jangling his car keys in his hand.

I stopped. I hadn't thought about the fact we were going to the same workplace. It would be a novelty not to have to walk. I could even have time for an iced coffee on the way. It was tempting. But then the thought of being right next to him in his tiny car brought me to my senses. I shook my head.

'Wouldn't want to be seen arriving with you, I have to maintain my street cred somehow,' I said lightly as I went into the hallway to slip on my shoes.

Aiden snorted as he followed me out. 'There is one thing you haven't got, Olivia, and that is street cred.'

When I turned around, my shoes on, his smirk was broad.

'Don't say I didn't offer,' he said, and with a wave he opened the front door and walked out briskly.

I looked out of the door after him, and my heart sank.

'Oh, crap.' It was pouring. Absolutely tipping it down out there. And I bet he'd assumed I would refuse a lift without knowing that.

Dan appeared behind me. 'I'll order you an Uber,' he said as he saw the rain, and before I could protest, added, 'I need you to help me film a video for a brand when you get in tonight.'

I smiled. 'Okay, deal.'

'Liv, I know Aiden acts like he doesn't care about anything but he's really nervous about this new job.' He looked up from where he was typing on his phone. 'It's a promotion, a new workplace – it's a big change. He could do with a friend there, you know?'

I was taken aback. I supposed I'd been thinking too much about what Aiden working at my university would mean for *me*. I had been annoyed he was invading not only my work space but my home too. I hadn't really thought about the fact it was a new job for him and how he might be feeling about it all. It was a big shift. I knew because I'd done it not so long ago. Moved to London. Changed where I lived and where I worked.

'Okay, I'll let him sit with me at the cool kids table,' I replied with a grin, remembering what Dan had said about it being like we were off to school together.

Dan chuckled. 'I'm afraid I'm with Aiden on this one: that isn't where you'd be sitting.'

I sighed. 'I wish I could argue but I did used to eat in the school library because the cool girls intimidated me.'

Dan waved his phone. 'The Uber's here. Have a good day. See you later for filming!'

I called out a goodbye to him and hurried out through the rain to climb into the taxi. London in the rain had a kind of romance about it – when you were safely dry, of course; otherwise it was a complete pain in the bum.

Gazing out of the window, I watched the city roll past me behind the droplets sliding down the glass. I was still nervous about Aiden being at the university too but I realised that his nerves must be much worse and I knew if the roles were reversed, I would want his support. It did require a brain rewiring though to consider supporting Aiden. We'd been at loggerheads for so many years, after all.

When I arrived at the university, I hurried into the main building, thankful I didn't need to leave again until tea time as it looked like the rain was in for the day. I walked to the library and smiled to see Stevie was already there, hanging up her raincoat and letting down her hair which had been tied up.

'Lovely day, isn't it?' I said as I joined her behind the front desk.

She groaned. 'I got soaked walking from the Tube. I didn't get a chance to get us coffee on the way either so I'm grumpy, I warn you now.'

'Want me to get you some?'

'I would love you forever. And when you're back,' she said, her eyes lighting up, 'we can discuss your chapters because I've read them.'

'How much caffeine will I need to get through that?' I asked nervously.

Stevie grinned. 'Let me go through the emails and open up, then we will talk.'

I could tell she was enjoying making me wait so I just shook my head and slipped out to head to the university coffee shop. I got us two large coffees and hurried back, hoping she wasn't going to keep me in suspense much longer. When I came back into the library, I could hear voices. It was early for students so I wasn't surprised to see Stevie was talking to staff instead. I almost spilled my coffee though when the two men at the desk turned around and I realised that it was Jasper and Aiden.

'Morning, Liv,' Jasper said with a warm smile. 'We were just asking where you were.'

'I missed getting coffee on the way in so Liv offered to be my saviour,' Stevie explained.

'It was mostly selfish as I wanted one too,' I said, walking behind the desk to hand her one of the cups. I lifted my eyes and noticed Aiden watching us with interest. 'So, how can we help you?'

I'd decided the only way to get through this was just to act like Aiden was any other professor here.

'Aiden needs you to order a set of books for one of his courses. I thought we'd stop off here while it's quiet before he sits in on one of the film lectures. He's just going to be observing this week, get everything sorted before diving in and taking over the department.' He clapped Aiden on the back. 'He's going to be a real asset to the university, I'm sure. He's already come up with a great way to get to know everyone in his department, both staff and students.'

'Oh, by doing what?' Stevie asked then took a sip of her coffee. She glanced from Aiden to me and back again. She was smiling a little too broadly for my liking. I could tell she was going to have a lot to say once they'd both left.

'A film festival on Saturday. The plan is to set up the projector in the main lecture hall and people can drop in all day to watch one of the four films I'll be showing. I did it at my old university and it went down really well so I thought it would be a great ice breaker here.'

'What are the films?' I asked him, curious in spite of it being Aiden behind the idea. It did sound like a great way to introduce himself.

'I was going to ask for suggestions for a theme for me to pick from, then the films will be a surprise on the day,' Aiden said. 'I'm going to leave a box outside my office and people can drop their ideas into it.'

'I love it,' Jasper said. 'And we'll all come along, won't we?' he said, looking at me.

I felt torn. I loved movies but an event run by Aiden? I was supposed to be trying to avoid him, not spending even more time with him. But Jasper looked so hopeful.

'I can't, I'm afraid,' Stevie said, looking disappointed. 'I'm going home to my parents' for the weekend.'

'Oh, that's a shame,' Jasper said. 'How about you, Liv? We can't let Aiden down, can we?'

'It's not like you have a hot date this weekend, is it?' Aiden chipped in.

My blood heated up. He loved to point out I wasn't dating anyone. Well, I would wipe that smile off his face. Before I could stop myself, I blurted out, 'It sounds fun. Why don't we go along together, Jasper?'

Aiden looked surprised, which made it worth it. Beside me, Stevie's eyebrows rose up into her forehead. I kept my gaze on Jasper, hoping I hadn't misread his friendliness towards me.

Jasper beamed at me. 'I think that's a wonderful idea. It's a date.'

I smiled back but then reality hit me. I had asked Jasper out on a date. A man who I hadn't seriously considered going out with. And he looked so happy. I shot Aiden a glare. This was all his fault. As usual. Aiden ignored me and showed Stevie the book he wanted to order, and I had the distinct feeling the only person annoyed by what had just happened was me.

I really hadn't thought this through.

11

I left Stevie helping Aiden as a group of students needed me to find a long list of books for them and when I returned, he'd gone.

'They had to have some really obscure medieval books,' I said to Stevie as I stepped behind the desk. 'They looked terrified by the size of them, poor things. All finished with Aiden then?' I asked as casually as I could manage.

Stevie spun around in her chair to face me. 'You just asked out Jasper!'

'Okay, calm down, we are in a library,' I reminded her as her incredulous tone had earned us some annoyed looks. 'And you told me that I should date Jasper, may I remind you?'

'Well, yes, but I didn't think you'd ask him in front of me and Aiden, who – I must say – looked pretty shocked.'

'Shocked?' I smiled. 'Good. He always thinks he knows exactly what I'm going to do.'

'Shocked and *disappointed* if you ask me,' Stevie continued. 'Whereas Jasper looked like all his Christmases had come at once.'

'Aiden was not disappointed!' I said, shaking my head. 'But I'm glad I wiped the smile off his face when he said that I didn't have a hot date for the weekend. I have one now! Well, a date anyway.' I wasn't sure Jasper could be described as hot, if I was honest.

Stevie eyed me. 'So, you're more excited by getting one over on Aiden than actually going on the date with Jasper?'

I stared at her. 'Well, not exactly...' I fudged, flustered at the piercing look she was giving me, as if she was seeing something I wasn't. 'Jasper is nice, I already said.'

'But do you fancy him?'

'I'm not sure,' I admitted. 'Is that bad? Should I cancel?' I was getting nervous now.

'Well, you can find out on your date; that's what the point of them is. I'm just not sure you asked the right person to go with you though.'

'What do you mean?'

'Your pages! I read your three chapters and...' Stevie picked up a book and pretended to fan herself with it. 'I'm swooning already. You have to write more and give it to me as soon as you can.'

I broke into a smile, the worry about my date fading away with her praise. 'You really liked it? You think it has legs?'

'I really do, I promise I'm being honest.' Stevie leaned in closer. 'But I think I'd better check... You *do* know the characters you've created bear a striking resemblance to some real-life people?'

'What do you mean?'

'Adam. In the book,' she hissed. 'He's just like Aiden.'

'Okay, I know I gave Adam his accent – I admit it can be sexy, but it's a shame that it's Aiden's accent. Sometimes when he talks, I want to shut my eyes...'

'This is going to be a problem Aiden working here.'

'I know, he's so annoying. My brother told me to be nice to him, which is completely alien to me.' I watched as Stevie huffed and folded her arms across her chest. 'What's wrong?'

'You are not getting it, are you? Adam, the love interest in your book, doesn't just have the same accent as Aiden – he *is* Aiden. They are exactly alike! You have based the character on him. Why won't you admit it?'

I gaped at her. 'I did not! I wrote a character that I would find sexy. Good looking, tall, athletic, a sexy accent and because it's hate-to-love, he winds Lily up, pushing her buttons and...' I trailed off, realising I wasn't helping my case at all. I was making it a whole lot worse.

'See?' she said triumphantly. 'You even called him Adam. And Lily? I hate to break it to you, Liv, but you've put yourself into that story. And I'm no therapist but maybe there is some fantasising going on there about you and—'

'Don't. Even. Say. It,' I instructed, holding my hand up to stop her from finishing her sentence. 'Nope. You have it all wrong. I have written a novel. It's fiction and my characters are not real.'

'Are you trying to convince me or yourself?'

'You don't understand. I do not fantasise about Aiden!' My traitorous Darcy/Aiden dream floated through my mind.

'It's okay if you do,' Stevie said. 'He is good looking, it's not like it's something to be ashamed of.'

'It's mortifying,' I snapped at her. I could not let myself fancy Aiden. Not after what had happened before. I couldn't tell Stevie the reason why though, so I stood up abruptly. 'We need to get back to work.'

'I'm sorry, I was only teasing you,' Stevie said, looking worried. 'I really did enjoy your first three chapters. It's such a good start to a story.'

I bit my lip. 'Maybe I shouldn't carry on with it,' I said, uncertain about it now she had linked Adam to Aiden. I'd thought that I was only using my knowledge of hating someone as inspiration, but it turned out Aiden had more than inspired the love interest in my book – he *was* the love interest. I was annoyed at myself. But it had come so easily. I finally had the inspiration I'd been waiting for. I was loving writing this book. Why did Aiden have to ruin everything?

Stevie reached out and touched my arm. 'It's okay, Liv, Aiden can inspire your love interest, it doesn't have to mean anything in real life. I didn't mean to freak you out.'

'I'm not freaked out,' I insisted. 'I know he's definitely not my real-life love interest so it's fine. I'd better get on with work though.'

I hurried off so she couldn't stop me, going to shelve some books off the returns trolley. As I worked, I tried to shut out what Stevie had said but, of course, I couldn't. She was wrong about me fancying Aiden. I knew my book was just a story. I told myself it didn't matter that my main character bore a striking resemblance to my enemy. I bet authors used people they knew in real life to help create characters all the time.

And Aiden was suddenly in my life a whole lot more so, if you thought about it, it made sense that he had seeped into my book. That was where he would stay anyway. Nothing to worry about.

But as I shelved books, a tiny part of my mind, the part of me that still remembered what I had thought about Aiden when we'd first met, the one I tried to ignore at all costs, reminded me of what Stevie had said just now.

Aiden had looked shocked and disappointed when I asked Jasper out.

Disappointed.

'Shut up, shut up, shut up,' I whispered to my annoying brain for planting the thought when I knew it shouldn't be there at all.

Thankfully, a student asked for my help then so I could focus on that, and I managed to push Aiden and my book out of my mind.

* * *

The rain clouds faded away by lunch time so I took the salad I got from the university cafeteria outside to try to get a dose of vitamin D. I tilted my face to the sun then frowned as a shadow appeared across the bench I was sitting on.

As I opened my eyes, hoping it wasn't yet another grey cloud, a face came into focus.

'You're blocking my sun,' I complained.

'Never. I'm as hot as the sun,' Aiden said, but moved so warmth hit my skin again. He waved the sandwich in his hand. 'I see we have the same idea.'

I hesitated, almost telling him to leave me in peace, but I remembered Dan's plea as I'd left the house earlier.

'You'd better join me then but over here so your big head doesn't keep blocking my light,' I replied, gesturing to the space beside me.

'Why are you being offensive about my head now?'

'You said you're as hot as the sun! Honestly, I'm surprised your head can actually hold your ego,' I said, reaching up to tap his temples with my fingers.

Aiden waved my fingers away and our skin touched for a moment. I felt a jolt, which made me quickly drop my hand and look down as though my salad was suddenly very interesting to me. I peered out of the corner of my eyes just as Aiden opened up his sandwich. I really hoped he hadn't noticed how his touch had affected me.

'My ego is perfectly normal sized, as is my head, thank you,' he retorted. 'So, are we going to talk about the elephant in the room?'

'We're outside.'

Aiden rolled his eyes. 'Why do you always have a terrible come-back? I'm talking, Olivia, about you asking a man out. I wanted to check you were okay – you haven't got a fever, have you?' he said, attempting to check the temperature of my forehead. 'You're acting very out of character. Maybe I should call Dan.'

'You'll ruin my hair, stop it!' I quickly ducked away from his hand, worried about how more skin contact with Aiden would make me feel. 'And maybe it isn't out of character – you don't know. Maybe I ask men out all the time!'

Aiden snorted. 'I may not see you much but I talk to Dan every day, and I get the gossip from him. Although when it comes to you, there is never any gossip.'

Ugh, I hated the fact that he was right.

I sighed. 'Fine, okay, it's not a normal occurrence but Jasper is nice and he's quite shy – I knew he'd never ask me out so I thought why not?'

'He's nice?' Aiden raised an eyebrow as he took a bite of his sandwich.

'There's nothing wrong with nice,' I said, though I wasn't sure if I was trying to convince him or me. 'Anyway, it's just to the film festival. I probably would have seen him there anyway, it's not a big deal. Let's change the subject. How is your first day going?'

Aiden looked suspicious. 'That's a normal question to ask me. I don't trust it.'

I shrugged as I took the final bite of my salad. 'I know it's tough on your first day, not knowing anyone...'

'I know you.'

'More's the pity.'

'It's going fine, thanks. I really like it here, everyone has been friendly, and the facilities are great.' He smiled and I could see he was enjoying himself. 'I'm going to be able to put my stamp on the courses. Oh, here.' He held out a piece of paper. 'I'm asking people to leave suggestions for the theme of the film festival in the box outside my office. I thought you'd want to join in.'

I stared at the card. 'Why?'

'Because you love telling me what to do,' he said, passing it over.

'That's true and I do have excellent movie taste,' I replied. I swivelled around to face him then. 'I'm always here in the library, you know, if you need me,' I said.

'Is that a threat or a promise?' he asked, looking back at me, the sun making his green eyes seem even brighter than usual.

'I'm not completely sure,' I said, holding his gaze even though I felt a strong urge to look away.

'I guess I'll find out,' he said. Then he stood up so suddenly I let out a gasp.

'Why are you so melodramatic? I have a meeting. I'll see you at home later, roomie,' he said and with a grin, he walked off as quickly as he had appeared.

I took a breath before getting up and hurrying back to the library. I shivered as I stepped back inside out of the sun and paused in the doorway, looking at the card in my hand. I grabbed a pen out of my pocket and wrote down a suggestion for the theme. On my way back to the library, I dropped the card into the suggestion box Aiden had left outside his office.

I glanced at the name plate on the door – *Professor Rivers* – and shook my head. It was still so strange to think of him as a professor, of leading the department here, of him being serious full stop.

I supposed I'd see him actually working when I came to the film festival on Saturday.

While I was on a date with Jasper.

It was going to be quite a day.

12

I wasn't working in the library again until Thursday so I was able to write more of my book. Adam and Lily started working together at his beach café and they were both very much in the 'pretending we hate one another' phase, which was a hell of a lot of fun to write. I hardly saw Aiden as he was spending so much time settling in at his new job and going out for drinks with colleagues in the evenings, which I tried not to be jealous of. Since starting at the university, I'd found there was a definite split between administrative staff and the lecturers and professors, which was why Stevie and I had become such good friends. Aiden belonged in a different camp to us, but then again, maybe that wasn't such a bad thing. If it wasn't like that, I would be seeing him a whole lot more so I let him get on with it.

On Wednesday, I helped Dan take some photos and a video for a brand at a new restaurant in Notting Hill. It was very aesthetic but the portions were small so when we came home, we decided to make pasta together.

'So, are you still staying over at Theo's on Saturday?' I asked casually as I pulled ingredients out of the fridge and Dan put his apron on. I had been unsure how much to mention Theo as Dan didn't seem to want to talk about it. I pulled out two glasses and poured us wine.

'Yeah. He's been working flat out to finish his latest piece so he can show it to the gallery. Saturday will be the only time I can see him.' Dan started to chop vegetables while I took a sip of my wine. 'Theo wants to just chill at his flat so you'll have to navigate your date without me,' he added with a sly grin.

I sighed. 'I'm never going to hear the end of me asking Jasper out, am I? I thought Aiden was bad enough...'

'I'm sorry. I think it's great. And it's a work thing anyway so less pressure, right?'

'Right,' I agreed, then bit my lip. 'Although I suppose we will be surrounded by colleagues, which could be awkward if it's an epic fail. I bet everyone will gossip about it. Apparently, a couple of years ago, two married professors got divorced and the whole staff took sides. It turned ugly and they both ended up quitting. People still talk about it now.'

Dan looked at me. 'I hardly think you need to worry about getting a divorce. Don't do what you usually do and talk yourself out of this before it's even something.'

'I don't do that!'

'You know you do,' he replied. 'Pass me the onion. Can you get out the cheese? We need all the cheese.'

I got out the cheese and started to grate it. I thought about what Dan had just said. I supposed there was some truth to me dismissing potential dates. It was always easier to tell yourself it wouldn't work out so why even bother trying? I had always believed if I met someone special, I'd know instantly. I sighed. 'Okay, I promise I will give this date with Jasper a chance.'

'At least there won't be much talking required as you'll be at a film festival.'

'True. I still think it's so strange Aiden running an event at my university. Stevie told me that everyone is talking about it. Loads of people seem to be going.'

'I'm glad he's settling in well.'

We heard the door open.

'Speak of the devil,' I muttered, finding myself grating the cheese even harder.

'Hello, hello, something smells good,' Aiden said as he walked into the room.

I glanced over my shoulder. He still had his work suit on and his hair was tousled from the breeze outside. He looked a little stressed, a slight crease visible on his forehead.

'Enough for three?'

'Of course. You can add some bacon into it if you want?' Dan said. 'Liv, pour the man a glass of wine, he looks like he needs it.'

'Actually, I do,' Aiden said as he perched on a bar stool. 'I was in a five-hour department meeting today. Five hours of my life I'm never getting back.'

I watched as he took his tie off and slipped off his jacket. He tossed them onto the sofa then pushed the sleeves of his white Oxford shirt up.

'Here,' I said, unable to take my eyes off his movements.

'Thanks, Olivia,' he said, for once no hint of mocking in his tone. He took the glass and gulped two mouthfuls down. Then he looked at me properly. 'Why are you wearing that dress to cook in?'

He gave it the once over. I'd found it in a vintage shop down the road – it was pink gingham and I was wearing it because the restaurant we'd been to was mostly decorated in pink. My hair was in waves and I had pink lip gloss on to complete the look. It was very cottagecore.

'I couldn't be bothered to change after Dan took me out. It worked perfectly for the pictures.' I picked up my phone and showed him a particularly good one Dan had got of me in one of the pink booths. 'Dan matched too but he said he didn't want to get pasta sauce on his shirt.' I showed him Dan's pink shirt in another picture. Then I gave him a twirl. 'I felt like I was about to run through a meadow full of flowers most of the day, which is a vibe. You just have no fashion appreciation,' I said, going back to my cheese grating.

'I didn't say I didn't like it,' Aiden said. 'I know you like to dress to fit where you're going, right down to the smallest detail. What, pray tell me, are you planning to wear on Saturday?'

I handed Dan the plate of cheese and breathed in the garlicky tomato smell of the sauce he was mixing. It smelled delicious.

'That's a good question actually. Can you give me a hint to the theme you chose – what films are we going to be watching?' I asked, leaning against the counter in front of him.

'I could tell you,' Aiden said, also leaning on his chin. I could have sworn I noticed his eyes dropping to the neckline of my dress for an instant. But then I told myself I must have imagined it because I did not want to think about him noticing anything below my neckline. 'But then I'd have to kill you.'

'Well, I hope you've made good choices; the whole university will be judging you.'

For a second, he seemed to look nervous and I felt bad. Then he grinned. 'Or they will be too busy watching you and Jasper to focus on the films.'

Now it was my turn to look nervous.

'Don't put her off,' Dan warned as he added the cheese to the saucepan. 'She's already telling herself this date is a bad idea. And she hasn't been on one for ages.'

'Thanks, dear brother,' I said dryly, then took a big glug, finishing my wine off to help calm myself. I looked at the bottle, then at Aiden, and decided I'd better not have any more in case I let down my guard too much and gave him some sort of ammunition to use against me. 'Why are you so obsessed with my date anyway?'

'I'm only saying there's a lot of gossip about the two of you at work,' Aiden replied with a shrug. 'I don't care. I just don't see it.'

'Oh, really?' Dan asked. 'She's worried he's too nice.'

'He *is* nice,' Aiden said. 'I don't think there's much chemistry.'

'Like you know about chemistry,' I said with a snort. 'Jasper is very handsome and intelligent and he's really kind.'

'Well, I hope he's good enough for you,' Dan said. 'Is he, Aiden?'

'I hardly know him,' he replied. 'But I think you should be worried for the man, not Olivia. I reckon she could eat him for breakfast.'

'I'm not some 1940s femme fatale,' I hissed. Aiden looked like he was about to argue, but I continued speaking before he could. 'When have I ever broken a man's heart?'

Dan nudged me. 'Your last boyfriend? He was smitten. When he asked you to go on a family holiday, you broke up with him instead.'

'Well, that was crazy. I'd only met them once. A holiday with someone else's family?' I shuddered at the very thought.

'I'm kind of with you on that,' Dan acknowledged. 'But still, he was head over heels.'

'She's too picky,' Aiden said.

'Hang on,' I said, holding my hand up. 'One minute you're telling me Jasper is too nice and we have no chemistry then you say I'm too picky. Which is it?' I demanded, irritated with the both of them.

'Generally, you're too picky but this time, you seem to have chosen the kind of man your mum would like,' Aiden replied.

He was probably right, but I couldn't admit that I'd mostly done it just to wind him up so all I could do was smile. 'Well, good. Maybe I've realised I'm being too picky. Maybe Jasper is just what I need. Boyfriend material, unlike *some* people.' I gave him a significant look. I'd been surprised to see him have such a long relationship with his ex, Zara, convinced he'd mess it up. I was still reeling to discover he hadn't.

'More like old married couple material. I can picture you both now wearing matching slippers and watching the *Antiques Roadshow* together wondering what "chemistry" even is,' Aiden said, his voice dripping with sarcasm.

'Well, we might not have spectacular chemistry yet, but at least I know he wouldn't cheat on me,' I snapped, my temper getting the best of me. I saw pain flash across Aiden's face at the mention of his ex and I wished I could take it back, but then I decided he shouldn't dish it out if he couldn't handle it. He was criticising Jasper but it wasn't like he was any better. He really had no place giving me relationship advice.

'Right, anyway, dinner is ready,' Dan said, clearing his throat over the sudden awkwardness.

I helped him dish up, and when I turned back, Aiden had finished his glass of wine and was typing on his phone.

Not wanting to get into another argument with him, I said, 'I promised I'd FaceTime Stevie so I'll take this into my room.' It was a lie.

I carried my plate out of the kitchen before they could stop me.

This just proved that the sooner Aiden found a place to move into, the better. We never had dinner together or talked about our personal lives, and it clearly wasn't something that we should get used to.

I tried to ignore the tiny pit of sadness in my stomach I felt about that fact and tucked into my pasta. As I sat on my bed, I wondered what Aiden and Dan were talking about in the kitchen but knew it was better for all of us that I stayed where I was.

13

I worked in the library Thursday and Friday but the days were long and dull as Stevie had that time off and there was a backlog of overdue book emails to send so I was mostly stuck at the desk. I usually enjoyed the library when it was peaceful but I had so much restless energy for Saturday that I couldn't relax.

I also felt blocked with the book I was writing. I needed a moment between my leading lady and her love interest that would provide a shift in their relationship, and readers would know that there was more to what was happening than they first thought. It had been a long time since I'd had that kind of moment with anyone and I couldn't come up with anything, maybe because I was so nervous for my date. I wasn't sure if it was something that might happen with Jasper or not. Or if I wanted it to.

So, by the time Saturday arrived, I was on the edge of a meltdown about it all and I woke up early after a rubbish night's sleep.

'Thank God for concealer,' I muttered to myself as I caught sight of the dark circles under my eyes. I sleepily went into the kitchen for coffee and found Aiden already in there, wearing shorts and a T-shirt, and drinking water. He'd evidently been to the gym and he looked far too bright-eyed and bushy-tailed for my liking.

'You're up early,' I said, walking over to the coffee machine.

'I have to get to the university early to set up so went to the gym first thing. I'm just going to have a quick shower then head off.' He finished his water, watching as I made my coffee. 'Rough night?'

'I couldn't sleep. And don't say it's because I'm nervous about my date,' I warned.

Aiden smiled. 'I wouldn't dream of it. I'll leave you to your coffee in peace. See you at the festival.' I eyed him suspiciously as he walked off. He was cheerful and not being horrible; it was worrying.

I took a gulp of the hot, strong coffee, hoping it would revive me. At least most of the day would involve sitting and watching films; no physical exertion was needed.

When I heard Aiden leave the bathroom, I went in and had a steamy shower before walking into my room and standing in front of my wardrobe. As I had no idea what the theme was for the day, I decided I'd just channel Audrey Hepburn, one of my all-time favourite film stars. Plus, I wanted to be as comfortable as possible.

I pulled on cigarette-style trousers, a black boat-neck top to match and ballet flats. I added a pearl necklace, perfume and a pop of red lipstick, hoping that Audrey Hepburn would lend me her poise today because I really would need it. I grabbed my black vintage bag, which I'd found in a charity shop, and then headed out.

'You look very chic,' Dan said. He was scrolling on his phone while he ate breakfast. 'Aiden has already gone.'

'He said he had to set up. I'm going to walk in. I said I'd meet Jasper by the coffee cart to caffeinate before we go in. I need all the coffee today so I'm happy with past me for making that suggestion.'

Dan looked at me. 'You do look a bit tired.'

'I didn't sleep well.'

'I hope you're not nervous about today? Dates should be fun, not stressful.'

'I'm a tiny bit in my head about it,' I admitted. 'It's always so easy in romance novels or in films. A couple meets, it's cute, they have an immediate spark – it helps that they're both stunning, of course – and then they navigate the tiny obstacles thrown in their way to live happily ever after. Real life is not like that. When I first met Jasper, he blushed and I babbled about a book he hadn't even heard of!'

'That sounds cute,' Dan argued. 'I'm not going to tell you real life is like a book because I know only too well it isn't,' he said. 'But don't sabotage yourself before you even get there. Don't put so much pressure on it. If it doesn't go well, what does it matter? It's one day, Liv. You are such a hopeless romantic, you look at every man you meet as either the Darcy to your Elizabeth or someone who's not even worth getting a coffee with. There is some grey in between. You might even have fun.'

I went over and gave him a kiss on the cheek.

'I know, you're right. I should give Jasper a chance and not think about whether there is a future. There doesn't have to be. We can just have a lovely date. And so can you with Theo,' I reminded him.

'We've kind of forgotten that, with all our talk of the future. So if anything, please learn from us and don't do that.'

'Do as you say, not as you do?'

'Exactly.'

I paused before I left. 'I hope you can work it out. I think you and Theo belong together. And that's even scarier than feeling like I do – that you'll never meet anyone you belong with.'

'I'm not going to argue with that,' he replied. 'I'm bloody terrified. God, what are we like?'

'Okay, let's make a promise to not be scared. Let's get through the day not worrying about the future.' I held out my pinkie finger.

Dan grinned. 'Deal.' He made a pinkie promise with me. 'Enjoy the films. Text me an update later.'

'Will do.'

I headed out and was happy to see it was a pleasant morning in the city so I could enjoy my walk to the university. I needed the fresh air to help wake me up and it was always nice to do this walk when I didn't have to rush. Everyone around me seemed to be having a lazy Saturday stroll too and I even received a couple of friendly smiles, which was unusual. There was a cool breeze, promising that autumn was on the way, but for now, I would enjoy not having to wear a thick coat. Dan had been right when he said I looked at potential love interests with a sceptical eye, that if they weren't sending me long-term relationship signals, there was no point in getting involved at all. It hadn't exactly worked out for me this far though. I was still single and had never had a serious relationship.

What if I was being too picky? Aiden had annoyed me with all those things he'd said but his words had left a mark.

The university came into view then and I could see the coffee cart opening up for the day. People were already strolling into the building. There was a buzz in the air. We didn't have many events like this; plus, everyone was curious about the newest member of the faculty.

I saw Jasper waiting for me, wearing a pair of trousers, a grey jumper, shiny black shoes and black-framed glasses. I supposed he'd need them for the films. As he walked towards the cart, I eyed him as objectively as I could. He was a good height. Not as tall as Aiden but taller than me and he had great hair. It was thick and fair and framed his face nicely.

Jasper lifted a hand in a wave and smiled broadly. He looked really pleased to see me, which was sweet.

'Morning, Liv. You look lovely,' he said when I reached him. 'I wasn't sure how cold it would be in the theatre so I thought I'd better wear a jumper.' He ran a hand through his hair.

He was nervous; I sensed it immediately. Which again, was sweet.

'Good idea. It looks cosy. Shall we get a coffee then find seats? We want a good view.'

'I asked Aiden to reserve two for us so we don't need to worry.'

I wondered where Aiden would lump us.

We went to the cart and Jasper paid for our drinks: a latte for him and an iced coffee for me.

'Shall we?' Jasper led the way inside the university, towards the theatre at the back of the main building.

It was an impressive room. Seats rose around in a semi-circle with a table in the middle where Aiden was fiddling with a projector. A huge white screen at the front of the room hung from the ceiling. The seats were filling up with mostly students but a few staff members had also come along, a couple of whom went over to talk to Aiden. Jasper gestured to a row of seats where he spotted our names written on card. Before I followed, I glanced over at Aiden. He was wearing jeans and a shirt with a tie, mixing his usual work attire with what I usually saw him in. I lifted my eyes away up to the white screen, on which some holding text was displayed:

Welcome to our first annual film festival

This year's theme is:

Kissing in the Rain

I let out a gasp.

Aiden had used my theme suggestion! Films that had scenes

where characters kissed in the rain. I'd put it in his suggestion box. Had he chosen it at random? Or had he recognised my handwriting? I couldn't help but hope he had. Either way, he had loved the idea so much he'd chosen it for today. I smiled. I couldn't wait to see the films he had picked.

14

'Welcome everyone,' Aiden said ten minutes later when everyone had settled into their seats. 'Thank you for coming. We'll have people dropping in and out all day, and feel free to skip a film if you need yet another coffee,' he said. I was sure his eyes rested on me when he said that last part. 'As you know, I've just started here as the new head of this department and I'm really excited to get to know you all this semester. My office door is always open if you want to talk about anything.'

I looked around and all the students were listening to Aiden, rapt. I'd been wrong when I thought he could never be serious – he had the room in the palm of his hand.

'I had some brilliant suggestions for themes today but I was struck by an unusual one that asked for movies that have scenes where the characters kiss in the rain. I took this as a challenge as I'd never really thought about it before, and you'll realise over the next few months I do love a good challenge.' His eyes twinkled. 'So, sit back, relax and enjoy these films, but if you're in my class, I'm expecting a healthy debate on them on Monday so don't relax too much.'

A few students tittered at that.

Aiden nodded and someone turned the lights right down as the first film started.

Breakfast at Tiffany's.

'I wore the right outfit then,' I said excitedly to Jasper. I loved this film, and the scene at the end in the rain with the cat was so emotional.

'Oh yes, it isn't as cold as I thought it would be in here,' Jasper hissed back, leaning in so I could hear him over the film starting.

I stared at him. Oh dear, that was a failure of communication. I eyed him curiously, wondering how old he actually was. I'd assumed four or five years older than me but now I was wondering if he might be even older.

'I assume this one meets with your approval,' a voice on the other side of me said.

I jumped in my seat as I turned to see Aiden's face lit up by the projector screen. Of course he'd reserved the seat beside me. I should have guessed when he'd looked so cheerful this morning.

'Aiden,' I said through gritted teeth.

Jasper leaned over me to speak to him. 'Thank you for saving our seats. Such an unusual theme to choose. I'm intrigued. I've never seen this film.'

I tried not to let my mouth fall open. At least we were in semi-darkness.

'No problem,' Aiden said, leaning over me to reply, his arm brushing against mine. I pulled my arm away instantly.

'Why are you always so jumpy?' Aiden asked as he leaned away again and Jasper turned his attention back to the film. 'Anyway, can you guess my other choices? I bet you wish you could change outfit for each one.'

I hated that he was right.

'You should have warned me to wear waterproof mascara, what

with this film and another one I assume you must have chosen as it is *the* best kissing in the rain scene.'

'So, if a man wants to kiss you in the rain they have to give advance notice so you can tailor your makeup accordingly?' Aiden whispered back.

As the light was so dim and he couldn't see, I let myself smile at that. 'I'd allow it as a spontaneous moment.'

'I doubt Jasper has ever considered kissing someone in the rain,' he whispered.

I elbowed him and he gasped dramatically, at which a couple of people looked over.

'Perhaps he's been waiting for the right woman.' I then turned pointedly to talk to Jasper. 'Audrey Hepburn was just so elegant, wasn't she?'

'Old movies are always quite slow, aren't they?' he whispered back.

I picked up my coffee and sipped it to save myself from responding. Aiden chuckled softly beside me so I knew he'd blatantly been listening.

As the film played, I sat there feeling unnerved – in between Jasper, who I wasn't sure I was at all compatible with, and Aiden, who was enjoying every uncomfortable moment.

I wondered if I should smash a panel to set the fire alarm off to get myself out of here.

* * *

After the first film finished, Aiden said there would be a half-hour break so everyone could have a quick refresh and to allow for new people to arrive. We blinked as the lights came back on fully and everyone stretched out and started talking in that way you always do after a long film.

'What did you think?' I asked Jasper, relieved Aiden had left us alone to sort out the next film.

'It was okay. The ending was good,' he said with an easy smile. 'I suppose I usually just watch documentaries so it made a nice change. Are you hungry, shall we get something to eat?'

'Good idea,' I said, trying not to be scandalised that he thought it was just okay. People had different opinions about films, I told myself. It wasn't something to discount a future over, right?

We went outside and I suggested we avoided the cafeteria as I knew we'd see everyone we knew. Instead, we walked just off the university site to a small café I'd been to a few times. They made delicious pastries and cakes there, just what a Saturday called for.

'Find us a table; what would you like?' Jasper said.

I thought I'd better avoid more coffee as I might get jittery so I asked for tea and a slice of chocolate cake, and then left him at the counter and found a table by the window. I took my phone out of my bag. I'd had it on silent and saw on the lock screen I'd had two messages come through: one from Stevie asking for an update and one from Dan saying he hoped I was having a good time.

Then, as I was reading, one came in from Aiden.

You won't want to miss the next film. I'll give you a clue...

A second message arrived. It was a pumpkin emoji.

I stared at my phone. Aiden rarely ever sent me messages. And I'd never seen him use an emoji before. I put my phone away as I saw Jasper was heading back, my mind racing with what the film could be.

'Thank you,' I said, taking my cake and tea from him. He sat down with his toasted sandwich and an orange juice. 'I don't usually have cake for lunch but it's so good here.'

'It looks it. I try to avoid sugar as it stops me sleeping,' he said.

'So, how are things in the library? I didn't get a chance to pop in much this week; we've had so much admin to do lately.'

We chatted about work for a while as we ate. It felt comfortable, like the other times we'd chatted around the university.

'I think people are enjoying the film festival,' I said once we'd run out of things to say. 'Aiden sent me a clue about the next film but I haven't worked it out. A pumpkin emoji. What do you think?'

Jasper looked confused. 'A pumpkin?'

'Could be a nod to Halloween, but I can't think of any films that have a kissing in the rain scene.'

'I have no idea,' he said with a shrug. 'So, Aiden seems to be settling in well. He said he was staying with you?'

Oh, did he?

'Well, it's my brother's flat and it's only until he finds a place of his own,' I said. 'He's my brother's best friend. We don't really hang out.'

'I didn't get that impression,' Jasper said with surprise. 'Aiden spoke of you as a close family friend and made it sound like you spent a lot of time together. I think he's grateful to have you here. This job is a step up for him and he admitted he's a little bit nervous. I think he'll do great but I know your opinion means a lot to him. To me too, of course.'

I was the confused one now. 'Aiden said that?' I knew Dan had said Aiden was nervous but I really hadn't thought that me being here would have helped him. I'd assumed he was as annoyed as me that we now had to live and work together.

'I told you when I showed him around that he said you'd spoken so highly about working here, it had encouraged him to come for the interview,' Jasper replied.

Knowing I hadn't spoken to Aiden since I'd started working in the library, I assumed he had taken that opinion from Dan telling him that I was enjoying my new job. That meant they spoke about me when I wasn't there. I would ordinarily be annoyed on learning that, feeling sure Aiden was trying to find out things he could use as ammunition, but Jasper was saying he'd used it to make a big life decision for himself.

I sipped my coffee to cover not knowing what to say. I couldn't tell Jasper we were enemies now Aiden had spoken of us being friends.

I had no idea what to make of what Jasper had just told me. Questions swirled in my mind. My opinion was important to Aiden? He was grateful I was around for his new job? Did Aiden really see it that way? There had been a time when I had hoped Aiden would be as important to me as he was to Dan but I'd had to forget about that. And since then, I'd kept as far away as I could.

'I love that Aiden is so passionate about films, like you are about books,' Jasper was saying, drawing me back to the here and now. I forced Aiden out of my head. There was no point in thinking back to our past. I was on a date with someone else. Who I needed to focus on.

'Well, how about you? What are you passionate about?' I leaned on the table and gave him an encouraging smile.

'I don't think I have anything. I enjoy my work, I like watching documentaries like I said, and I like walking around the city.'

'Oh, me too! What are your favourite places?' I said, grasping hold of something in common. Jasper started to describe a walk around Hyde Park he liked to go on and the rest of lunch flew by.

We walked back to find Aiden by the door to the theatre talking to a couple of the professors. All eyes turned curiously to the two of us.

'Ah, here they are,' Aiden said. 'We wondered where you'd disappeared to.'

'We had some food at a charming café nearby,' Jasper said,

smiling at me. 'Liv says she's worked out the film you're showing next.'

'Oh, you have?' Aiden raised an eyebrow.

'The pumpkin didn't mean it was Halloween themed but Cinderella. More specifically, the teen modern spin on it, featuring a very cute kissing in the rain scene – *A Cinderella Story!*'

One of the professors, I think he was in the English department but I hadn't spoken to him much, shook his head.

'How can you show that at a film festival?' he said to Aiden.

'We're working to a very specific topic today,' Aiden replied. 'Someone suggested films with kissing in the rain scenes. Olivia is right, and the scene is great because it is the culmination of a theme throughout the film, the fact the story takes place during a drought.'

'I love a teen reworking of a classic,' I said, giving the professor a haughty look. 'Especially the Shakespeare ones like *She's the Man* or *Ten Things I Hate About You*, not to mention *Clueless* being based on *Emma*. Maybe you could use them on your course so students understand the classics a bit better?'

The professor looked thoroughly horrified.

I turned to Jasper. 'Let's find our seats.'

I laughed as soon as we were out of earshot. 'Some of the professors here are really snooty. I've probably read just as many of the classics as him but I only work in the library, he's an academic. Yawn.'

Jasper seemed unsure as to what to make of what had just happened. 'The library is very important to this university,' he said firmly.

Okay, so we didn't have the same sense of humour but that was okay too.

'Thanks, Jasper, I think you'll enjoy this one.'

'I'll just go to the facilities, won't be a minute,' he said, leaving me to sit down.

Aiden came over instantly. 'There goes our invite to the English department drinks,' he said with a grin. 'I only went to the one on Monday because I thought you'd be there. You didn't tell me the lecturers all hide out in this dingy pub where they slag all the admin staff off all night.'

'I'm glad I've never been invited then. Honestly, it's like being back at school sometimes. You probably shouldn't be seen talking with me now I'm the enemy.'

'As if I care what they think. And I can't really avoid it, roomie. You know what, the next drinks, you're coming along – it'll be a huge scandal.' Looking thoroughly delighted by that idea, he strode off to start the next film.

I shook my head. Aiden could always be counted on to stir up a little bit of trouble and I could always be counted on to pretend I didn't like it, despite loving every minute.

The lights dimmed again and the film started. A figure came over and sat down next to me.

'It's much fuller now,' I whispered to who I thought was Jasper.

'These are the only free seats,' Aiden whispered back.

Startled, I watched as Jasper came in and sat down on the other side of Aiden.

I turned. The rest of the row was full up. Aiden had claimed the seat between us.

'What are you doing?' I hissed at him, which earned me a couple of 'shhhh's – I realised it must be annoying when I did the same thing to people in the library.

'What? He wasn't here,' he whispered back.

I couldn't see him clearly but I would have bet all the money in my bank account that irritating smirk was on his face again.

15

'Your boyfriend has fallen asleep,' Aiden leaned over to whisper as the kissing in the rain scene was about to start on the screen ahead. I'd always found *A Cinderella Story* super cute but I'd had trouble concentrating with Aiden stuck in the middle of me and Jasper. That and the fact my first date with him really wasn't going at all well.

I glanced over and sure enough, Jasper was asleep. Film festivals were definitely not his scene (pun intended!).

'He's bored out of his mind next to you; I'm not surprised,' I whispered back. 'Why are you so intent on ruining my date?'

The film distracted me for a moment as Hilary Duff got the guy just as it started to rain. I watched, thinking as I always did that kissing in the rain was so romantic. You didn't care about anything happening around you, or your ruined hair and makeup, because you were swept up in the moment, kissing the man you loved. That was all that mattered.

I sighed. Why did that never happen to me?

Aiden leaned over. 'If I was trying to, I wouldn't have had to try too hard. Your date is asleep, Olivia!' He looked so pleased with himself. I really wished I hadn't finished my drink so I could throw the rest of it all over him.

I snapped. 'So, I'm so boring I send all men to sleep, is that what you think?' I turned back to the film, crossing my arms over my chest, fuming. When Aiden started to say something else, I ignored him and watched as the final moments of the film played.

When it had ended, I jumped up and pushed past Aiden's legs. I reached down and touched Jasper. 'Wake up, the film has finished,' I said as the screen went blank and someone turned the lights up. Aiden said my name and started to reach for my arm as Jasper woke up, but I ignored them both.

Tired of this so-called date, I walked out of the aisle and headed for the exit, furious with Aiden and myself for letting him get to me. And a little bit furious with Jasper too because he didn't seem at all bothered by Aiden sitting in his seat and had then slept through the film.

I marched out of the university building, letting the double doors swing behind me and bang against the wall. Outside, the sky had turned an ominous grey and I had no umbrella or coat. This day really wasn't going my way.

'Liv!'

I turned to see Jasper coming outside behind me.

'I'm so sorry I fell asleep,' he said, looking sheepish.

'I think that's the first time I've had a date fall asleep on me!'

'Oh God, it was nothing to do with you... I was up late working and films always make me sleepy. I should have taken you some-where else for our first date. I'm so sorry,' he said, looking aghast at what had happened.

I shrugged. 'It's okay,' I said, but I was disappointed my first date in so long had gone this badly.

'I really feel terrible,' Jasper continued. 'I've been wanting to ask you out for a while. Could I have a second chance and take you out for dinner soon?'

I hesitated, not sure if there was any point, but he looked so apologetic that I gave a tight nod.

'Yeah, maybe. I think I've had enough films for the day though. I'm going to head home.'

'Professor Davies needs to talk to me,' he said, hovering a little awkwardly.

'You go back, I'm fine,' I insisted, quite happy to head home alone. 'Rain check.' (I really was on fire with the puns today!)

'Definitely.' Jasper leaned in and my body stiffened. He gave me a quick peck on the cheek and I exhaled in relief as he walked away.

I turned to go but heard the doors open again.

'Olivia,' Aiden said, coming outside, his hands in his pockets. He looked up at the sky. 'I think it's going to rain. Want a lift home in the break before the next film? Or are you going to stay? I've picked two classics for the afternoon – *Four Weddings and a Funeral* and *The Notebook*.'

I stared at him incredulously. 'After what you've been like all morning, you honestly think I'd go back in there with you? I get that you enjoy making me miserable but I thought you'd behave more professionally in front of someone who is the assistant to our boss!'

'Jasper is fine, I just spoke to him. He feels bad for falling asleep. He knows we're old family friends.'

I threw my hands up. 'We are not friends!' I didn't understand how Aiden was so conveniently forgetting what had happened between us that had made us enemies.

The heavens opened then in a lovely burst of irony and it started to rain. In a very unromantic way.

Aiden walked closer. 'Look, I knew you weren't really into Jasper. I was trying to help.'

'You never help. And how do you know that anyway?'

He shrugged. 'I can see it. I told you – you have no chemistry.'

'You have no idea who I have chemistry with,' I replied, stepping closer until we were inches apart. My heart was hammering in my chest. I'd never felt so riled up by someone. I pushed my damp hair off my face. 'You just wanted to ruin my date because you don't want to see me happy.'

Aiden's mouth fell open. 'You can't really think that. I just know you won't be happy with him.'

'Oh, right. Okay then, if you're such an expert then tell me – who would I be happy with?' I challenged.

We stared at one another, the air between us thick with tension. The rain was coming down in earnest now but we both ignored it.

'I...' Aiden started but his words faded away. He shook his head, as if he wasn't sure what to say. 'Olivia...'

The way he said my name sent a shiver down my spine. He sounded breathless. Like I'd knocked the wind out of him.

I sucked in a breath as I looked into his eyes. My stomach gave a very big flip as I heard his ragged breaths. I was furious with him. But the heat under my skin felt like something else entirely. I had no idea what Aiden was feeling right now. But the way he was looking at me suggested he might be feeling the same heat...

'Olivia,' he said again but this time he half-growled it. His eyes had turned as dark as the sky above us. I watched him shift on his feet. Was he thinking about closing that gap between us? Did I want him to?

I swallowed hard. My body felt like it was on fire. I was pissed off at him but couldn't deny that he looked so gorgeous, his hair damp from the rain, his chest rising in time with mine. Why did he have to look so good?

There was a hum of energy between us and it was both terrifying and exhilarating. I wanted to run but I wanted to stay and never leave too.

There was a clap of thunder then, which startled us both.

I looked away and came back to my senses. I inhaled and reminded myself who I was speaking to.

And thankfully, the spell was broken.

'I have to go,' I said, not realising until I said the words that that was exactly what he'd said to me the last time we'd had a moment like this. I was glad that this time it was me who was going to walk away.

I spun around and took off across the courtyard.

'Wait, Olivia, you'll get soaked!' he yelled after me, but I carried on. I couldn't face staying with him a moment longer. I had to get away. Before I did something I would regret. I had been torn between slapping Aiden and grabbing hold of him and kissing him. Both completely out of character.

Why did he do this to me? It was like he had a button he could press that left me a complete mess.

As I walked, the rain washed over me slowly, calming me down like a much-needed cold shower. I finally realised I was getting soaked. When there was another clap of thunder, I took cover in an archway of a building and watched as people dashed about madly trying to find cover, putting up umbrellas or frantically trying to hail black cabs which were hard to see through the thick sheets of rain. I stood there trying to catch my breath, wrapping my arms around myself as the dampness settled on my skin. My clothes were stuck to me. My hair clung to my cheeks. My heart was pounding.

I didn't understand what had just happened. My feelings were a jumbled mess.

I pulled out my phone and ordered an Uber before I gave myself a cold, and as I waited for it, I told myself to stop thinking about Aiden. But it was impossible. He was all I could think about. My whole body was attuned to him. I had been so angry with him. But mostly because out there in the rain, I had wanted him.

And it was a feeling I'd worked so hard to supress over the last few years, but it had spilled out. And now it was all over me just like the rain.

There had been a moment back there where I'd wondered if he felt the same. If he had wanted me too.

My mind slipped back to ten years ago as I remembered he'd had the same look in his eyes as he had just now. It had made me think he wanted to kiss me. But I'd misread that look once before.

I shook my damp hair. Longing trickled through my veins. But I couldn't let myself feel it. Not after what had happened last time.

'Crap,' I said out loud, my voice covered by the storm. The storm that mimicked my turbulent feelings. Closing my eyes, I went right back to that night.

The first time I'd met Aiden.

16

TEN YEARS AGO…

It was a Saturday night in July when I'd first met Aiden. I was seventeen and after reading a Felicity Fowler book, I was hooked on romance novels and the idea that one day I'd find my soulmate. Dan and Aiden were two years older than me and Dan had been talking non-stop about the new friend he'd made at the cinema he had a part-time job at. Someone they worked with was throwing a party so Dan invited me and my best friend at the time, Katy, to come as well.

I was so excited to be at what I saw as a 'grown-up' party and I spent hours getting ready with Katy. I wore skinny jeans and a black corset-style top with my hair loose, and I did my eyes smoky and spritzed my mum's perfume all over me. Mum dropped me and Katy at the party as Dan had gone straight from the cinema and was meeting us there. It was high summer and the air was thick with humidity and promise.

'Liv!' Dan called me over when we arrived, and we weaved our way through teenagers drinking cheap alcohol. Everyone around us was talking at high volume over the pulsing bass coming from two speakers in the living room. I even remember there was a Miley

Cyrus song playing, that was how vivid the memory of that night still was.

I walked over to Dan, with Katy, and looked at the guy he was standing with. It was like the world suddenly slowed down as Dan leaned in to shout an introduction to the friend he had been talking about non-stop all summer. I was only half listening as I looked up at Aiden, already so much taller than me, and when you're that age someone two years older and taller always sparks your intertest.

Our eyes met and there it was. The moment all my favourite books talked about. Sparks flew as I looked into his green eyes and took in his dark hair and smile.

'I've heard a lot about you,' Aiden said, holding out a hand for me.

Shaking his hand felt really grown-up. I took it eagerly, hoping my palms weren't sweaty from the sticky summer heat, and when his skin touched mine, it felt like his hand had always belonged in mine.

'Me too,' I shouted back, wishing he would keep holding on but he let go to say hi to Katy. I wished that she wasn't wearing her pretty black dress, longing for his eyes to come back to me.

'Drinks?' Dan suggested and he set off for the kitchen, the rest of us following, Aiden then me then Katy. I watched his back, thinking that he was the best-looking guy I'd ever met. My heart sped up in time with the beat of the music as Aiden handed me a paper cup with beer in and Dan suggested we went into the garden as it was so hot.

Outside, the music was at a better volume. Everyone had spilled onto the lawn as the sun just started to dip in the sky from the warm day.

'I still feel like I smell of popcorn,' Dan complained.

'It never washes out properly, does it?' Aiden agreed. Now I could hear him properly, the Irish accent that Dan had mentioned sounded like the sexiest sound I'd ever heard.

'Do you like working there?' I asked, eager to get him to speak to me.

'I thought I liked films but this guy is obsessed,' Dan said with a grin that suggested this was a familiar conversation between them.

'Liv is book obsessed,' Katy said. I resisted the urge to glare at her, knowing that none of the boys at school were impressed by my love of books.

'Oh yeah? Who is your favourite author?' Aiden turned to look down at me.

'Either Jane Austen or Felicity Fowler,' I said. 'They are both amazing.'

'I just saw a film about an Austen fanatic – *Austenland*,' Aiden said.

My eyes widened. I couldn't believe this gorgeous guy had seen that film. 'Oh my God, isn't it so much fun?'

'There's Sam,' Katy suddenly said. 'I'll just say hi.'

'I'll get us all more drinks,' Dan said, disappearing as well.

I stared at Aiden. We were alone and behind him, the sun moved further towards the horizon, the sky turning a pretty pastel pink. The music in the house slowed down too. 'I love it when the sky looks like this,' I said, looking up.

'It looks like candyfloss.'

'Yes.' I looked at Aiden in surprise. 'I always think that. Although I hate the stuff after I was sick at Thorpe Park when I went on a roller-coaster after eating too much.' I wished I could sink into the ground as Aiden raised an eyebrow and my cheeks turned the same colour as the sky. Why did I tell him that?

Then Aiden chuckled. 'That stuff should come with a warning label. Let's sit and watch the sunset. I've been on my feet at the cinema all day and at the risk of sounding like my dad, I need to sit down.'

'I got a job at the bookshop in town for the summer so I know how you feel; standing all day is the worst,' I said, following him to a bench at the side of the garden.

'Dan said you love it.'

I nodded eagerly. 'I do. It's great to work with something you love all day, isn't it?' I said as we sat down.

Aiden looked across at me. 'That's it, exactly. Whenever someone asks me what I want to do, I always say something in film.'

'I'm the same with books.' We grinned stupidly at one another. I could feel my heart still hammering in my chest as Aiden held my gaze.

I wished I was like a character in a romance novel and could just lean in and kiss him. Then I watched as his eyes dropped to my lips and I knew he was thinking the same thing. I held my breath as Aiden scooted a little bit closer on the bench. Hope soared in me that Aiden could feel the same electricity in the air as me.

'So, do you think we can do it?' Aiden asked softly, leaning in closer so I could hear him. 'Make our dreams come true?'

'I think we should give it a bloody good try,' I said firmly. 'We don't want to end up bitter and hopeless.'

Aiden's lips curved into a smile that made me catch my breath. 'I understand now why Dan talks about you so much.'

'Me too. About you,' I added, flustered.

Aiden reached out. 'You have a hair on your lip gloss.' He brushed it away and I felt my knees tremble, glad I was sitting down. He was close enough to kiss me. Was he going to kiss me? It was all I could think about. Everything went hazy. The pink sky, the party, it all slipped into the background, just leaving Aiden's eyes gazing into my own.

This was it. Finally, I'd get the romantic moment I'd been

longing for.

I leaned in, closing my eyes, ready to feel fireworks, and then…

'I have to go,' Aiden blurted out. He jumped up and my eyes flew open. I leaned back in shock and embarrassment. 'I have to go home. I forgot… I'm sorry,' he said, and turned and rushed back into the party as if there was a fire he was running from.

My face flushed the colour of a lobster. I must have completely misunderstood that moment. I'd been thinking romance, and Aiden had been thinking about how to get away from me. I was humiliated.

After a few minutes, I went back into the party to find Katy and Dan, and to my further embarrassment, I saw Aiden hadn't left at all. He was talking and drinking with his friends.

'Liv! There you are!' Katy slipped out of the crowd and grabbed my hands. 'I couldn't find Sam. Where did Dan go? And his friend? Aiden. How lush is he?'

I looked over her shoulder and saw Aiden's eyes flick to mine. He could hear what she was saying. He was smiling. Was he making fun of me to his mates? Telling them that Dan's silly little sister had tried to kiss him?

I pretended to lean in but shouted back to Katy. 'Ugh, Aiden is the last boy I'd want to kiss,' I told her firmly. I knew calling him a boy when he was nineteen like Dan would add more fire to my burn. I looked again and saw Aiden had turned away. I felt some satisfaction at rescuing my humiliation but the moment of triumph was short-lived. I watched as Aiden joined a group of girls and after a while, he put his arm around one of them. My heart sank. Aiden had clearly not fancied me at all. I felt so stupid for even thinking that he might. For hoping something would happen between us.

And I told myself when I got home, I was right to have said he was the last boy I'd want to kiss.

I'd been telling myself that for ten years.

17

Ever since that night, our interactions had been snarky. Aiden always gave as good as he got. Perhaps he liked the idea of me wanting him even though he didn't feel the same so when I'd made it clear I didn't, he was annoyed.

We've been at war ever since either way. And today was the cherry on top of the cake with how annoying he'd been with me and Jasper.

Then we had that moment in the rain and I wondered if Aiden felt differently about me. But I was glad I had escaped before I got carried away all over again because I had no desire to relive the night we met, to make that same mistake again.

My Uber arrived then, and I dived in thankfully. I couldn't wait to put this shit day behind me.

* * *

The flat was dark, as if it was night time, and disconcertingly quiet when I got home. With Dan staying at Theo's, I was dreading what would happen when Aiden came back from the film festival. I took a deep calming breath as I closed the door. I wished I'd never picked kissing in the rain as the theme for the festival. It had made the whole day just weird.

I went into my room and took off my damp things and pulled on a jogging set. I blasted my hair with the dyer then tied it into a ponytail and pulled on a pair of cosy socks. Finally warm and dry, I went into the kitchen and turned on the lights to make myself a cup of tea.

My mind was still a jumble from the day and my heart was still working at a faster than normal rate. I tried not to picture Aiden's face in the rain but it was impossible. The fire in that look. The darkness of his eyes. That heat between us. I knew I had to forget it though. There was no way it was plaguing Aiden right now. I assumed he'd gone back into the film festival as if nothing had happened. Would he think of me when the next kissing in the rain scene came on?

'Nope,' I said to the empty flat. He wouldn't so I shouldn't. I felt restless though. The moment had left my body thrumming with energy.

I leaned against the counter to sip my tea. The rain was thrashing against the window. I felt like I had to do something.

Then, inspiration struck.

The way that I knew how to make sense of things was to write them down. And I had been stuck with my book, wondering how to create that first moment between my characters. But now I had real life experience to draw on. I knew how to write heat between my characters. If Stevie thought I had based my characters on real people then I would lean into it. Because in real life, nothing could happen between me and Aiden. But in my book, I could create whatever the hell I wanted between us.

Between my characters, I meant.

I grabbed my laptop from my room and curled up on the sofa,

draping a throw over me, and started to write. Slowly, with the help of my cup of tea, I warmed up and my pulse started to slow down. I poured out everything I was feeling into the story, frantically typing out the scene, my nails tapping on the keys, loud enough to cover the sound of the rain.

Lily storms into the kitchen. 'What was that all about?' she demands of Adam as he plates up food. He had just been completely rude to a customer.

'I don't like him,' Adam says with a shrug. 'He was flirting with you.'

'Why would you care even if he was?'

Adam turns to her. 'You were flirting back. It was irritating.'

'I wasn't, but who made you the flirting police? What the hell is wrong with you?'

Adam steps closer. Lily leans against the counter, hitching her breath at his sudden closeness. 'I didn't like it.'

'Why?' Lily's pulse starts to race. She looks into his eyes. They are almost black. His chest is rising and falling with ragged breaths like hers. There's electricity in the air. Lily feels light-headed like she suddenly can't take in enough oxygen.

'You are driving me crazy,' Adam says then. He puts his hands on the counter behind her, on either side of her body.

It would require just a slight shift for him to put those hands on her hips.

Lily craves his touch but she wishes she didn't.

'You have been rude to me since the first day we met and I don't know why but I'm sick of it,' she says, trying to hold on to her anger and not let it slip into desire.

'Right back at you.'

'You started it! With the volleyball...'

Adam closes his eyes for a moment then opens them again. 'I'm trying to keep you away from me. It's better for us both.'

Lily gapes at him. She hadn't expected that. She knows the sensible thing is to turn and walk away, just like he wants, but her body is screaming at her to stay. To pull him closer. She stares at him, her heart pounding.

'Shouldn't I get a say in that?'

She's wrongfooted him again. They stare at one another, heat building between them until the kitchen phone rings out shrilly, making them both jump. The spell is broken and they step apart but both of them know that something has shifted between them.

* * *

I woke up with a jump when the flat door opened. After I had poured my feelings out into my book and sent the scene to Stevie to read, my energy was all but drained, and due to my bad night's sleep and the eventful day, I had accidentally napped. Opening my eyes, I saw the light had dimmed further. It was still raining but clearly the sun had set while I was sleeping.

I heard Aiden walk in. He stopped when he saw me. I held my breath.

'I'm sorry,' he said after a moment. 'Are you okay? You must have got soaked.'

'Fine, I'm all warm and dry now.' I struggled to sit up. 'I fell asleep.'

I reached over to switch a lamp on.

'It's so dark,' I continued. 'It's like we've suddenly hit autumn today.'

I couldn't meet his eyes. I was scared of how my body would react to him if I did. And I was embarrassed. And hated the awkwardness. I wished I had retreated to my room before he'd come home.

'Look,' he said. Reluctantly, I turned around to see him holding up a paper bag. 'I, uh, got us a takeaway. A forgive-me gift. I really am sorry.'

'What is it?' I asked, standing up.

'Chinese – vegetable dumplings, spring rolls, noodles, rice and the cucumber salad,' he said, waving the bag. 'I asked Dan what to get and where to go. He said this is your favourite.'

He looked so hopeful, it was impossible to resist.

'I can't say no to that,' I said, my stomach rumbling on cue.

Aiden broke into a wide smile and began to pull the containers and chopsticks out.

'A drink?' I said as I went into the kitchen.

'After today, hell yes,' Aiden said.

I put the plates out, which Aiden started loading up with the food, and then I got him a beer from the fridge. I poured myself a glass of wine and joined him on the bar stools.

'You're about to have the best Chinese you've ever had,' I said as he picked up his chopsticks. Aiden had got himself sweet and sour chicken, but the rest of the feast we shared. I grabbed a spring roll and took a big bite.

'My expectations are high,' he said as he picked up a mouthful. He moaned. 'Mmm, that is really good. How did you find this place?'

'TikTok, of course,' I replied. 'Dan is always on the lookout for new places to try but this is the best takeaway we've discovered so far.' I paused. 'When you texted him, did he seem okay?' I asked, still unable to believe Aiden went to the effort of asking Dan what food to bring back for me. It didn't make me forget what had happened today but I appreciated that he was trying to make it up to me. He certainly had never done that before. But I supposed we now lived together and things would have been so awkward if he had just ignored our argument.

My mind annoyingly flashed back to him staring at me as it

rained. I was dying to know if he had felt the charge between us but I could never ask him that.

'I think so,' he replied after he'd had some time to think about it. 'Dan said he and Theo were going out for drinks. By the way, I said this was to thank you for your support today, I didn't tell him...'

'That you'd been a twat?' I filled in as he trailed off sheepishly.

'Thanks. I deserve it though,' Aiden said. 'When you go out with Jasper again, I promise to be miles away.'

He lifted his bottle up. I wasn't sure why I felt disappointed by his toast but I clinked my glass against it and then took a long sip.

'He suggested dinner,' I said as I chewed on a mouthful of food. I glanced across but Aiden's expression remained neutral. 'I don't think a film festival was his idea of a good time but it was sweet he wanted to come with me and support you.'

Aiden groaned. 'You're making me feel worse. You're right, he's a good guy.'

'Did the rest of the afternoon go well?' I asked, changing the subject.

'I think so. Everyone was sobbing at the end of *The Notebook*.'

'Even you?'

'I don't have a heart of stone, Olivia,' he replied, the twinkle back in his eyes as he looked across at me.

'I remain unconvinced.'

'Hey, I didn't fall asleep before seeing if Hilary and Chad would live happily ever after.' He held a hand up. 'I'm sorry. No more Jasper jibes, I swear.'

'You just can't help yourself, can you?' I said, shaking my head, but annoyingly there was a smile on my lips.

'Teasing you is my favourite activity,' Aiden said then.

I met his gaze. 'It's not mine!'

'Isn't it?' he challenged. He was smiling now.

My heart picked up speed all over again. In case I said something I couldn't take back, I picked up a prawn cracker and threw it at him. Somehow, he caught it in his mouth.

'That was actually impressive,' I said.

Aiden pretended to take a bow, at which point my phone vibrated with a voice note from Stevie followed by a series of emojis and exclamation marks. I assumed she'd read my new chapter and the rundown of my day I'd messaged her. I quickly turned my phone over so Aiden wouldn't see.

Aiden clocked the movement but didn't say anything. Maybe he would assume it was from Jasper.

'So, am I forgiven for today?' he asked. 'Dan won't come back from Theo's to find you've packed my bags and thrown them and me out on the street?'

'Well, now you're just giving me ideas.' I put my chopsticks down. 'I'm so full; that was just about good enough for me to forgive you.'

'I'll be on my best behaviour from now on.'

I snorted. 'I don't believe that for a second. I know you, Aiden Rivers, and you're always trouble with a capital T.'

I got up to clear away the dinner things.

Aiden watched me for a moment. 'You know, I'm not really. I just think you bring it out in me. You have ever since we first met as teenagers.'

Turning, I tipped our rubbish inside the bin so I could hide the sudden flush to my cheeks. Aiden never talked about us meeting. Neither did I. Slowly, I turned around. 'You know it was you who started this...'

I trailed off then, not sure how I'd ever describe what *this* was.

He stared at me, looking confused. 'What are you talking about? You—'

My phone rang, interrupting him. We both looked at it. I was relieved at the distraction. I really didn't want to talk to Aiden about that night at the party. I wanted to forget it. Like I wanted to forget today had happened. I grabbed the phone.

'I have to take this,' I said, seeing that it was Stevie. 'Look, it's all fine, okay? We don't need to go over the past, it is what it is,' I said then I answered her call, moving past him into my bedroom. I could feel his eyes on my back as I walked away.

I sank against my bedroom door.

'I couldn't wait for you to reply to my voice note,' Stevie said. 'We need to debrief the whole day!'

'I have no idea what just happened,' I said, to her as much as to myself.

'Well, all I can say is poor Jasper,' Stevie said. 'If your chapter is anything to go by, the moment you said you had in the rain with Aiden blew your first date with Jasper out of the water.'

I sighed. The chemistry between me and Jasper was non-existent when you compared it to the heat I had felt with Aiden.

'I need to tell you something about Aiden...' I said. I had to explain about our history and why I had to shake off this pull towards him. It would only end in tears.

And they would be mine.

18

I was in the middle of another dream.

I was wearing a ball gown. One of those pink tulle ones that made you look like a toilet roll holder. I hitched up both sides and tried to run but I was wearing pink stilettos and as I moved, it began to rain. I looked behind me. There was someone chasing me and I was desperate to escape from them, but what with the shoes, the hinderance of the dress and the rain, I was making slow progress. And whoever was behind me was gaining ground.

'Olivia!' My name rang out, echoing though the rain to reach me. The call was full of anguish. Desperation. Whoever it was, they were trying to reach me as badly as I wanted to get away.

'Olivia!'

I realised I recognised that voice. I couldn't escape it.

'Aiden,' I whispered, sure it was him chasing me.

'Olivia!'

My name broke through the dream. A hand shook my shoulder and I started awake. I gasped as my dark bedroom suddenly flooded with light. My breathing ragged, I blinked, trying to get my eyes to adjust after being woken up.

'What the hell?' I gasped, clutching my chest underneath my duvet.

'I'm sorry I scared you,' Aiden said. He was leaning over my bed. 'But I had to wake you up.' He waved his phone. 'Theo just called.'

'What?' I said, still trying to pull myself out of my heavy sleep. I grabbed my phone. It was full of missed calls and messages. My blood ran cold. I looked at Aiden and saw now he was worried.

'What is it?' I asked, my voice coming out as barely more than a croak.

'It's Dan,' he said. 'There has been an accident. Theo is with him at the hospital,' he hurried to reassure me as I gasped and sat bolt upright in bed. 'I don't know what happened. Theo was in a state. But I think a motorbike knocked Dan over.'

'Oh my God,' I said, feeling sick. I pulled back the duvet. 'Where is he?'

'I'll take you to the hospital.' Aiden stepped back as I stood up. He already had jeans and a jumper on. He turned to go then looked back. 'Theo said Dan's hurt but he'll be okay.'

I nodded but panic was setting in. I dashed around trying to find clothes and barely registered Aiden walking out. I grabbed my leggings and threw on a jumper, then I pulled on trainers, picked up my bag and tugged my coat off the hanger as I rushed out.

'Does my mum know?' I asked. Aiden was hovering by the door, his shoes and coat on, keys in hand. I hurried out and he followed me, locking the door behind us.

'Theo said he called her – I think she's on her way too. My car is over there,' he said, pointing. We walked over to it quickly.

We jumped into the Mini and he set off immediately towards the hospital. I chewed on my lip as I watched the world blur past the window. This part of the city was silent, everyone in bed. I glanced at my phone. It was 2 a.m. The rain had eased to a light drizzle but the pavement was dotted with puddles. Above us, there was no sign of the stars.

'Did Theo say anything else?'

'I think they were leaving a club and a bike clipped Dan as they crossed the road.'

'God, I've always been scared of the traffic here. I never actually thought though...' I turned to Aiden, his profile lit by lampposts. I swallowed hard. It felt like there was a lump lodged in my throat. 'What if it's really bad?'

I couldn't bear even thinking it. Ever since our dad left, Dan had been the man in my life. We had always been close but we became even closer after that. We were best friends. And I had been so happy since I moved in with him in London.

Aiden glanced over at me as we stopped at a red light.

'He will be fine. Don't worry.' He reached over and gave my hand one quick squeeze. The light turned green and Aiden let go. We looked away as if it hadn't happened.

Aiden parked outside the hospital and I set off for the double doors without waiting for him to lock the car. I was directed to A and E, and Aiden caught up to me.

We spotted Theo pacing the corridor. He turned when he saw us and looked relieved.

'I'm glad you're here.'

I rushed up to him and he pulled me into his arms.

'How bad is it?' I asked as he hugged me tightly.

'I don't know for sure, I'm waiting for the doctor.' Theo pulled back. 'It all happened so quickly. The bike came around the corner like lightning. He clipped Dan as he turned, and he fell down. It was terrifying. I called an ambulance. People rushed over to help. The bike drove off though.'

'Bastard,' Aiden said from behind me. 'Was he conscious?'

'He blacked out for a minute but then he came to and was talking. He was clutching his leg though. He was in agony. Oh, here's the doctor.'

We turned as she approached us.

'Dan is up and talking so you can go and see him. He has a broken leg and will be in plaster for at least six weeks. He also has mild concussion from falling onto the pavement and bruised ribs so he's on strong painkillers. But no lasting damage,' she reassured us. 'He will be fine.'

'Oh, thank you!' I grabbed her hand to shake it. 'Thank you.'

She smiled. 'It's okay. Go on through but not for too long. We'll keep him in overnight then hopefully he can go home as long as he gets lots of rest. No walking around for at least a week then he can try crutches.'

After another round of us thanking her, we let the doctor go and hurried into Dan's room. A nurse told us we could stay for twenty minutes then he had to go to sleep. We found Dan propped up in the bed, his leg stretched out in plaster. He looked deathly white but he smiled when he saw us.

'Thank God you're okay,' Theo said, rushing over to grab his hand.

'Had us worried for a moment there, mate,' Aiden said, walking to the other side of the bed.

Dan's eyes met mine as I hovered in the doorway. As soon as he looked at me, I felt a tear of relief roll down my cheek.

'Liv, it's okay, I'm okay,' he said, beckoning me over.

'Sorry, I should be reassuring you,' I said as I leaned over to try to hug him. He winced so I pulled back. 'Sorry. Are you really okay?' I said, wiping my tears away.

'Yeah, they gave me the good stuff,' he said, trying to smile, but then he winced again. 'This is shit though,' he added, gesturing to his leg. 'And my head is pounding. Teach me to not check my phone as I cross the road.'

'He was going way too fast,' Theo said. 'I wish I could have stopped him driving off.' He sank into the chair by the bed. 'It was terrifying.'

'I can't believe someone would drive off like that after hitting someone,' I said. I perched on the edge of the bed. 'You're lucky. Really lucky.'

'I know.' He patted my leg. 'Can't get rid of me that easily.'

'Always with the bad jokes,' Aiden said from behind me. 'What will your followers say?'

'I already posted a video,' Dan said.

'Jesus,' Theo muttered, but he kept hold of Dan's hand, gazing at him like he couldn't quite believe he was real so I knew he wasn't really bothered.

I sniffed and Aiden held out a tissue.

'Thanks,' I said. 'Can we get you anything?'

'I'm just tired,' Dan replied. 'Don't worry, I'll be fine.'

The nurse came in then to tell us we needed to go in five minutes but we could come back for morning visiting hours. Theo asked if he could stay the night, but she said that wasn't allowed.

'I'd better phone your mum. I'll tell her what the doctor said and get her to come to the flat and not here,' Theo said, getting up to go into the corridor.

'I don't want to leave,' I said, standing up reluctantly.

'I'll just be sleeping,' Dan said.

I leaned over and kissed his cheek. 'Don't scare me like that again.'

'I won't.'

'Rest, okay? Do everything they tell you.'

'I promise.' Dan looked at Aiden. 'Look after Liv, okay?'

I was about to protest I didn't need looking after but Aiden replied too quickly.

'Of course.' His reply was so serious I glanced at him in surprise, but he kept his eyes on Dan. 'Text us if we can bring you anything in the morning. We'll come as soon as they let us.'

Theo walked back in. 'Your mum is about twenty minutes away. She'll come to your flat,' he said.

Dan nodded, looking like he was half asleep already.

'Love you,' he mumbled to us.

'We love you,' I said as Theo leaned down to kiss him. Aiden gave him a wave then we all walked out of the room.

'What a night,' Theo said, rubbing his head.

I touched his arm. 'Come back with us? See Mum. Have a coffee or something stronger.'

'Something stronger sounds good,' Theo replied. 'I hate leaving him.'

I wrapped an arm around his waist. 'Me too.'

'He's in the best place,' Aiden said. 'Come on, I'll drive us home.'

I'd been so annoyed at Aiden invading our flat but, in that moment, I felt relieved that he had been with me tonight.

19

'Dan looked so small in that bed,' I said as I sank down onto the sofa.

Theo took his jacket off and sat beside me. 'I know. Watching him fall on the pavement...' He shook his head. 'It was horrible. He was so brave the whole time. Trying to act like he wasn't really in pain.'

I nodded. 'When we were younger, he fell off his bike and I was so scared, he acted like he hadn't hurt himself at all to not worry me. That's Dan all over.'

'Drinks.' Aiden came in, holding out a glass of wine for me and Theo, and opened a bottle of beer for himself. 'What a night.'

I saw his hand shake a little bit as he took a long gulp. I realised he'd held it together to drive us but he must have been as worried sick as me.

'To Dan, getting healed quickly,' I said, raising my glass then taking a long sip. It must have been well past 3 a.m. but I didn't feel tired. Maybe it was adrenaline. 'Thanks for looking after him, Theo. Thank God you were there and could call the ambulance.'

'I just went into auto pilot but I was scared stiff,' he admitted. He rubbed his chin. 'You realise in those moments how much people mean to you.'

I reached over and squeezed his hand. 'You really do,' I said. 'He'll be fine. If he's been filming for TikTok since, we don't need to worry.'

They both chuckled at that.

Then there was a knock at the door.

'Mum,' I said, jumping up to answer it. She pulled me into her arms as soon as she saw me. 'He's okay. He's okay.'

'It's the thing you worry about most as a mother, getting a phone call saying one of your kids has been hurt,' she said, pulling back. I could see she'd been crying like me. Like mother like daughter. She blew out a puff of air. 'Thank goodness he'll be okay. Getting him to rest though won't be easy...'

She walked on through into the flat and I shut the door behind her. I could smell her familiar floral perfume, which was comforting. It didn't matter how old you were, sometimes you just needed your mum around. I felt better that was she here, and I knew Dan would as well.

'Theo, Aiden. Two of my favourite men in one room,' Mum was saying as I followed her in. She hugged them each in turn. 'Drinking, are we? Got any gin, love?'

'I'll make it,' Aiden said. He winked as he walked past me.

I shook my head. He had always loved my mum and she loved him. It was very annoying.

'You got down here quickly,' I said.

'No traffic at this time of night,' Mum replied as she curled up in the armchair. She was, as usual, in her yoga leggings and matching top, with a long cosy cardigan over it. Her grey hair was highlighted with blonde streaks and her blue eyes were always bright. We got our dark hair and hazel eyes from our father. She was the same height as me, with a figure that I'd always envy thanks to her lifestyle.

Aiden handed her a gin and tonic.

As she sipped at it, she asked Theo again what the doctor had said about Dan.

'I'm so glad he wasn't alone when it happened,' she said. 'You got him help quickly. Thank you, Theo. You're always there for him.'

Theo cleared his throat, embarrassed.

'I try to be,' he said softly. I wondered if he and Dan had talked about what was going on between them before the accident or not. I hoped they were working things out. The way he'd looked at Dan earlier, I was sure he was still head over heels for him.

'I can't wait to see my boy,' Mum said. 'I'd better not drink any more of this otherwise I'll miss morning visiting hours. Oh, we should take him some things with us.'

'Let's pack a bag now then try to get a bit of sleep before going in,' Theo suggested. And with that, they went into Dan's room to sort things out.

Aiden came over to the sofa as I poured myself another glass of wine.

'Probably a mistake like Mum says but...' I said.

'You've had a shock, it's fine.' He leaned back on the sofa. 'You were in such a deep sleep when I woke you up.'

'I was dreaming,' I replied, hoping he wouldn't notice me blush behind my glass. That was the second dream I'd had about him. At least he'd been fully dressed this time.

'Hmm,' he replied, then took another gulp from his beer. 'I have no idea how I'm going to sleep. Mind if I put something on?' He nodded to the TV.

'No, good idea, might make us sleepy.' I curled up with my wine as Aiden flicked through Netflix. I had a feeling he was scrolling past anything romantic and I was relieved. He settled on an old thriller I knew we'd both seen.

Half an hour later, Mum and Theo came out with a bag sorted for Dan. Theo said he was going to head home and we arranged to meet him at the hospital in the morning. Mum said she'd sleep in Dan's room and told us not to stay up to too late.

I laughed. 'We're not teenagers, Mum.'

'I still like to look after you all, you know that.'

She said goodnight and left us alone.

'Oops,' I said when I went back to the bottle of wine and realised I'd finished it. 'I'm going to pay for this,' I said with a giggle.

When the film had finished, Aiden turned off the TV. 'I guess we'd better go to bed too.'

'Is that a proposition?' I enquired with a raised eyebrow.

Aiden made a half-snorting, half-coughing noise. 'You definitely have had too much wine if you're trying to flirt with me.' He jumped up and held out two hands. 'Come on, I'll help you up.'

'Are you going to put me to bed?' I asked. I hadn't realised how light-headed I was feeling from the wine.

'I'm going to help you get up; you can put yourself to bed.'

I actually wasn't sure I could get up myself so I took Aiden's hands in mine and let him pull me from the sofa.

'Don't fall back again,' he said as I swayed. 'You really are a lightweight; maybe I *am* going to have to put you to bed.'

'You know what? You could give me a piggyback there,' I said. 'I'm not entirely sure I can walk.'

Aiden raised an eyebrow. 'Really? Or are you just feeling lazy?'

'Better safe than sorry,' I sing-songed.

Aiden tutted. 'Drunk Olivia, I forgot what this is like.' He turned around. 'Okay, fine, if it gets you to bed.' He bent down and I climbed onto his back. 'You're going to hate hearing about this when you're sober.'

'Don't tell me then,' I said, hooking my arms around his neck. Aiden held my legs around his waist and I clung on as he started to walk. 'This reminds me of Dan's twenty-first,' I giggled as we walked with difficulty to my room.

'God, that's burned into my memory. You wore shoes that cut your feet so I had to do this all the way home from the party,' Aiden replied. 'Luckily, after that, you didn't get drunk in front of me much.'

'I was embarrassed,' I said. 'I always embarrass myself in front of you. Like now,' I said, regretting this idea as my skin burned wherever I touched him.

'It's been a hard night, it's fine,' he said. He looked behind at me and grinned. 'I will use this for many years to come though to embarrass you.'

'Of course you will,' I said as we reached my room. 'Okay, you can put me down now. I can make it the rest of the way.'

But he ignored me, pushing open my bedroom door and carrying me in, turning around and depositing me backwards onto my bed.

'Just being a gentleman.'

I was sprawled out on my duvet. 'Yeah, very gentlemanly.'

Aiden grinned. 'Anything else, m'lady?'

'Are you trying to be Mr Darcy because I'm not falling for that again.'

'Again?'

I waved my hand to dismiss the question. I was not drunk enough to spill the beans about my Aiden/Darcy dream.

'Just let me sleep, please. I need to be somewhat human to visit Dan in a few hours.' I grimaced at the thought. I should not have had that last glass of wine, that was for sure.

'I don't know if that's ever possible for you,' Aiden replied. I picked up a pillow and threw it but it missed him completely. He laughed. 'Right, I'll wake you up if you're still asleep when we need to go and see Dan.'

'That's nice of you.'

'I can be nice,' he said. 'You just never notice.'

I pouted. 'I don't think I can get my jumper off.'

Aiden's mouth twitched. 'I think you'll do just fine.'

'I thought you were being a gentleman?'

'I am. That's why I'm not going to help you take your clothes off. No matter how much I might want to,' he replied.

As he saw my mouth fall open in shock, his smile broadened.

'What? You can flirt with me and I can't flirt back? I thought you believed in equality between the sexes.'

'Wait...' I groaned as I struggled to sit up on my bed. 'My head is too fuzzy for this.'

'I should remember this if I'm losing a battle in our ongoing war: get you drunk and then you can't argue back.'

He started to walk to the door.

'I'll still have the last word either way,' I called after him.

Aiden paused in the doorway. 'I always count on it, Olivia. Now, go to sleep or you'll blame me for how bad you feel later on this morning.'

'Okay then, thanks for...' I trailed off, not sure what to exactly thank him for. 'Looking after me,' I finished.

Aiden looked at me. 'I promised Dan I would.'

'Oh, yeah, of course,' I said, wondering why his answer made me feel so bad.

'It's a tough job though, Olivia,' he added with one of his trademark smirks. 'Get into bed, okay? Sweet dreams.'

'Night,' I said even though it was definitely morning now.

He left me alone and I flopped back against the pillows with a sigh. I felt frustrated and I wasn't entirely sure why. I knew I'd regret this whole encounter once the wine buzz left me, but I had enjoyed it. I couldn't deny that.

Sighing, I managed to sit up and pull my jumper off, not wanting to get off the bed. The room was spinning a little bit. I threw my clothes on the floor, and not being bothered to find any night clothes, I curled up under the covers in my underwear.

I couldn't believe I'd asked Aiden to help me get undressed. What was wrong with me? Why was I trying to play with fire? I didn't want to get burned again. But I seemed to not be able to help myself. Aiden living here was turning out to be the worst kind of torture. I tried to blame the dramatic night or the wine – anything else but the fact that ever since our moment in the rain, it felt like Aiden was a magnet and I was a paperclip helpless to resist being pulled towards him.

And the worst part? I wanted him to pull me closer.

Completely confused, I rolled on my side and willed sleep to obliterate this night from existence.

20

I woke up with my head pounding. I cracked one eye open. My mouth was dry too from the wine I'd consumed.

Rolling over, I looked at the time on the clock on my bedside table. It was 9 a.m. I'd managed less than four hours' sleep.

The whole night washed over me like a cold shower.

Dan... Aiden helping me to bed... What a crazy few hours...

I sat up suddenly and groaned as the pain hit me. I needed to sort myself out so we could get to the hospital.

I shuffled out into the kitchen where Mum was making a hot drink.

'Coffee?' I asked hopefully.

'I'm having a herbal tea,' she replied. She looked at me. 'Oh, dear.'

'Yep,' I said, slipping past her to make a coffee. I eyed her. 'You're dressed already?'

'I wanted to fit in a yoga routine before seeing Dan so then I had a shower and got dressed. Shall I make us eggs? You need fuel. We both do.' She went to the fridge. 'I still can't believe what happened.'

'Poor Dan,' I said as I made my coffee, hoping it would revive me. 'He'll really struggle with a cast on his leg for so long.'

'I was thinking,' Mum said as she started to crack eggs into a bowl. 'The doctor said he needs complete rest for the first week so why don't I take him back to Hampshire with me? That way, he won't be tempted to do anything and I can look after him.'

'I think that's a really good idea,' I said. 'When I'm at the library, he'd be alone here so it makes sense.'

'Great, I'll pack some more of his things and then he can't argue. Now, before we focus on Dan and visit him, tell me, are you okay here? I haven't seen you face to face not over a phone screen since you moved in with your brother.'

I smiled. 'It seems like I've lived here longer than I actually have; it feels like home.'

'London suits you. Dan said you were thriving and I can see you are. Well, apart from the wine hangover.'

'I love working in the library,' I said. 'Stevie has become such a good friend and it's fun living with Dan again.'

Mum pulled out a saucepan. 'Shall I make enough for Aiden too? I don't know when he'll be back from the gym.'

'He went to the gym? What, did he have like two hours' sleep?' I shook my head. That was madness in my book.

'He likes to look after himself.'

'I look after myself!'

'Are you doing your yoga every day and meditating?' she asked over her shoulder. I sipped my coffee. 'And how many cups of that are you drinking every day? What about journaling?'

'No, but I have started to write my novel finally,' I said, eager to give her one positive. Because she was a wellness goddess, it was very hard to impress her with my lifestyle.

'Ooh, lovely, what's it about?'

'A man and woman who hate each other when they first meet

but start working together and they're going to end up falling in love, obviously.'

'Obviously. Well, I can't wait to read it. I bet you've written a dishy love interest.'

I hid my face behind my coffee cup.

'And what about real-life romance? You said you were going out with someone from work when we last spoke?'

'Jasper, and I had a date yesterday but Aiden was there and—'

'Aiden?' She looked up in surprise. 'Why was he on your date?'

'It was a university event. He sat with us,' I said, grimacing before drinking more coffee. 'So, we're going to go out again and then I'll see. He's nice though.'

'Aiden?'

I snorted. 'Jasper. The guy at work.'

'Aiden is now a guy at work.'

'Hmm. A pain at work and at home,' I said automatically. It was my default position when it came to Aiden. I thought back to our interaction last night and blushed as I remembered making him help me into bed.

'But I'm such a handsome pain.' A voice behind us made us jump. Aiden strode in. 'Stacey, are you cooking breakfast, because I would love you forever if you are.' He turned to my mum, avoiding any eye contact with me. He was wearing shorts and a T-shirt with trainers and looked remarkably fresh considering how little sleep we'd all had. It was really unfair.

He held three takeaway cups.

I swallowed. I felt bad that he'd heard me calling him a pain even though that was what I always did. I wasn't exactly sure why I felt bad though. My head felt fuzzy again.

'I am. Sit down and let me finish the breakfast,' Mum said, waving us both to the bar stools.

'Okay, thanks,' he replied. 'I picked these up on the walk back from the gym for us.' He gave Mum one and told her it was a herbal tea then he slid a cup across to me as he slowly sat down on a bar stool, still avoiding eye contact.

'Oh, this beats my homemade coffee,' I said, grabbing the Starbucks cup. I took a sip. 'This is my favourite,' I said, turning to him in surprise. An iced latte with an extra shot and vanilla syrup was my go-to order. 'I didn't know you knew what I liked.'

'I was with Dan once when he picked you up one,' Aiden said, finally looking at me. 'Mine is a mocha with an extra shot if you ever want to return the favour.'

Aiden had memorised my coffee order. I didn't know what to say.

'Here we are,' Mum said, and handed us a plate of scrambled eggs, avocado and toast. 'I was saying to Liv that I'm going to get Dan to come back with me; that way he can have complete rest for a week like the doctor told him he needs. I can look after him, what with you both being at work and Theo having his paintings for the gallery to finish.'

Aiden nodded. 'He won't rest otherwise.'

'And I know you'll both be fine here together,' Mum continued brightly.

I stopped eating. I hadn't thought about the fact that Mum taking Dan home would mean we'd be alone here. Dan came first, of course. But it meant a week with just me and Aiden. I wondered what he thought about it, but when I looked over, he was eating his breakfast as if nothing was wrong.

'So, how are you finding it in London, Aiden?' Mum asked him.

Aiden looked up and smiled. 'Good so far. I really like the new job. And knowing Olivia doesn't seem to have destroyed my street cred at the university too much.'

'Hilarious,' I said. 'There goes your invite to have lunch with me.'

'I'd rather sit with the cool kids anyway.'

'They just don't want to sit with you,' I fired back.

'Oh, I missed this,' Mum said then and to my horror, her eyes started to tear up. 'I'm okay. Sorry. It's just been a hard few hours. And I miss you all. This reminds me of before Liv went away to university and I'd make you all breakfast after a night out. You two bickered like that back then and Dan would always be the peacemaker. I wish he was here.'

I reached over to squeeze her hand. 'He'll heal in no time and he'll be back here to referee, don't you worry. Well, until Aiden moves out anyway.'

'Don't rush,' she said to Aiden. 'Liv will need you this week with Dan being away. And I feel so much better knowing you're here together.'

'I don't need looking after,' I protested again.

'I'm going nowhere anytime soon,' Aiden promised as if I hadn't spoken. I looked behind Mum's back at him and he winked.

I sighed. With no peacemaker here, this week was going to be interesting.

After breakfast, we got ready and headed off to the hospital, taking the things Theo and Mum had packed for Dan. Sunday was grey and quiet in the city, as if time had slowed down just for a few hours. It felt the most peaceful that London ever gets. I tried to take some deep breaths as we drove to see Dan. It had been a crazy few hours of worry and I felt hungover from it – and the wine. My brain felt as cloudy as the sky.

Dan, thankfully, looked so much better when we went in to see him. Awake and propped up in the bed, he had some colour back in his cheeks and was having a cup of tea. Theo was already there in a chair beside him and looked as shattered as me.

'Oh, darling!' Mum rushed in to hug Dan and as soon as she did she started crying again.

'Mum, I'm okay, I swear,' he said, smiling at her tears. 'Honestly, you and Liv can cry for England.'

'We are both too sensitive for our own good,' she said, brushing his hair back. 'Now, have they given you enough pain relief? Did the doctor say you can leave today? I have a plan that I'm not letting you say no to...'

Mum continued talking nineteen to the dozen, telling Dan her plan of having him come to stay. I could see he wasn't a big fan of the idea but we all pressed him into accepting, knowing it was the only way he would rest and recuperate properly.

Mum went off to find a doctor to get Dan discharged and soon after, Aiden's phone rang and he left the room as well, saying, 'I'll just tell Zara I'm here.'

'Zara?' I asked as I watched him go. 'She's calling him again?'

'I think they've been talking,' Dan said, wincing a bit as he moved in the bed.

'Why? Once a cheater, always a cheater.'

'It's probably more complicated than that,' Theo said. 'But I hope he doesn't get hurt again.'

'Aiden's a big boy,' Dan said. 'Anyway, Liv, I didn't get to ask you about your date with Jasper. How did it go?'

'Great,' I said, throwing on a smile because I could feel Aiden coming back into the room, forcing away the disappointment I felt that he'd been talking to his ex. I needed to show everyone, including myself, that I didn't care. 'He suggested we go for dinner as our next date.'

'Well, that's good because you weren't sure—'

'How's Zara?' I cut him off, looking curiously up at Aiden.

'We're going for a drink this evening,' he said, putting his phone back into his pocket. 'You'll be okay at home on your own, won't you?' he asked me. 'I can rearrange if not?'

Was I imagining the challenge in his eyes?

'Of course,' I said in such a bright voice I was sure I wasn't convincing anyone. 'I'll love having the place to myself.' I turned to Dan. 'And I'll see Jasper at work tomorrow and we can plan our dinner date. It'll be great,' I added.

'Great,' Aiden muttered.

Dan and Theo exchanged a look. 'Well, I'm glad you'll both be great while I'm away at Mum's,' he said. 'I'll miss you all though. Don't do anything too fun without me, will you?'

21

By the time I finally got back to the flat, I was exhausted. And sad. Saying goodbye to Dan and Mum had been hard – Theo had been upset too but wanted to be alone – and so Aiden had driven us home. It had been a silent journey. I couldn't stop thinking about him seeing his ex and perhaps his mind was on that too. I didn't understand why he would want to even talk to her, let alone go for a drink. And even more so, I wasn't sure why it was annoying me quite so much.

We walked inside the flat and looked at one another awkwardly. Aiden put his hands into his pockets.

'Right, well, I'm going to get ready and go out for that drink. What will, uh, you do?'

'I'm knackered so heading to bed early with a book sounds perfect to me. I'll make some food first, I guess,' I said, walking to the fridge so I could focus on something other than him. But then I turned around, deciding to ask what was on my mind. 'Why are you seeing Zara? After what... what happened?'

'She's going through some things right now. She needs someone to talk to and we have a lot of history. I can't just abandon her,'

Aiden said quietly. 'Why do you care? You've never been interested in my love life before.'

I turned away and opened the fridge. I was worried that if I carried on looking at him, I might burst into tears. I blamed the exhaustion that had settled into my bones.

'I'm not. I just... never mind. Have fun. I'll see you at work tomorrow.'

'You excited to see Jasper?' Aiden asked, seemingly not about to make a move to leave.

I looked over my shoulder. 'Why are you so interested in my love life?' I snapped.

'I just don't think you should settle for second best,' he replied.

'Well, right back at you!'

We stared at one another. Anger bubbled up under my skin.

'You should go and get ready for your date,' I said finally.

'Fine. Enjoy your night alone,' he replied with a shrug.

'Oh, I will,' I called to his retreating back as he stalked away. 'It'll be so relaxing here without you!'

He slammed his bedroom door shut and I sagged against the fridge, leaning my head against the cool metal. Why did he get to me so much?

'Ugh,' I said to myself, then turned back to the fridge and pulled out a tub of houmous. I grabbed a bag of crisps then went to the sofa, ready to demolish the lot.

Ten minutes later, Aiden came out. He was wearing dark jeans and a shirt that showed off his arm muscles, and I could smell that he'd put on his aftershave. His hair was smooth and he'd shaved too, keeping just a faint line of stubble that suited him so much my heart squeezed.

'Do you need anything before I go?' he asked as he grabbed his keys.

'Nope,' I said, not looking at him. 'I'll be just fine.'

'Great,' he replied and then stalked out.

I had no idea why he was pissed at me – he was the one seeing his ex-girlfriend.

Once the door shut I let out a breath. At least I wouldn't need to deal with him for the rest of the night. I didn't want to think about him out with her so I went into my room and climbed into my pyjamas and instead of watching a movie, I pulled out my laptop. Writing some more of my book felt like the only way I was going to stop myself obsessing about Aiden being out with Zara. Maybe the best way to not think about his date was to fantasise about my two characters on a date together instead.

Lily has been thinking about the moment with Adam in the kitchen ever since it happened. She feels drawn to him and the harder she tries to stay away, the more she wants to get closer. He won't tell her why he said she should stay away from him, why he has this barrier up between them, why he won't admit that there is something there, so she decides to find out for herself and asks Adam to meet her at the beach.

When he arrives, he's surprised to see her on a blanket, a picnic basket beside her. 'Sit with me. Please?'

Adam hesitates.

'Just sit. It's a picnic, that's all. I won't jump on you or anything,' Lily says, frustrated.

Adam stares at her then finally laughs. 'The strangest proposition from a woman I've ever had,' he says, but he sits down.

I type frantically, picturing Adam and Lily on the beach together. The waves lapping behind them, the breeze blowing gently in Lily's hair, the way Adam notices how beautiful she is. Then Lily asks him why he was so rude to her when they first met.

'I'd had such a bad day. I found out my dad has been cheating on my mum,' Adam finally admits. 'I saw him with her. He begged me to not to tell my mum. Then I had to go and play volleyball with my cousins. But I

shouldn't have been rude to you. It wasn't your fault I'd had the day from hell.'

'I'm sorry. About all of it.'

'I just don't think I could give you anything right now with all this family drama going on. And I worry... What if I'm like him, Lily? What if I hurt the people I love the most? Just for kicks.'

Lily shakes her head. 'You are nothing like him.'

Adam really wants Lily to be right about that. The way she is looking at him makes him feel that maybe he could be different. That they could be different. And even though there are a million reasons not to, Adam just can't help but lean in and brush his lips against hers.

Lily lets out a small gasp and pulls him closer, deepening their kiss. The kiss they had wanted since they had first met, even if they hadn't been able to admit it to themselves until this moment. When they draw back, both of them are smiling.

I stared at my laptop. Lily and Adam had kissed. But instead of relief, I felt even more longing. I closed my laptop sharply. I was finding it harder than I thought to get that moment with Aiden in the rain out of my head. It had been ten years since I'd thought about Aiden kissing me, but now it was all I could think about.

I wanted Aiden to want me the way Adam wanted Lily in my book.

And I was just like Lily. I wanted Aiden like she wanted Adam.

'Oh, God,' I whispered.

Curling up, I turned out my light and tucked my legs under my duvet. I couldn't deny it any more. My love interest was Aiden and my leading lady was me. And I was telling the story I wished I could live for real. I wished me and Aiden were on the same page like Lily and Adam were.

We hadn't been on the same page since the night we met.

But things were different somehow. I could feel it. As though living with Aiden and seeing him more, and him being there when

Dan got hurt, had shifted our relationship. I remembered what he'd said to Jasper about me. I think I knew that he didn't really hate me, not like I'd told myself he did for years.

But more than that, I wasn't sure. And after our argument and him going out to see his ex, it wasn't like I could ask. I was annoyed at myself for wanting Aiden, annoyed at him for making me feel that way but then going out with his ex, and frustration about the whole thing meant I struggled to go to sleep. Tossing and turning, I got more pissed off about the whole situation and decided that hating Aiden was far easier than liking him so I really should go back to doing that.

It wasn't until I heard the front door open, and Aiden creep in, that I could finally relax. I hated that it was because I was happy he hadn't stayed with Zara. He'd come home.

And once I knew that, I could drift off to sleep.

Ugh.

* * *

Monday morning arrived far too soon. My grumpy mood hadn't faded. I woke up before my alarm with Aiden still on my mind.

I staggered into the shower and turned the water as hot as I could stand it. I was so annoyed with Aiden for making me think about kissing him while he was out with his ex. And the fact I'd stayed awake to hear him come back like a loser. I wanted to piss Aiden off like he had pissed me off.

Maybe I'd let pettiness get to me but when I got out of my long shower, I went to the airing cupboard and turned off the hot water with a satisfying flick of the switch, knowing I'd used it all up.

Then I got dressed, pulling on an outfit to try to improve my mood – my favourite pencil skirt that hugged me in all the right places, a fitted camel jumper and my four-inch-high boots so I would be as tall as possible. I let my hair loose over my shoulders and finished the look with my clear-lensed glasses.

Once I was ready, I went into the kitchen to make a coffee, deciding to turn on the speaker and find a Taylor Swift break-up song to blast out – and sing along badly to.

It only took a minute before Aiden stomped in.

'Jesus, Olivia, are you trying to wake up the whole building?'

'Oh, is it too loud?' I asked, feigning innocence.

Aiden grabbed the speaker and turned it right down. 'Is this to get me back for Harry Styles? You could have picked any other morning but no, after the weekend we've had and after me not sleeping more than hour, today is the day, huh?'

He looked at me and seemed to take in my outfit. His brow furrowed further.

'I don't know what you mean. I was just in a good mood so decided to listen to some music.' I smoothed down my skirt, wondering why he seemed to be staring.

'Yeah, right. You're always grumpy in the mornings so don't pretend.' He finally looked away. 'I'm going for a shower,' he said, walking back out, muttering to himself.

I smiled into my coffee cup and waited.

'Fuck's sake, Olivia!' The yell came two minutes later.

'A cold shower is good for your circulation,' I yelled back.

I felt a tiny bit better, I couldn't lie. It really was the small things in life, wasn't it?

I finished getting ready and thought Aiden might drive off without me but he was waiting in the hall when I walked out.

'Ready for work?' I asked brightly.

He gave me a withering look. 'No. It's my first lecture and I look and feel like shit. I'm going to make a great impression.'

I stared at him. I kind of felt bad now, which was annoying. 'Oh, shit, I'm sorry,' I stuttered, the plan of making myself feel better by sabotaging him back-firing.

'I suppose I deserved it after doing it to you,' Aiden said. 'Want a lift? Call it a truce? If we carry on this battle I won't survive the week.'

'Okay, truce,' I agreed. We left the flat and headed towards his car. 'We don't have Dan to keep an eye on us so we'd better not let things get out of hand,' I added as I climbed into his Mini.

Aiden slid in beside me.

'I dread to think what we could get up to,' he said, but he was smiling now. 'We'd better be on our best behaviour. If you can manage that, Olivia.'

'I told you, I only get into trouble with you around.'

'I quite like being a bad influence on you.'

'And to think they pay you to teach and shape students' minds.'

'I'll have you know I have much knowledge to impart,' he said as he started the car and pulled out of the space. 'I'm very serious and wise, you just don't see it.'

'Maybe I'll sit in on one of your lectures then to see this other side to you because I have to be honest, I can't picture it.'

'No way. I wouldn't be able to concentrate at all if you were there.'

I bit my lip so I wouldn't smile. I liked the idea that I distracted him. 'That sounds like a challenge.'

Aiden groaned. 'We said truce, didn't we?'

I held my hands up. 'Fine, fine.'

He gave me a look as if he didn't fully believe me. He seemed to decide it was best to change the subject. 'So, are you ready to see your boyfriend?'

'How was seeing your ex?' I countered, trying to keep my voice casual. I gripped the seat, my knuckles turning white. I really hoped he hadn't kissed her. Hope was dangerous though, I knew.

'Maybe we shouldn't discuss our love lives any more,' Aiden suggested.

The university came into view then.

'I hope my lecture goes well,' he said quietly.

I was always thrown when he said something that wasn't a joke.

'Fake it until you make it. You look the part, you're halfway there,' I said as he parked in the staff car park. I gestured to his grey suit and tried not to picture myself loosening that tie of his.

Aiden switched off the engine and raised an eyebrow.

'That was close to a compliment, Olivia.'

'I can be nice too,' I said, taking off my seatbelt. I didn't get out of the car though.

Aiden remained where he was too.

'I don't get to see it often; I'd better make the most of it.' He looked at my outfit. 'Librarian chic again today.' He smiled.

'I have to look the part,' I replied, smoothing down my pencil skirt on my thighs. His eyes watched the movement.

'Is my tie straight?' he asked softly.

It was perfectly straight but my fingers itched to touch him anyway. I reached out and moved it crooked then straight again. I smiled.

'Perfect.'

'Perfect,' he echoed, holding my eyes with his. His pupils were dark again. I bit my lip and his eyes flicked to my mouth. I wondered if he could tell I was holding my breath or not. Finally, he leaned back. 'We'll be late if we don't go in.'

'You're right,' I said, smiling to hide my disappointment.

I had to get out of the car before I said or did something that would betray what I was feeling right now. I yanked the door open and jumped out, breathing in the cool morning air. Aiden got out too and we looked at one another over the roof of the car.

'I hope it goes well. That's what nice people would say, isn't it?'

Aiden grinned. 'Yes. And they would say back – have a good day.'

I smiled. 'I'll see you later then.' It sounded like a question.

'See you later.'

We parted ways and I realised, as I walked to the library, that somehow my grumpy mood had evaporated.

22

Stevie was pacing back and forth when I unlocked the library door.

'Lock it again, quick,' she called. I hastily locked the door behind me. 'We have ten minutes and I need an update!' she said, waving two coffees in my direction.

I smiled. 'I don't know if ten minutes is long enough.' I took the coffee she held out and had a sip. 'Okay, so after I filled you in on the film festival, things have got even crazier...'

I told her about Dan's accident, rushing to the hospital with Aiden, Dan thankfully being okay, my mum taking Dan home, and how I was now living alone with Aiden.

Stevie's eyes widened. 'Oh my God! Thank God Dan is okay. That sounds so scary. I hope he heals quickly. Send him my love when you call him next, won't you?'

'I will,' I promised. 'Stevie, you need to help me. Last night, Aiden went out with his ex and I started writing more of my book and... I think you might be right. About my characters. I think I might have based them too much on me and Aiden because suddenly all I can think about...' My face flushed as my words came out in a rush. Then I shook my head. 'Nope, I can't say it!'

To her credit, Stevie didn't gloat that she'd told me so. 'You fancy Aiden?' she checked.

'Oh God, this is a nightmare! I can't stop thinking about kissing him.' I clamped my hands over my mouth as if I could suck that sentence back in.

Stevie's lips twitched but she didn't laugh. 'Okay. Breathe, Liv. Have a sip of coffee.' I did as she said. 'I know you've known him a long time and have thought about him in a certain way but it isn't a nightmare if you like him now. I can see why. He's really good looking, Liv, and I don't know, when you're together, it's like there are...' She trailed off as I stared at her. 'Don't kill me. But sparks. Chemistry. Whatever you want to call it. You guys have it.'

'I don't think arguing can be described as chemistry,' I replied hotly, even though I had felt sparks lately. A whole bucket-load of them. 'That's what we do. We argue. I told you what happened when we met. We don't kiss.'

'But you said yourself you wish you did,' she pointed out. I must have looked horrified as she held a hand up. 'Okay, let's just say that writing your book has made you see that Aiden isn't as bad as you thought and that instant attraction when you first met him, maybe it's been there under the surface all these years and now spending all this time together, it's bubbling up. Is it really that terrible? I mean, this could be something great, right?'

I let that sink in and I was stumped on how to argue back for a moment. 'But,' I said triumphantly, 'as you just said, I was attracted to him but he ran away rather than kiss me back then. He might feel the same way now.'

'And how would that make you feel?'

Disappointment washed over me. 'Why am I making the same mistake ten years later?' I groaned to myself and to Stevie. 'He's just going to disappoint me all over again.'

'Not necessarily. You're both grown-ups now.'

I shook my head. 'But he went out with his ex-girlfriend last night.'

'Maybe because he has no idea you fancy him,' Stevie suggested. 'You went on a date with Jasper and agreed to another one, don't forget.'

'You're right,' I said, trying to feel enthusiastic about our next date. 'Jasper. I need to focus on Jasper. He likes me and wants to go out with me. He's nice. And he's safe.'

'Safe?'

'I know he won't run instead of kissing me,' I said. 'I need to give things a try with Jasper, don't I? Aiden is just like my book, right? Just a fantasy.' I tried not to think about how the fantasy of Aiden excited me more than the reality of going out with Jasper again. My heart really was a traitor.

Stevie sighed. 'I keep on saying it but the lady does protest too much when it comes to Professor Rivers.'

I groaned. 'I wish I was writing my own love story. I'd make it a much smoother journey for sure. Why is it so much more complicated outside of a book?'

'Tell me about it.'

'Can we talk about someone other than Aiden please?' I begged her.

'Okay, I won't mention him any more,' Stevie promised. 'Tell me more about what you wrote for your book. Can I read the new chapters?'

It was a relief to go back to my fantasy world. I was happier there. 'Okay, I'll send them to you. My characters have now kissed for the first time.' I refused to let myself think about what kissing Aiden would be like. 'They have realised that they like each other so now I just have to write them falling in love and living happily ever after.'

'You're right. I wish it would be that easy for us,' Stevie said. 'Well, I'm looking forward to reading them.'

'And I shall look forward to my second date with Jasper,' I declared. 'And after that, Aiden will be out of my head once and for all,' I replied firmly.

'All I'll say is you'd better arrange the second date with Jasper quickly if you're going to be alone with Aiden for a whole week. You don't want to have to have too many cold showers.'

We looked at one another and even though the situation wasn't at all funny, we burst into laughter and carried on until we had to unlock the library doors and let the students in for the day.

* * *

I phoned Dan at lunchtime. He was settled back at Mum's house where she was fussing over him. She was constantly bringing him food and drinks and they'd done an hour's mediation. But I could tell he was resting so this had been the best plan. He asked if me and Aiden were surviving without him and I told him not to worry, wondering what he'd say if he knew what I'd been thinking – and feeling – about his best friend. I hated having secrets from my brother, but this one I knew I couldn't share. I asked him if he'd spoken to Theo and he said they were going to FaceTime later. I was relieved he was okay, and decided that if Dan could heal himself this week, maybe I could too.

So, I sought out Jasper. I found him on the way to the cafeteria. He waved happily and I returned the wave but seeing him didn't give me butterflies in my stomach.

'I wondered when you wanted to have that dinner?' I said to him.

Jasper smiled. He did look nice when he smiled, I decided. 'I'm free tonight. Why don't we go to that Chinese you're always talking about?'

I hesitated. That was the takeaway Aiden had bought me to apologise and I was supposed to be focusing on dating Jasper. But the food was too good to turn down. 'Sure,' I agreed. 'We can meet when we finish work and walk there together.'

I was glad I'd worn a smart outfit today; it was perfect for going out after work. We agreed that he'd collect me from the library at six when my shift finished.

The day passed by quickly as the library had been busy. As the clock on the wall ticked closer to six, I pulled out my compact mirror and touched up my lipstick.

'I know I said go out with Jasper again quickly but I didn't think you'd pick tonight,' Stevie said with a laugh.

I turned to her. 'I need to give it a chance. And forget about...' The words died on my lips as Aiden himself strode into the library.

Stevie cleared her throat. 'I'll just tidy those books over there,' she said, jumping up from her chair and dashing out from behind the front desk before I could stop her.

'What's up with Stevie?' Aiden asked when he reached the desk, leaning his elbow on it and looking over at me. He nodded in her direction. She was taking a book off the shelf then putting it straight back, blatantly looking over at us.

'Who knows with Stevie,' I said with a shrug. 'Did you need something?'

'Well, a few lecturers asked me to join them at the pub so I thought we could piss them all off and have you come too,' he said with a grin.

My heart lifted at the idea of an evening with Aiden but then I remembered my plans.

'I can't. I'm, um, having dinner with Jasper.'

Aiden's face didn't change. 'Oh, right.' He shrugged. 'Never mind, maybe next time.'

I nodded. 'Sure. Thanks for asking me.' We looked at one another. 'I just feel like I need to give him a second chance,' I blurted out. 'You're always saying I'm too picky, right?'

Aiden opened his mouth but then shook his head. 'See you at home,' he added, then turned around and strode back out.

My chest sagged. I had the distinct feeling he was disappointed in me. But I was sure that was just because he knew I wasn't that excited to see Jasper again. Maybe he thought I'd hurt Jasper. Which I really didn't want to do.

Stevie returned. 'Liv, maybe you shouldn't go if you feel...' She trailed off. 'Maybe you should tell Aiden...'

'Nope,' I cut her off firmly. 'I'm not telling Aiden anything. He told me this morning we shouldn't discuss our love lives and he's right. He can go back to his ex and I'll go on my date and everything will turn out fine. I just need to wait for him to move out and then I can forget about all this.'

'It's been ten years since you almost kissed,' Stevie said. 'And you still haven't let it go.'

'I really wish I'd never told you about that night.'

Stevie held her hands up. 'I'm just saying. I don't think about anyone I kissed when I was a teenager. There's something between you two. If I can see it, feel it, then Aiden can too.'

'I'm not making that mistake again,' I insisted, grabbing my bag and jacket. 'Wish me luck with the man that actually wants to go out with me.'

As I passed by her, she touched my arm. 'I just want you to be happy. You deserve that love that people write stories about,' she said, gesturing to the books around us.

'I know, thank you. You do too.' I gave her a hug. 'I'll message you later.'

I looked as the doors opened and Jasper arrived right on time.

'Have fun,' she called, giving Jasper a wave as I walked over, and we left the library together. Outside in the corridor, I glanced around but Aiden had long gone. I wondered whether I'd have arranged this dinner date with Jasper if I'd known he was going to ask me to go to the pub. I knew I wouldn't have. But I needed to stop myself from getting hurt and this was the best way to do that.

'Ready?' Jasper asked as he held the main doors open for me.

'Absolutely.'

23

The Chinese restaurant was around the corner from Dan's flat, a cosy place with low lighting and small booths for people to eat in. We were sharing a bottle of wine and I felt the age difference between us. Not just because he was older in years but because of his temperament; he had an adult air about him that I wasn't at all convinced I had myself yet. I was still figuring things out but Jasper seemed to have already done that.

'I was in a meeting with the vice chancellor most of the day,' he was saying. 'He's so disorganised, I have to remind him of everything he needs to do.'

'I would make such a bad assistant. I'm like him, I always seem to be a few minutes late and if I don't have a list with me in the supermarket, I forget everything. He's lucky to have you being so organised.'

'He works hard so I don't mind but sometimes it can be frustrating.' Jasper shook his head. 'It's a cliché, isn't it, complaining about your boss?'

'Technically, I see you more than him, my actual boss, so I'd better not complain.'

'You have complaints?' he asked.

I shook my head. 'No, I don't.'

And I didn't. The date was going much better than the film festival. With no interruptions, the conversation was moving much more smoothly and the food here was good enough to help elevate the evening.

'So, how did you get into working for a university? I don't really know much about your background,' I said to him.

'I've always lived close to London and after university, I wanted to move properly to the city. I've loved it since I was a child coming on school trips. There is so much to do and see. I love the history and the architecture.'

'Aren't the buildings here in Islington so amazing? I just love it here.'

'Me too.' We smiled at one another. 'I went to our university myself.'

'I didn't know that,' I said.

'I studied history, which won't come as much of a surprise to you, and my lecturer needed administrative assistance so I stepped in and worked for him through my studies. Then afterwards, he offered me a job and I worked my way up. How did you end up in our library?'

'I studied English literature and I always had this dream to write my own book but, you know, it's not like it's a job you can just apply for. I knew it would be a long, hard road. I wrote all through my studies and won a short story competition but I needed to make money. I got a job in a local bookshop but I wanted more time to write. So, my brother suggested I come to London. He said I didn't need to work but I wanted to find something part-time. I'd helped out at the library when I was at university so when I saw the vacancy in the library, I applied. I just love working with books. Writing though is what I really want to do. Hopefully one day.'

'Are you writing something now?'

'I'm trying to write a romance novel.'

'Oh, right. Is this research?' He looked a little bit alarmed.

'No, don't worry,' I replied with a laugh, but my cheeks heated up as I thought about who my actual research was. 'I'm really enjoying living in London,' I said, changing the subject.

'And now there are three of you? Aiden said he was staying with you and your brother?'

I nodded, wondering how Aiden was managing to invade this date too despite not being here. 'Just until he finds his own flat. He and my brother have been best friends for ten years.'

'It's lovely he has you both here. The vice chancellor was so pleased with the film festival. The students seemed to love it and he loves events that bring everyone together.'

'I'll tell Aiden,' I said. 'So, are your family still close by?'

The meal went by quickly and Jasper was good company. I didn't see much of a different side to him than the one I knew at work though.

As we stepped out into the night, he offered to walk me home as I was so close by, so I accepted and we set off through Islington. It was dry outside but there was a cool breeze in the air, making me glad I had a jacket with me.

'This is me,' I said as we turned onto my road. I gestured to the converted townhouse ahead. I could see the lights weren't on so I assumed Aiden was still out with his colleagues. We stopped outside. 'Thank you for this evening – the meal was lovely. And for walking me home,' I said, turning to face him. It was dark now and his face was dimly lit by the lamppost behind us but I could see him smiling.

'It was a lovely evening.' Jasper stepped closer. 'Perhaps we can do it again?'

He leaned down then and hesitated close to my lips.

I hesitated too. But I had to try. I smiled and he pressed his lips against mine. It was tentative, and he kept his hands stiffly by his sides. I didn't deepen the kiss and he didn't try to.

Jasper pulled back then and nodded formally. 'Well, thank you again, Liv. Goodnight.'

'Goodnight,' I said, and I turned around and walked into my flat.

I waved before I closed the door and sighed. That had not been great. I'd felt nothing. It had been like kissing my brother.

'Damn it,' I said out loud. I couldn't pretend there was any future for us. He was so nice but I just didn't fancy him. I had no idea if that would have been the case if there wasn't someone else in my life I was lusting after. But I couldn't pretend that Aiden smiling at me wasn't more exciting than that kiss.

I pulled out my phone and recorded a voice note.

'I'm back home. We had such a lovely meal and we get on fine. But when he kissed me, I didn't feel anything. No butterflies. No fireworks. No spark at all. Ugh!'

I sent it to Stevie and she replied with one just seconds later.

'Because he's not the person you really want to kiss right now!'

I groaned. I hated that she was right. 'But I can't do anything about it! I can't tell Aiden I want to kiss him. God, even just thinking about doing that makes me want to run in the opposite direction. You know, like one of those cartoon characters that leaves the outline of their body in the door. Why?'

Stevie had the answer instantly. 'Because love is *scary*. It means putting yourself out there. Opening your heart. And you could get hurt.'

'I'm sorry.' I knew she was talking from personal experience. Stevie had had her heart broken a few years ago, she'd told me. I knew that had been far more serious than any of my relationships. Maybe I had been guilty of choosing fictional love stories over taking a chance on a real life one. Maybe, like Dan, it had been seeing my mum lose my dad and him leaving us. The idea of committing and then having my heart broken was too scary. Or maybe I just hadn't met anyone special enough to even consider doing that.

'It's okay. I get how you feel, that's all I meant. But I don't regret putting myself out there for someone who I felt a connection with. And you feel it with Aiden. You'll never know what might happen, good or bad, unless you take a risk.'

'I can't tell him, I can't give him that satisfaction. He has to make the first move.' Aiden had rejected me once; I wasn't going to let him do it again no matter how much I wanted to kiss him.

'Okay, well, he won't if you never put yourself in a date-like situation with him.'

'What should I do?'

'Channel some main character energy. Pretend you're Lily in your book. What would she do?'

'She'd probably go to the pub where Aiden is tonight.'

Instead of another voice note, Stevie messaged me a gif of someone saying, 'Go, go, go!!!!'

I laughed out loud. I wasn't sure if having a friend like Stevie was a good thing or not. She was encouraging me to do something I wasn't sure was a good idea at all. But I really wanted to do it. I didn't want to sit in the flat by myself waiting for Aiden to come home. And it was a work thing. It wasn't like it was a date. I was just popping by to say hi to colleagues on my way home. No one needed to know I'd already been home first.

Before I chickened out, I went straight back out of the door. I knew the pub they always went to and it wasn't far. I could just say hello and leave again if Aiden wasn't pleased to see me. But I hoped he would be.

I walked quickly down the road towards the lit-up pub. I could still feel the trace of Jasper's lips on mine. It had been the furthest thing from the epic kiss I was looking for. The kind of kiss my characters in my book had. That was what I wanted. And I had no idea if I'd ever get that from Aiden but something told me that if sparks could fly when we were just talking then maybe if we did ever kiss, it could be something special. And that was scary but it also spurred me on to find him tonight.

As I pushed the door open, the noise and warmth of the pub enveloped me. A fire had been lit and there were the sounds of laughter and clinking glasses around me. I looked through the crowd and saw at the back table a group of lecturers including Aiden. I went to the bar first. I needed Dutch courage for this. I ordered an espresso martini and carried it over to where they were sitting.

'Hi, everyone,' I said loudly over the noise as the eyes at the table turned on me.

'Liv!' Priya cried, breaking into a smile. 'It's lovely to see you.'

I was relieved to know someone else here other than Aiden. It helped to relax my nerves a bit. 'Yeah, I just thought...'

'I'm glad you came,' Aiden said when our eyes met. He scooted over. 'Sit down. Charles was just telling us about his new research paper,' he said. His eyes twinkled.

I sat down, relieved to be out from under their gaze. It was obvious that, apart from Aiden and Priya, everyone was wondering why I was there.

Aiden leaned over and whispered into my hair, 'It sounds like the most boring thing you'll ever read in your life.'

I spluttered some of my drink. Eyes turned to me again. 'It's strong,' I said and cleared my throat.

Under the table, I nudged Aiden with my leg. He didn't look the slightest bit remorseful.

As Charles – who I thought was one of the physics professors –

continued to drone on, Aiden turned to me again. 'Your date finished early.' He picked up his beer and took a sip.

I looked into his green eyes, bright under the lights. There hadn't really been room for me at the table so we were squished together. I enjoyed the warmth of his body next to mine. I wondered if my proximity was causing him any pleasure or not.

'Hmm.' I leaned in so my mouth almost touched his ear. I could feel his body tighten. So, he was aware of how close we were as well.

'We went early to be fair, after work. And it's not a dessert place.'

'Did he walk you home?'

Because he'd turned to speak into my ear, we weren't looking directly at each other, which made it easier even though I could feel my heart hammering inside my chest.

'Yes.'

'But you didn't want to invite him in to the flat?'

'On the first date? I'm shocked, Mr Rivers.'

'Professor Rivers,' he corrected.

I tried not to think about how sexy that sounded.

'Anyway, not after the way he kissed me...' I stopped, realising I'd been too honest once again. Why couldn't I keep my mouth shut around Aiden?

Aiden paused again. Then he leaned in so close, his mouth definitely touched my ear. I shivered involuntarily.

'You didn't like the kiss?'

24

'Okay, what are you two gossiping about over there?' Priya called out, breaking through mine and Aiden's conversation.

Aiden drew back from me, and I hoped my clearly heated face would be put down to the log fire and not him asking about my kiss with Jasper.

'Just the rumour about the vice chancellor.'

'I heard that,' one of the other lecturers said. 'Apparently, his wife has left him for her personal trainer.'

I hadn't heard that so I leaned forward to hear what everyone had to say about the big boss. I wondered if Jasper knew but I doubted he indulged in university gossip.

'Well, I hope this won't put him off funding my project,' Charles said with a sigh. He really did have the dullest voice. I wondered if any of his students stayed awake during his lectures. 'I need him in a good mood next week to approve my proposal.'

'Just don't mention anything to do with fitness,' Priya told him. I saw her holding back a grin.

'Why would I?' Charles asked, confused.

I snorted into my drink. Charles really didn't have much of a sense of humour.

'I spoke to Dan at lunch,' I said to Aiden, careful not to lean in too close again and rouse the others' interest in us. 'He sounded much more like his usual self.'

Aiden nodded. 'We messaged for a bit. I think he's loving being looked after by your mum. He deserves it. I still can't believe that bike hit him like that and drove off. He was so lucky.'

I shivered again. 'I know. Thank God. I don't know what I'd do without him. Thank you, by the way, for staying so calm. I think I might have freaked out a lot more if you hadn't been with me.'

Aiden smiled. 'You can always call me in a crisis.'

'But we don't speak on the phone,' I said, remembering what I'd told my mum when Aiden was with me in the bookshop. My heart though gave a little jump at his offer.

'We know each other well enough; you can call me about anything.' He sounded serious. Then he leaned in again. 'Especially if you need rescuing from another bad date.'

'It wasn't a bad date,' I hissed back, never wanting to agree with anything he said.

'Just a bad kiss.' He grinned.

I shook my head. 'It was nice.'

'Ouch,' Aiden replied. 'Nice is not good feedback, Olivia. Do you really want *nice* kisses for the rest of your life?'

My eyes flicked to his lips. I was sure he noticed. I took a breath before I was able to speak. 'No, I really don't,' I admitted. I leaned away from him, shocked at myself for being that honest. And flirty. Out of the corner of my eyes, I saw him watching me as he finished his beer.

Priya said she needed to get up early for a morning lecture, and the others started gathering their things and getting up. A suggestion was made to order Ubers and then we all left the pub together to climb into the waiting cars. Aiden and I lived close enough to walk but maybe neither of us was sure about being alone just yet so we got into one together.

I tried not to think about Aiden's thighs pressed up against mine as we drove to Dan's flat but it was impossible not to. After the flirting in the pub, we were now both silent as the others chatted, and I longed to know what he was thinking.

'Good night guys!' Priya called cheerfully when we arrived and I climbed out, followed by Aiden. We waved and watched the Uber drive off.

Aiden turned to me. 'So... uh, shall we?'

He looked a little uncertain, and it was a relief that it wasn't just me suddenly very aware it was now just the two of us.

I nodded and we walked up to our front door, Aiden unlocking it and stepping back to let me through. I didn't know what to say. I was scared I might just blurt out the fact I wanted to kiss him. I switched on the lights inside and kicked off my shoes while Aiden took off his jacket, and we wandered through to the kitchen.

Aiden coughed as if announcing he was going to stop the silence.

'So, as you can see, you haven't really been missing out on work drinks,' Aiden said as he threw his keys into the bowl on the counter.

I chuckled a little bit nervously. 'No, maybe there's a reason admin and teaching staff keep apart, after all.' I wondered how I could pick up our flirty banter again but my confidence had dwindled with every minute since we'd left the pub. Around the others, it had felt safer and easier to flirt with Aiden. And he'd flirted back. But now it just felt awkward.

'As long as you don't lump me with them. Well, some of them are okay – I like Priya and Gabriella, but Charles...' He rolled his eyes.

'Same,' I agreed, stuck on how to navigate this. Maybe I needed to forget the whole idea. I felt like a balloon that someone had stuck a pin in. One minute, I'd felt the possibility between us again, then the next it was like nothing had happened. God, what if I'd been imagining all of it? I wrapped my arm across my chest.

Aiden walked over to the sofa and flopped down, putting his feet up on the coffee table. 'Why are you being weird?' he asked, looking over. 'You look tense.'

'I'm not!' I said, dropping my arms, knowing that I was incredibly tense.

'Are you worried about how to let Jasper down gently?'

I supposed that was less humiliating to admit to than being nervous about how to flirt with Aiden again. 'Well, I am now you've mentioned it.'

Aiden smirked. 'He's a big boy, he can handle it. And to be fair, maybe your kiss didn't rock his world either.'

'Hey, my kisses... Ugh,' I said, stopping myself. 'Why do I always let you wind me up?'

Aiden's smirk turned into a grin. 'You have always been easy to wind up. I would say it's one of my favourite activities.'

'I'm glad I amuse you so much.' I tutted. Some of my tension dissipated with the familiarity of bickering with Aiden.

'Why are you still standing over there? Come and sit down. Or do you need your beauty sleep?'

I rolled my eyes but took the opportunity to sit next to him.

'You weren't this quiet in the pub,' Aiden said after a moment. He raised an eyebrow like he was challenging me. Maybe he was trying to work out why I'd been flirting.

Oh God. My nerves were like a volume button being turned up. But I needed to know if I was imagining this thing between us or not. I turned to him. 'I have to ask you something.'

'Uh oh,' Aiden said. Then he saw my face and he pulled his legs off the coffee table. 'Sure. What's up?'

'Did you know the theme you chose for the film festival was mine? Kissing in the rain?'

Aiden looked at me for a moment then nodded. 'I recognised your handwriting. Although I'd have worked it out from the idea alone anyway. Only a hopeless romantic would choose that. It takes one to know one.'

'Okay. But why did you choose it?' I asked, then held my breath for his answer. Was he going to tell me the truth?

He exhaled. He seemed to be considering whether to make a joke or not. He sat upright so he was mirroring my position. I looked down. Our thighs were an inch apart.

I lifted my eyes slowly to meet his again.

'Honestly?' he asked gruffly.

'Yes. Please,' I said, hoping he couldn't hear how hard my heart was beating again.

'I wanted to make you happy.'

I exhaled then. I folded my hands in my lap to stop them from reaching out, grabbing his shirt and pulling him on top of me. Because, well... SWOON.

'You... you did?'

Aiden cleared his throat. 'I mean, I know you didn't want me to move in and...' He trailed off and shook his head. 'I chose it to make you happy. And I knew that when you walked in and saw the theme up on the projector, it would make you smile. And that thought made me smile.'

'God, Aiden.' My whole body felt like a coiled-up spring just waiting to be released. I had no idea what I would do if that happened though, so I got up and started to pace in front of the coffee table.

'What did I say?' Aiden asked. 'Why are you pacing? Now I'm really nervous.'

'You're nervous?' I stopped and spun around to face him. 'You tell me that you did that to make me happy and all I want to do, all I want to do is...'

I threw up my hands, unable to say the words.

Aiden sprang up then and walked over to stand in front of me.

'What do you want to do?' he asked, his voice gruff again. He stepped closer, looking down at me, his green eyes darkening.

I looked up at him. My whole body wanted to lean in towards him. It craved his. Aiden was the drug I was not allowed to try, and it only made me want to do it more.

'We need to talk,' I blurted out.

Aiden raised an eyebrow. 'I thought we *were* talking. Or did you have a deeper subject in mind? Climate change, world peace or—'

'Aiden,' I said, reaching up to put a finger on his lips. 'Can you not be annoying for one minute, please?'

He smiled against my finger. 'I thought you found me charming, not annoying?'

'No, I definitely find you annoying.' I took my finger away. I looked at him. 'And occasionally charming. Always annoying though.'

'Hmm, noted,' he replied. 'So, what do you want to talk about then?' He drew the words out, his accent sounding sexier than ever.

'Um...' It was getting hard to think. Aiden had never been closer. I just needed to stand on my tiptoes and our lips would meet. Could he tell my body felt like it might spontaneously combust if he didn't touch me?

Aiden seemed to think for a moment then he reached down and this time, he touched my lips with his fingertip. My breath hitched and I knew he heard it. He smiled.

'I don't want to talk.'

Then I clamped my hand over my mouth. I hadn't meant to admit that.

'No?' Aiden said. 'What then?'

When I was silent, he reached out and gently prised my hand away.

'Olivia, you need to tell me what you want,' he said softly. He looked pained then, as if I was torturing him. I kind of hoped I was, so he would know how it felt. 'I really wish I knew what you were thinking right now,' he murmured.

'I need to stop thinking,' I murmured back.

'Okay, so what do you want to do instead of talking and thinking?'

I looked at his lips. 'What do you want to do?' I challenged, remembering what I'd said to Stevie about needing Aiden to make the first move.

'Isn't it obvious? I want to kiss you, Olivia.'

The sound of my name on his lips was the spark my body needed. I couldn't stop the fire now even if I wanted to. I saw a flash of surprise on his lips before I grabbed a fistful of his shirt and pulled him towards me, closing the tiny gap between us.

Our lips met and I couldn't stop the noise of appreciation in the back of my throat as we kissed. Aiden's arms wrapped around my waist, pulling me closer, his mouth gently parting my lips with his, his tongue finding mine and exploring it like I was a treasure he'd been searching all his life for.

I let go of his shirt and moved my arms around his neck, pulling him further down towards me as our kisses turned hungrier. We moved even closer.

My body had taken over. I was powerless to resist how much I wanted him. My heart pounded against his chest. I felt the muscles in his chest against my body. I felt my nipples under my jumper harden.

Aiden's lips broke from mine. I gasped breathlessly as he moved to my neck and began to kiss me under my ear then down my neck to my collarbone. I trembled, willing him to move his lips lower and lower.

'I definitely prefer this to talking,' Aiden murmured, breaking me out of my trance.

My brain kicked back in. I was finally kissing him. *Aiden*. And God it felt so good. He tasted so good. He had lit me up from the inside out. I had wanted sparks. I had wanted butterflies. I had wanted fireworks. I'd longed for a kiss like this. And now I had it, I didn't know what I'd do without it.

This was just like my book. Lily and Adam's arguments had been peppered with sparks and they had finally given in and kissed and that was what I had wanted so badly to happen with Aiden. But that had been a fantasy. This was reality. And it was confusing as hell.

I had spent so long thinking of Aiden one way and now I was in his arms. I pulled back. 'We're kissing,' I said, my mind reeling while my body craved more.

Aiden's lips curled into a smile. 'Oh, I'm aware.'

I stepped away from him. 'But we hate each other!' I went back to the sofa, slowly falling down onto it. 'I mean, you're my nemesis,' I said, looking up at him, hoping he might explain this epically hot kiss to me. Because I was stumped.

Aiden looked back at me, running a hand through his hair and taking a visible breath. I couldn't help but feel pleased our kiss had also affected him. My legs would be shaky if I wasn't sitting down. 'But isn't this what you wanted? I mean, tonight, at the pub...' He trailed off, looking as uncertain as I felt.

'Yes,' I said quickly.

'Well, that's a relief.' Aiden came to sit beside me. 'So, why the freaking out?'

I touched my lips. They were still tingling from his. His after-shave was all over me. My whole body was attuned to his. I turned to face him on the sofa. 'Yes,' I repeated firmly. 'But this is *us*,' I said. 'We don't ever do *this*.'

'We've been missing out,' Aiden replied. 'Don't you think?'

I smiled. It did feel that way. It felt weird, yes, but also like, why had we not been doing this all along? 'Yes... No,' I said, remembering why we hadn't been doing this all along.

'Olivia, you need to let me in to that mind of yours. What's wrong?' Aiden said gently, reaching out to brush his hand across mine.

My mind was back to when we were teenagers. I had thought Aiden rejected me that night but now we were kissing like that had never happened. But I still remembered how embarrassed I'd been and how that night had shaped our whole relationship. I just couldn't relax and enjoy this change without knowing if Aiden remembered it too. Because I really didn't want to make the same mistake again.

Aiden was stuck in this flat with me, he'd had his heart broken by his ex who he'd gone out with again; maybe he was confused and I was just a distraction? I didn't want to wake up tomorrow and find Aiden acting like nothing had happened. 'Why didn't you kiss me?'

'I was kissing you,' Aiden said, confused.

'No, why didn't you kiss me back then?' I asked. 'The night we first met. Why didn't you kiss me that night?'

25

Aiden blinked. 'What do you mean?' he asked.

'Why didn't you kiss me back at the party the night we first met? Ten years ago? We were in the garden and I thought you felt... what I felt and I leaned in, hoping you were about to kiss me, but then you suddenly ran off back to the party like the idea of kissing me was repulsive.' It was hard to bring it up after all this time but I felt like I owed it to my younger self to find out what he had thought that night, and why things were so different now.

Aiden shook his head. 'That's not what happened.'

I looked at him incredulously. 'It's exactly what happened! I tried to kiss you and you rejected me. Which is why this' – I pointed between us furiously – 'is confusing. My head is all over the place. I mean, it's been ten years of us fighting, you treating me like I was the last woman you wanted.'

'Is that what you really think?' Aiden asked, his voice soft.

'You rejected me that night,' I insisted.

'No, no,' he said, shaking his head. 'I wanted to kiss you that night but I didn't think...' He trailed off. 'You wanted me to?'

'You really are going to pretend you didn't know that?'

'It wasn't like that. I didn't think you even remembered, that you ever thought about that night. Let me explain.' Aiden took hold of one of my hands and my whole body responded to that innocent touch. His thumb rubbed the back of my hand and I felt myself calming down instantly. 'Okay, so that summer... I met Dan working at the cinema and I liked him instantly. The job was pretty crap apart from getting to watch the films for free but he made it fun. We became such good mates so quickly.' Aiden smiled at the memory. 'He told me so much about you. He was always talking about his sister. I knew how close the two of you were, and I was really looking forward to meeting you. Then I got to the party, and he introduced us and I thought, "Oh God, I'm in trouble."'

My mouth twitched. 'You did?'

Aiden lifted our entwined hands. 'Look at you. I thought you were so funny, so sweet, so... unique.'

I raised an eyebrow. 'I thought you saw me just as Dan's annoying little sister.'

Aiden's lips curved into a grin. 'I mean, you still are.'

I glared at him.

'Sorry, it's a habit. No, I really liked you and I thought you were cool. But I was nervous. I was nineteen, I hadn't lived in England for long, Dan had become my best friend and there I was lusting after his sister who I was sure thought I was frankly a twat.'

'I mean, you still are,' I retorted.

'I'm regretting this story, Olivia.'

'I'm sorry!' I gestured. 'Please, do go on. You really were nervous?' I was sceptical. Aiden had always been the confident one, the one who never seemed bothered by anything.

Aiden muttered under his breath but he continued. 'Anyway, so yes, I did feel that connection too, I did want to kiss you but I was young, inexperienced and I didn't know if you wanted to, plus I was thinking about Dan. What would he say if I kissed his little sister? There's a guy code about these things.'

'A guy code?'

'I'd never had a close mate like that before. Dan was so protective of you. He always said he'd kill any guy who hurt you. And rightly so, I would too,' he added. 'I didn't want to lose him if I kissed you. I thought the safest thing to do was to walk away and talk to him about it first.'

'You could have told me that! You jumped up like you'd been burnt and ran inside,' I said, thinking back to how humiliated I'd felt in that moment.

'I'm sorry. It was purely a cowardly move.'

'Huh,' I said, processing that.

I had been so sure I'd been rejected for something about me, I hadn't thought about Aiden being my brother's friend. I had only been seventeen and just as inexperienced and confused as Aiden had been, and my heart had felt stamped on. I had seen that night one way for ten years; it was hard to re-adjust the story in my head.

'I thought you didn't want me,' I admitted. 'And it hurt.'

'Shit,' Aiden said. He squeezed my hand. 'I realised my mistake when you came back into the party. I was going to go and talk to Dan when I heard you and your friend talking about me. You told her that I was the last guy you'd ever want to kiss.'

'Oh,' I said sheepishly. 'Yeah, I remember that.'

'Well, that made me think twice. You didn't want to kiss me so that was that. I'd blown it. So, I decided I should just forget about you. But you're kind of hard to forget.'

'You were horrible to me after that,' I pointed out.

'I was trying save face. I was embarrassed! I hoped you liked me back but hearing you say that, I thought I had to make sure you had no idea I fancied you,' Aiden said. 'And you can't tell me you didn't give back as good as you got.'

I smiled sheepishly. 'I wanted to make sure you knew I didn't fancy you.'

'Hmm, it worked for ten years,' Aiden said, pulling me a little bit closer so our legs touched on the sofa. 'You might have ruined the act now though. Even so, I've always loved our back-and-forth banter.'

'You seriously enjoy arguing with me?' I asked, raising an eyebrow.

'Don't you enjoy it?' he asked, looking at my lips again.

I shook my head. 'No. Yes. Sometimes. I don't know. It's very confusing. I want to hate you. I've tried very hard to hate you.'

'I have some idea. You have a cutting tongue when you try, Olivia,' he said. 'But sometimes you have this smile on your face when we argue. And I noticed when I looked at you, which was most of the time by the way, you'd sometimes sneak a look at me too. And it would give me just a little bit of hope to hold on to that you didn't completely hate me. That maybe you enjoy all the arguing too.'

'I'm not sure I agree with that.'

'No? What about at the film festival?' He reached out to brush back a strand of my hair. 'You can't tell me you didn't enjoy arguing with me there. More than being on a date with Jasper.'

'Were you jealous I was there with Jasper?'

'Yeah, of course,' Aiden said. My heart lifted. 'We've been spending more time together than we ever have and I realised that all the teasing hadn't changed the fact I still fancy you like crazy. I thought maybe the film festival was a chance to see if you'd ever see me as anything more than your brother's annoying best friend. I used your theme and thought we could hang out there, but then you asked Jasper to go with you.'

'A knock to your ego,' I said, smiling at the thought of him wanting to be with me there.

'I knew if you really liked him then I'd have to forget the whole thing but it gave me a little bit of hope when you didn't seem to have much fun with him. Even when we're arguing, we always seem to have fun. Did you wish you were there with me and not Jasper?'

Aiden looked so hopeful that even though I did want to continue teasing him like I always had done, I couldn't deny it. I nodded. 'Yeah, and when we argued in the rain, I did wonder if you were going to kiss me.'

'God, I wanted to, but you were so angry with me, I thought you might slap me.'

'It was a toss-up in my head whether I wanted to slap you or kiss you,' I conceded.

'You made a decision in the end though,' Aiden said.

I thought about how I'd written the kissing scene in my book and how I'd longed for it to be me and Aiden kissing and not the characters in my head. I was not ready to tell him about how he'd inspired my book though. I moved on to tonight. 'When you asked me to the pub, I was annoyed I'd agreed to go out with Jasper again.'

'That was another blow to my ego,' Aiden admitted. 'I told myself I needed to stop thinking about you but it didn't work.'

'It didn't work for me either. As you know. I left my date and came to find you.'

Aiden smiled. 'Seeing you walk in tonight was the best surprise. Please tell me that you won't be going out with Jasper again?'

'I don't think we're compatible,' I said. I wanted to ask Aiden about Zara. About the fact he had met up with her again. I opened my mouth to ask but Aiden leaned in closer and the words died on my lips.

'I'm very relieved to hear that,' Aiden whispered.

We looked at one another and sparks flew all around us.

'Please can I kiss you again now?' he asked, still softly.

There was plenty of time to talk more. I needed his lips back on mine. I nodded and he pulled me towards him, and our lips met again. Aiden made a contented sound and I curved my body against his, the heat building inside me as I tasted him. I felt like I could keep kissing him forever. Aiden pulled me closer, lifting my legs so they draped across his lap, and it was my turn to sigh contently. My whole body felt alive from his touch. Aiden kissed me gently but also hungrily as if he wanted me as much as I did him.

Then I pulled away from his lips and trailed kisses along the stubble on his jaw line.

'Liv,' Aiden sighed.

I looked up at him. 'You never call me Liv,' I said, lifting my hand to touch his hair. It felt as soft as I'd imagined it would. I traced a line down his face with my fingertip before brushing it against his lip.

'It annoys you too much when I call you Olivia,' he said, that glorious smirk of his reappearing.

'Let me tell you a secret,' I said. I turned his head so I could whisper into his ear. 'I only pretend to be annoyed by it.'

'Now she tells me,' he said with a groan.

I laughed. 'I have to keep you on your toes.'

Aiden kept one hand on my thigh and with the other, he reached out and ran his fingers through my hair. 'You certainly do that. So, what now?'

We stared at one another. I wanted him. I knew now he wanted me. But that was equally a relief and scary.

'I think I need to process this,' I said, my pulse still racing from his touch. I gestured between us. I had spent so long telling myself I hated Aiden that now he'd kissed me, I felt like I was on the edge of a precipice, unsure whether to jump into the unknown or crawl my way back.

'Okay. Sure. Just tell me one thing?'

I was nervous. 'What?'

'Am I a better kisser than Jasper?'

I burst out laughing. Aiden was always able to take me out of my own head and make me laugh. 'I don't want you getting an even bigger ego than you already have.' I kissed him once on the lips. 'I still can't believe we both thought differently about that night for ten years.'

'We need to work on our communication.'

'I suppose I should go to bed,' I said, a little bit reluctantly. I knew if I didn't leave now and Aiden kissed me again, I wouldn't be able to tear myself away.

'I should too,' he agreed. He leaned in towards me, moving back my hair so he could put his mouth close to my ear. 'Sleep well,' he said, his mouth tickling my ear.

My body trembled. I was pretty sure I wouldn't sleep a wink. I wanted to jump right back into his arms and explore every inch of him but this was Aiden. I needed to be 100 per cent sure that this was what I wanted. Everything felt different, like the Earth had tipped on its axis. I felt light-headed and dizzy as I climbed off Aiden's lap and stood up.

'Sweet dreams,' I told him.

I turned around and left the room, willing myself not to look back as I felt him watch me walk away.

26

Back in my bedroom, I closed the door and leaned against it, breathing heavily.

'Well, that happened,' I said out loud.

I went through the motions of getting ready for bed, pulling on my white nightdress, brushing my hair and teeth, and wiping off the last of the day's makeup and moisturising my face before climbing into bed in what felt like a trance.

It was late now and I could see the outline of the silvery moon through my curtains. I touched my face. My cheeks felt hot after kissing Aiden. In fact, my whole body was still warm. I didn't think I'd ever felt like this before. I was giddy. Greedy for more. But if Aiden's kisses alone had made such an impact, what would doing more with him do to me?

'Don't get carried away,' I told myself. But it was hard not to. We'd finally kissed. After all this time. And I now knew he'd wanted to kiss me the night we met. I hadn't imagined that moment. I couldn't stop smiling. I hoped he was smiling in the room next door.

My phone buzzed on my bedside table.

I rolled over in surprise. Who would be calling me at this time? Suddenly worried it was Dan not well, I grabbed it without looking at the screen properly. 'Hello? Hello?'

'You said I never ring you so I thought I would say goodnight,' Aiden's voice purred into my ear.

'You already said goodnight,' I said, but I was smiling. Aiden's accent was even sexier on the phone. 'You missing me already?'

'I think I might be. It's kind of torture you being next door.'

'You deserve it after all these years.'

'Fair enough. I'll accept my punishment with good grace. But just know, it's killing me.'

'Why did you move in here?' I wondered aloud as I rolled onto my back and looked up at the ceiling, picturing Aiden doing the same thing.

'It was 100 per cent a practical solution to my accommodation needs.'

'Oh, really?'

'Well, when Dan suggested it, I did think about the fact I'd be in close proximity to you,' he admitted.

'I could have killed him when he told me you'd be moving in. I thought I was being punished. I'd be seeing you at work, at home...'

'You deserve it after all these years.' He repeated what I'd said.

'It was all your fault,' I protested.

'Most things are.'

Speaking about Dan reminded me about what Aiden had said the night we'd met. I was hesitant to bring it up but it was something to think about if we were going to carry on kissing. 'I suppose we need to talk about Dan and what he might think if we ever want to do what we did tonight again.' I cringed inwardly. I sounded like I was still a teenager.

There was a short pause. 'That's true. Listen, I know this is kind of complicated and we like to banter so I just want you to know before you go to sleep that I want to kiss you again, Olivia, but I understand if you want us to go back to... whatever it is we've always been to each other, okay?'

I wasn't used to this serious, sweet side of Aiden. He'd always kept it for everyone but me. I understood why now. Because he hadn't wanted to let his guard down. I'd been exactly the same with him. I just couldn't help but tease him one more time. 'Hmm. I'll have to get back to you on that.'

Aiden chuckled. 'Okay, you do that, Olivia. But you know what? Tonight was worth the wait for me.'

My smile got so wide, I probably looked hysterical. Thank God he couldn't see me. 'Oh, yeah?'

'You tell me. You were the one who came looking for me after your "nice" moment with Jasper,' Aiden said, his voice turning husky. Goosebumps appeared on my arms. 'Was this just nice?'

'I've told you before. You're not nice, Aiden Rivers.'

'And yet you're already thinking about kissing me again.'

'Am I now?' I asked, but under the covers, my body was screaming *yes*.

I could hear the smirk in his voice, as if he was fully aware that I was. 'Sweet dreams, Olivia.'

I blushed thinking about my Aiden dreams. 'Goodnight.'

I put my phone down and curled up in bed, letting the memory of our heated moment wash over me again and again. I didn't think I'd ever get tired of replaying it.

I wanted to run into Aiden's room and do things to him I'd never done with anyone before. I knew sleeping with him would be unlike any encounter I'd had until now and I wanted it, I wanted him, more than I'd ever wanted anyone. Maybe because I'd wanted him so much, no one else had come close. It felt like past relationships, always brief, never meaning anything close to what I was looking for, had only been the starters and Aiden was my main course.

But it was complicated. We still had Dan to think about. We worked and lived together. We'd been pretending to hate each other for ten years. I was still nervous about giving my heart to anyone. I also was desperate to give my heart to Aiden. But I knew I had to be careful.

Because this undeniable tension, this heat between us, could either burn brightly or implode.

27

When Aiden walked into the flat the following morning, I was in the living room on my yoga mat. In the Downward Dog position, I tilted my head to watch as he strolled in. He was wearing shorts and a T-shirt, holding a water bottle, his hair damp.

'You got up early,' I said.

It was only 7 a.m. and when I'd woken up, the flat had been empty. I wondered if he'd been hoping to avoid me and had gone to work, so I was relieved to see he had just been to the gym.

'I had lots of energy I needed to burn off,' he replied with a grin. 'Looks like you did too.'

'Hmm.' I moved out of the position, self-conscious with him watching me. I was in leggings and a crop top and neither left much to the imagination. I noticed his bare legs then.

'Stop ogling me, Olivia, I'm not a piece of meat,' he said, putting the water bottle down and walking over.

'You love it,' I replied, climbing up off my yoga mat. I stretched my arms above my head. Aiden stared. 'Who's ogling now?'

'Can we stop talking about ogling please, it's getting creepy.' He turned towards the kitchen. 'How about I make us some breakfast?'

'You can't cook.'

'I've lived on my own since I was eighteen, I can cook breakfast,' he scoffed. 'We have time before work, right?'

I rolled up my mat and propped it up in the corner then followed him into the kitchen. I was glad things weren't too awkward between us. And that we could openly talk about looking at each other. Before, I only ever let myself steal glances at him but now I sat on a bar stool and propped my chin on my elbow to watch as he pulled out food from the fridge. He could reach the top cupboard easily whereas I had to stand on tiptoes. I watched him, appreciating his muscular arms, his broad shoulders, the way his damp hair curled slightly at the nape of his neck.

'Showered after the gym, did you?'

Aiden looked over his shoulder and shook his head. 'You are shameless. Are you upset I'm not in a white shirt or something?'

I spluttered, my cheeks burning instantly.

'Why are you looking so embarrassed?' he asked, confused.

'No reason at all,' I said, waving my hand to dismiss the question. 'I just think that look would suit you, that's all.'

'I bet you do, Colin Firth fangirl.'

'Mr Darcy fangirl,' I corrected. 'What are you making me then?'

'French toast.' He watched my face closely. 'You look sceptical. But this is my specialty.'

His expression made me suspicious. 'Let me guess – this is the food you make if a woman stays over?'

Aiden stopped what he was doing and walked over to lean on the other side of the kitchen counter. 'My gran used to make me this every Sunday and she taught me,' he said. 'This is wholesome, so get your mind out of the gutter, Olivia.'

I bit my lip to stop myself laughing. 'I'm sorry. I just don't think of you as wholesome. That's really sweet though. You and your gran.'

'It's very manly, you mean,' he said, and with a wink, he went back to cooking. 'So, you haven't freaked out too much yet.'

'There's plenty of time, it's only seven o'clock,' I replied. 'It feels weird going to work like nothing has happened…'

'I told you last night, nothing has to change if you don't want it to,' he said. 'Here we go.' He carried over two plates and sat down next to me. 'But just so you know, I am having a very difficult time keeping my hands off you in that outfit.'

'Good,' I said, and smiling, I took a bite of French toast. I moaned. 'Oh my God, Aiden.'

'Jesus,' Aiden said. 'You'll be the death of me.' But he smiled too. 'You like it?'

'It's delicious.'

Without thinking, I leaned over and kissed him once on the lips. I pulled back quickly, unsure who was more surprised by the move – me or him.

'Delicious,' Aiden agreed. He went back to his breakfast. 'I knew you wouldn't be able to keep your hands off me.'

'You'll be the death of me,' I said, repeating his words. I took another mouthful. It really was good French toast. I could get used to this. Then I remembered something and turned to Aiden in panic. 'What do I do about Jasper?'

'I don't really want to talk about him.'

'No.' I nudged him. 'I went on a date with him last night,' I said, shaking my head. How had that only been yesterday? It felt like so much had happened since then. 'What do I say?'

'"Your kiss didn't rock my world"?' Aiden reached out and stroked my thigh. I tried to concentrate on what he was saying but his touch made it difficult. 'If you don't want to mention me, I mean we don't… haven't… God, why am I so incoherent today?'

I giggled, glad that he was having a hard time focusing too.

'Just say you don't think it will work out. If that's what you think.'

I realised then he was as unsure as me about this between us. We'd kept up this wall for so long.

'It definitely won't work out with him,' I said firmly. Reluctantly, I checked the time and climbed off my stool. 'I'd better get ready for work. And so should you.'

'Yes, boss.'

Turning to leave, I paused and looked back. 'Will I see you later, after work?'

'You want to go out somewhere?'

I shook my head. 'No. Just hang out here, is that okay?'

I wasn't sure how I was going to concentrate on anything but Aiden today but at least knowing he'd be here when I got home would make it somewhat bearable.

'Sure. We can have a movie night. Do you want a lift in?'

'Yes, please,' I said, happy I got to be with him for a bit longer.

Aiden smiled. 'I like you in this mood.'

'What mood?'

'Not hating me.'

I smiled back. 'Right back at you.'

I finally made myself leave him then. I was in a good mood, I realised. It was a relief not to pretend that I hated him any more. I still had butterflies in my stomach about what all of this meant but knowing he had wanted to kiss me all those years ago, and still did, made me happier than I thought it would.

* * *

The morning was crisp and clear, the kind of mornings I loved in London. The blue sky stretched out like the sea above the city. I looked out the window as Aiden drove, music playing on the radio, and when an Olivia Rodrigo song came on, I turned to him and smiled. 'This reminds me of when we sang along badly on the way to Dan's last birthday night out.'

'Badly? We could be backing singers.' Aiden started singing along again, and laughing, I joined in.

'No Dan to tell us we are breaking his eardrums,' I said.

'Send him a video of us to wind him up.'

I pulled out my phone and started recording a video of our singing, both of us bopping our heads in time as well.

Eventually, I had to put the phone down because I was laughing too hard. As we drove into the car park, I sent it to my brother, telling him we wished he was here with us. Then after I'd sent it, I wondered if it had been a good idea.

Dan messaged back instantly.

I'm glad to see you both getting on so well! But you're both still off key :)

I wondered what he would say if he knew just how well we were getting on. I had no idea how he'd react if he knew I was lusting after his best friend. That was definitely something Aiden and I needed to talk about but there was no point if we didn't see anything more happening between us. It felt so unreal. Like a dream. At least Dan was away for the whole week. Aiden and I could exist in a bubble until we chose to pop it.

'Okay then,' I said when Aiden had parked and turned off the engine, the music stopping suddenly. 'I'll see you later.'

Aiden leaned over and kissed my cheek. 'Have a good day, Olivia.'

There was no point pretending I minded him calling me that. It would be strange for him to revert to Liv now. It was like he had a special name for me. And that made me smile even harder.

'You too.' I climbed out of the car and headed inside, feeling his eyes on me as I left.

I could put off telling anyone about what happened between me and Aiden but I did need to talk to Jasper. I couldn't begin to think about doing anything else with Aiden until I'd spoken to him. I hoped he wouldn't feel too hurt.

Stealing myself, I knocked on his office door.

'Liv, good morning,' he said, smiling when I entered. I closed the door behind me. 'This is a nice surprise. Do you want to sit down?'

'Oh, sure.' I sat in the chair behind the desk and folded my hands in my lap. 'So, Jasper, I really did have a lovely time yesterday but I have to be honest—'

'We're better as friends,' Jasper said, finishing my sentence for me. He nodded at my surprised expression. 'I got the feeling last night there wasn't, hmm, what is the right word?'

'Chemistry,' I supplied. 'I'm sorry.'

'No, you're right. I think that's right.'

'Oh, good.' I breathed a sigh of relief. 'You really are a great guy.'

'Thank you. And you are wonderful too.'

I could tell he really wasn't all that upset. You needed a spark to work with. And we didn't have one.

'So, friends?' I asked.

Jasper smiled. 'Of course.'

I stood up. 'I'd better get to the library and let you get on.'

'I'll pop by later.'

As I left, I received a message from Stevie, who had the day off.

Are you going to make me wait until I see you to tell me what happened at the pub with Aiden?

I had completely forgotten about her pep talk that had encouraged me to find Aiden after my lacklustre date with Jasper.

Um… things may have progressed a little bit with Aiden.

She replied straight away.

OMG! And how do you feel about that????

Good. Bad. Excited. Scared. I can't believe I might like Aiden, Stevie. I am all over the place! All I know is when we kissed, it was nothing like any other kiss I've had before.

You kissed! Yessssss!! Liv, you deserve a kiss like that. Wow. I am going to need all the details. Ring me as soon as you can.

Smiling, I replied.

Thanks, lovely! I will xxx

Then before anyone came into the library and I had to focus on work, I sent a message to Aiden.

I spoke to Jasper. I told him it wasn't going to work out between us. He was fine about it. See you at home!

It took another thirty seconds to decide whether to add any kisses or not. In the end, I sent one.
Aiden replied instantly.

I'll check on him later in case he's sobbing into his spreadsheets
;) See you at home x

Rolling my eyes, I put my phone away and started to shelve the returns trolley.

28

It felt like the longest day at work. I had enjoyed the library since I'd started working there but today, I kept watching the clock. I just wanted to be back at the flat with Aiden. But I was also freaking out about it (I know, I know, I freak out too much about too many things but at least I own it) and I wondered if Aiden was at all nervous. We had never been this alone and after what had happened last night, I was running scenarios through my mind. Would we have dinner and watch a film? Would we talk about us? Or would we do what I really wanted to do and rip each other's clothes off and not worry about anything else?

Aiden had a late lecture, I knew, so when it was time for me to hand the library over to Jamal, I hurried home alone and decided that it was better to be prepared just in case. I dived into the bath and shaved my legs. I used my strawberry body scrub too and afterwards, my strawberry body cream. I pulled on my white nightdress and re-straightened my hair and touched up my makeup. Looking at myself in my bedroom mirror, I took a calming breath. I felt so on edge. Restless. Like tonight had the power to change everything or nothing at all. Depending on what choice we both made.

'No pressure or anything,' I muttered. I picked up my perfume to give myself a spritz when I heard a noise. I froze, realising it was the sound of the flat door opening. Aiden was back half an hour earlier than I had expected.

Walking out of my bedroom, I watched him go into the kitchen. He was loosening his tie and had a bottle of wine in hand.

'You're back early,' I said. 'I'm still getting ready.'

'I finished my lecture early as to be honest, half the students looked ready to drop asleep. They'd been in a three-hour seminar beforehand. I'm going to have to talk to Professor...' Aiden trailed off as he finally looked at me. He slowly put the wine down onto the counter as his eyes took me in. He stilled. 'You're wearing that nightdress.'

I looked down at the white nightdress edged in lace.

'What's wrong with it?' I asked, confused.

Aiden shook his head. 'You know it's see-through, right? Every time you've worn this since I moved in, I've tried really hard not to look at you.' His face twisted in agony.

I bit my lip, trying not to smile. I wasn't going to deny I loved the fact he'd noticed that detail. I was enjoying this.

'I have no idea what you mean. It's completely innocent.' I stepped closer. 'Don't you think?' I gave a slow twirl.

Aiden groaned. 'You love torturing me, don't you?'

'You can talk. Wearing this.' I reached up and slid my fingers up his shirt to his tie. I saw him swallow hard. I slipped the tie off of him and draped it round my neck. 'You know how many times I've wanted to do that?'

'That might be the sexiest move I've ever witnessed,' he replied, his gaze holding mine steadily. His chest was rising and falling along with mine. I liked the fact his pulse was speeding up too.

'I have other moves,' I promised.

'I'm not sure I'll survive.' We looked at one another. Once again, it felt like we were the only two people in the world. It was exhilarating being alone with Aiden and not having to hide the fact I fancied him. Like we were caged birds finally set free. 'I like being able to talk to you like this,' I admitted.

'What, flirting instead of our veiled banter?' Aiden joked. 'I'm not sure I can talk with you wearing that though. Do you want to get dressed and I'll pour us some wine? I know that you need to think about everything and...' He stopped as I stepped closer, putting my hand on his arm.

'Suddenly, I'm not sure I want to talk,' I said, looking up at him. It was something to do with his response to this nightdress and how good he looked in his work suit. Plus the fact we had an empty flat. I was tired of pretending. Of holding back. I had stopped myself from wanting him for so long. Now it was spilling out of every pore. This need for him. 'What do you think?'

Aiden pushed my hair back off my face, then touched my cheek. 'I think I would do anything you wanted right now.'

'Even something illegal?' I asked, smiling. I moved closer and his hands moved down to rest on my hips. The material of the nightdress was so thin I could feel how hot his hands were, matching the heat bubbling up under my own skin.

'I told you, you're trouble,' Aiden murmured. 'I think you could talk me into anything.'

'I'll have to remember that,' I said lightly.

I looked up and studied his face. His lips curved into that smile he shared only with me, his delicious green eyes smouldering down at me. There was a line of stubble across his chin that added to how sexy he looked right now. His hair was tousled from the breeze outside. I lifted a hand and ran my fingers through it. Then I lifted myself up on tiptoes so our faces were in line.

'For now though, I'd just take a kiss. If you want...'

Before I finished the sentence, Aiden's lips caught mine. He kissed me softly, as if I was precious. My whole body instantly lit up with his touch. I tried to get closer.

'Too tall,' I complained, pulling away slightly.

'Here.' Aiden deftly lifted me up onto the kitchen counter. 'Better?'

'Much better.' I parted my legs and he stepped in between them. Hooking them around his waist, I reached up and pushed at his jacket. He shrugged it off his shoulders then moved closer to kiss me again. Gentle, probing, then his tongue found mine. I let out a moan and the kiss deepened. I wrapped my arms around his neck and Aiden moved his to the small of my back, heating me up instantly. His mouth moved from my lips to my neck and across my collarbone then back up my neck to my jaw line, dropping gentle kisses all along the way. I gasped as a shiver ran down my body from his touch.

Aiden lifted his lips off me for a moment and smiled. 'See what that nightdress does to me?'

'Maybe you'd better take it off so it doesn't get you into more trouble,' I suggested.

'That sounds like more trouble,' he replied. His eyes were locked on mine. 'Are you sure?' he asked seriously.

'Yes,' I breathed.

'We can still open the wine, watch a movie, talk about world peace...' His eyes twinkled.

'I think we should do that later. Maybe not the world peace part though. Right now, we should go to my bedroom.' Then I hesitated, suddenly unsure. 'Only if you want to though.'

Aiden reached out to touch my lips with his fingertips. 'You have no idea how much I want you.'

'Show me,' I said, my nerves fading and my desire increasing.

'So bossy.' But with that delicious smirk of his, he lifted me up off the counter. I laughed as he carried me to my bedroom. 'Definitely preferable to you being on my back,' he said when we got there.

'I wanted an excuse to touch you,' I said, remembering my drunken request for a piggyback.

'Why do you think I agreed to it?' He laid me gently down on the bed, leaning over me. Then he gave me a long, lingering kiss.

I shifted beneath him so he sat up, letting me kneel on the bed next to him. I reached for the buttons of his white shirt and began to unbutton them.

'I do enjoy a white shirt.'

'You may have mentioned that,' he said, smiling.

His shirt open, I slid my hands up his chest, enjoying the feel of his muscles, tense beneath my hands. Then I pushed the shirt off him and onto the floor.

'Much better.'

'I'm at a disadvantage though,' Aiden said. 'Put your arms up.'

His eyes smouldering at me, I lifted my arms. Aiden reached for my nightdress and pulled it off me. His breath hitched and he tossed it onto the floor on top of his shirt. 'I'm glad I came back early. It would have been a crime if you'd had time to get dressed,' he said softly as he took in my bare breasts and white, lacy knickers.

'A crime.' I smiled. I liked the way he was looking at me. My cheeks flushed and my whole body thrummed with need. I wanted him to touch me everywhere.

Reading my mind, Aiden scooped a hand around my back and pulled me towards him. His mouth dipped down and kissed the hollow of my throat. I tilted my head back as he moved down my chest, leaving a trail of kisses, before moving sideways to press his lips to my breast. He moved to my nipple, taking it into his mouth. I let out a moan then, unable to keep it in.

He then carried on kissing down my chest towards my stomach, stopping just at the edge of my underwear.

'Aiden,' I murmured.

'You okay, Liv?' he asked, lifting his head up.

'Don't call me that. You call me Olivia,' I said, my eyes opening. Aiden's face lit up.

'My Olivia,' he said. He put a hand on the bed, guiding me down onto the duvet. 'You are the most beautiful woman I have ever met.'

'Aiden,' I breathed, squirming on the bed as he leaned over me again. I pulled his face down and kissed him. 'I need you to touch me. Please.'

'So demanding,' he said, but he put his hand on my cheek. He brushed it once delicately then moved his hand down to my breast then down my stomach then along my thigh. I trembled with anticipation. Aiden kept his eyes locked onto me and I couldn't tear mine away from him. He stroked me under my thigh and I let out a whimper. I couldn't help it. My body was filling with heat again. It felt like he was going to set me on fire. And I was happy to let him make me burn.

Finally, his fingertips found my knickers. He raised an eyebrow and I nodded furiously, lifting my bum up. Chuckling, Aiden slipped my underwear off. He murmured something under his breath – something that sounded like 'Jesus Christ.'

'Now I'm at the disadvantage,' I said, echoing his earlier words.

Aiden stood up and slipped off his trousers and boxer shorts all in one go. My eyes widened when I saw how much he wanted me. I bit my lip to stop myself using the words 'very big and very hard' but from the look on his face, he knew what I was thinking.

'Ogling me again, Olivia.' He tutted as he climbed back onto the bed.

'Yep,' I said, licking my lips.

Aiden leaned back over me. 'You sure about this?'

'Yes, yes,' I said. 'Are you?'

'I have never been so sure.' He moved his hand up my leg, stroking my thigh slowly then moving towards the spot where I ached for him. I moaned as he slipped his fingers inside.

'Aiden,' I gasped as he touched me. The ache inside me built further. 'Please,' I begged. 'Aiden.'

I tugged on his arm.

'What do you need?' he asked, curling his fingers inside me in a delicious movement that made me catch my breath.

I lifted my head to look at him. 'I need you to fuck me,' I gasped.

Aiden's eyebrow quirked. 'Olivia, I'm shocked,' he said, then he leaned closer. 'Say it again.'

'Fuck me, please,' I said with a laugh.

'Very polite.' He gave me a swift kiss. 'You're amazing. Hang on.' He let go of me and I whimpered. He disappeared for a moment but hurried back carrying a wrapped condom.

'I was worried for a minute,' I said.

When he came back to the bed, this time I pulled him to me and moved my hand down his chest, across his defined stomach and then to his thigh. Then it was Aiden's turn to gasp as I wrapped my hand around him. He throbbed with desire.

Aiden pushed back my hair to see my face properly. 'You're incredible. Can I fuck you now, please?'

I laughed at him using my line on me. 'Hell yes.'

Aiden unwrapped the condom and slipped it on. I made to move but he shook his head.

'I like this view.' His hands slid over my breasts. 'If you don't mind.'

I pulled my legs over so I could sit astride him.

'I definitely don't mind.' I moved on top of him. 'Is this okay?'

'Perfect,' Aiden said as he slid inside me and we both gasped at the friction between us. 'You are perfect.'

'You're not so bad yourself,' I said. I looked down at him

watching me with hooded eyes and I winked. He pulled me towards him and kissed me, both of us moving slowly together.

I had honestly always felt a bit underwhelmed in the bedroom before but not this time. My body had never felt so alive. I moved faster, wanting to feel more. I wanted Aiden even closer. I couldn't get enough.

'Olivia,' Aiden said urgently. 'Please tell me this feels as good to you as it does to me.'

I nodded, not even able to speak. I lifted myself back up and we gasped again as Aiden slid in even deeper. He reached for my hips and I placed my hands on that gorgeous chest of his.

'God, Aiden,' I said. 'I need more.'

He rolled us over then, flipping me onto my back. I lifted my legs and wrapped them around him as he thrusted deeper into me. He lifted my hands above my head and held them with his.

'So gorgeous,' he said.

'Faster,' I breathed, and he thrusted into me again and again, deeper and faster and I gripped his hands so tightly, I was sure I was hurting him.

I lost all awareness as we moved together, pleasure building and building inside me until it became almost unbearable, and then I felt the most delicious release. I let out a moan that I didn't think I was capable of producing.

'Fuck, Olivia,' Aiden gasped as he let out one last moan and collapsed on top of me. I felt him tremble as I released his hands. I threaded my fingers in his hair as we clung to one another, our hearts beating in quick time together.

He lifted his head to look at me. 'Okay?'

'More than okay,' I said with a contented sigh.

The sexiest of all his smirks appeared. 'Thank God for that.'

29

Aiden went to the bathroom then the kitchen and came back into my room with a bottle of wine and two glasses. He hovered in the doorway in just his boxers.

'You want to stay in here?'

I sat up, now back in my nightdress.

'It's cosy in here,' I said, not adding that it felt easier to be intimate with him in my room. I watched him shyly as he climbed into the bed beside me and poured us a glass each. My body was still tingling from him. I felt contented in a way I'd never felt before. Not just sexually satisfied (but FYI – wow!) but like I could finally relax.

'Here.' Aiden passed me a glass then looked across at me, propped up on the pillow. 'I haven't spent much time in your room before. You always escaped in here when things got interesting,' he said, teasing.

'I was worried I'd give myself away if I didn't,' I confessed. I took a gulp of wine. 'What do you think?' I asked, gesturing to the room with a questioning look.

Aiden took the room in. Dan had given me free rein to decorate or bring in anything I wanted. I had a huge bookshelf, of course (arranged by author) and a vintage dressing table and wardrobe. My bed had a white frame and was covered with a floral duvet cover that always gave the room a feeling of spring. On the windowsill were pictures in antique frames. Aiden's eyes went to them.

'Is that...?' He jumped out of the bed to go over and I appreciated the view of his bum as he moved. He picked up one of the pictures and then turned to look at me, the frame in his hands. 'You have a picture of me.'

'Not just you,' I said, sinking down into the pillows. It was of me, Aiden and Dan when we went to Disneyland Paris for Dan's twentieth birthday. Mum came too, as did Dan's boyfriend at the time. Aiden and I were both single so we hadn't brought anyone and honestly, it had been such a fun trip. Mum had made us take this picture, in front of the castle, telling us to squeeze in. Aiden had had his arm around me and I looked so happy; it was one of my favourites. If life got sucky, I always looked at it as a reminder that there would always be days that brought joy.

'I loved that trip.'

'Me too,' Aiden said, putting it down. 'I used to have a picture of us in my flat. It was that Christmas we stayed in a cottage and we had a Christmas movie night in front of the fire and we all wore ridiculous novelty pyjamas.'

I snorted. 'They were so ugly! You don't have it any more?'

Aiden walked back over. 'I moved it for Zara.'

'Oh,' I said. Zara. I had told Jasper we had no future yet I wasn't sure if Aiden had had the same conversation with his ex – or if he even needed to or not. And I was too nervous to ask.

This was all so new. I felt like I wanted to hold on to Aiden and never let him go, lest someone burst this bubble we'd created.

He climbed back into the bed beside me.

'I love that you have that picture.' He leaned towards me then hesitated. 'I'm still in disbelief that I get to kiss you. Unless you've decided to revoke my rights again?'

'Why would I do that?' I asked, surprised.

'Well, maybe it was just a one-time thing for you,' he began in a fake dramatic voice. 'Maybe you're now tired of my body. Maybe you've used me and now you'll cast me aside like a discarded potato.'

'Why would you discard a potato? Surely you'd just eat it?'

'Not if it's rotten,' Aiden pointed out.

I laughed, loving the fact I didn't need to hide how funny I found him and then I pulled him to me to give him a drawn-out kiss. His lips felt so good on mine. It seemed crazy we hadn't been doing this the whole time we'd known each other. I felt more comfortable with him than any other man but it wasn't a boring familiarity, it was a special one. A thrilling one. I wanted to tell him that I really hoped this wasn't a one-time thing, that this was something I wanted to do over and over again.

But before I could, my phone rang on my bedside table. I looked over at it and my eyes widened.

'Dan is FaceTiming me,' I said in horror. 'I can't answer it in bed with you!'

Aiden took a moment to reply as if he was weighing the situation up. 'Just call him back in a minute, say you were in the bathroom.'

'Okay, good plan.' I picked up my phone as the call ended. I looked at Aiden. 'Do we need to tell him though?' I asked nervously.

I wasn't sure what I was most nervous about. Telling Dan I'd slept with his best mate would probably mean having to admit I'd actually liked Aiden all along but had kept it a secret. Which Dan might be upset about. He'd be shocked, I knew that for sure. I also didn't know if Aiden wanted to tell him. Maybe he'd asked me if this was a one-time thing because that was what it was; that was what he thought was for the best.

'We don't have to yet, if that's what you want?' Aiden asked. 'He's at your mum's all week, isn't he?'

'Okay, good,' I agreed quickly. It was a relief to put it off. To not have to have a big talk about me and Aiden just yet. 'I'll go and call him,' I said, jumping up.

I walked to the door and looked back. Aiden was watching me and I wished I knew what he was thinking.

'Don't leave,' I blurted out before I walked out. 'I'll be right back.'

I sat down on the sofa and took a deep breath before calling Dan back.

'There you are,' he said with relief when he picked up.

'Why, what's wrong?' I said, instantly on alert.

'Oh, nothing, just Mum driving me crazy. I know she means well but she's hovering all the time and won't let me do anything – not even make a video for TikTok.'

'Well, I hope you weren't considering making a dance video,' I said, hoping I was coming off as normal. I was worried my voice sounded an octave higher than it usually did. All I could think about was Aiden waiting for me in my bed.

'I thought it would be funny with my cast,' Dan huffed.

'Dan!' I admonished him. 'Why don't you do a jokey video about being a bad patient? Sneaking around, trying to film a TikTok, or you could pretend to be a lord and ring a bell for Mum to make you something?'

'These are good ideas,' he said happily. 'I'm on it. Anyway, how are things there? You and Aiden getting on okay still? You should post that video of you both singing in his car, it was cute.'

I couldn't help but smile. Were we cute together? I hoped we were.

'That was to cheer you up, for your eyes only! He's out actually, I'm just chilling,' I found myself lying. 'Have you heard from Theo?' I asked, desperate to not talk about Aiden.

'We spoke this morning. It's going to be the longest time we've been apart since we got together. I told Mum, by the way...'

'What did she say?'

'She told me I'm being an idiot basically.'

I struggled to control my laughter.

'No need to agree! She said Dad hurt the hell out of us but was I really going to let that man ruin relationships for me from now on? And she has a point.'

'Wow. I mean, yeah, she does.' I wondered what advice she'd have for me about Aiden. If I ever dared to tell her about him.

'I'd better go. Mum has made some vegan, gluten-free dessert that I'm frankly scared to try.'

Laughing, I told him to send her my love and we hung up. I walked slowly back into my room. Aiden was still there propped up in my bed drinking wine. I blinked twice. 'It wasn't a dream,' I said, as usual blurting out my thoughts aloud when I really shouldn't.

A slow smiled spread across his face. 'I hope not.'

I rushed over, forgetting that I should probably try to play it cool, and climbed back into bed next to him. 'Hi.'

'Hi.'

'That was weird,' I admitted. 'Talking to Dan and not saying anything. About any of this.' I pointed between the two of us, hoping that there might now be an us.

Aiden reached out to stroke my arm. 'We don't have to figure it all out now.'

'We have until the weekend,' I agreed. I leaned in and kissed him. 'You taste like wine.'

'Is that bad?' he asked huskily, putting his arm around my waist.

'I just need to catch up.' I moved to get my glass of wine.

'Catch up like this,' Aiden said, pulling me back to him. I smiled against his lips and tasted him again. He slipped his tongue against mine and I let out a contented noise, letting him pull me down onto the bed. The world around us seemed to blur, leaving just the two of us on my bed kissing, as if we needed each other's lips to breathe.

30

Wednesday was my day off from the library, and I was really excited to get back to writing.

'Will you ever tell me what your book is about?' Aiden asked when he came out into the living room dressed in his work suit, holding his car keys, to find me on the sofa in my pyjamas, my laptop on the coffee table ready for me to start.

I took a sip of my coffee and shook my head. 'As you said about the film festival, I'd tell you but then I'd have to kill you.'

I wondered what Aiden would say if he knew how similar my fictional romance had now become to my real life. I was too embarrassed to tell him that he'd inspired my male character and the story, how I'd wished for him to see me as a leading lady, how he'd always been my love interest. This felt too new, too delicate, for me to admit yet. I didn't want to scare him away.

'Okay, I get it. But I feel pressure to live up to whatever romance you're writing,' he said.

'I'm open to any romance you want to send my way,' I teased. I put my coffee down next to my laptop and walked over to him. 'Your tie is crooked.'

'I know,' he replied with a grin. 'I made sure it was.'

Smiling, I reached up and fixed it for him. I breathed in his aftershave. It was a novelty being able to be this close and look at him without worrying he'd know exactly what I was thinking. This time, I hoped he did.

'You got out of bed before I woke up,' I said softly. I'd opened my eyes to light streaming in my bedroom and the sound of Aiden in the shower, and I was a bit disappointed to have missed a wake-up kiss. Although I do remember waking up a few times in the night, our bodies pressed together, and that helped a bit.

'You looked too peaceful. And I slept through my alarm so I had to hurry.' I let go of his tie and he ran his fingers through my hair. 'Has anyone told you how lovely you look first thing in the morning?'

I scoffed. 'Yeah, right.' I tried to step back but he held me close. 'I need a shower and to brush my hair,' I said, squirming.

'But I need a kiss. Pretty please?'

'As you've asked so nicely,' I replied, powerless to resist.

He touched my cheek and my heart instantly picked up speed as he moved down to touch my lips. I parted them automatically and he ran his fingertip across the surface before cupping my chin and drawing my face to his. I melted into him, tilting my face up to meet his in a delicious kiss. I forgot all about the fact I wasn't dressed and wrapped my arms around his neck.

Aiden lifted me off my feet as he kissed me and I squealed. Laughing, he put me down.

'If I don't stop now, I won't be able to at all,' he said, stepping back from me with regret in his eyes. 'Can I take you out tonight?'

'You want to?' I asked happily.

'I think we should have our official first date.' He reached behind him and picked up his leather laptop bag. 'If that's okay with you?'

We were still both dipping our toes in the water. When he kissed me like that though, I wished I could dive right in.

I nodded. 'Yes, please.'

'Okay, I'll pick you up after work. Be ready for seven?'

'I'll be here,' I promised, biting my lip to stop the grin that threatened to break out. 'Have a good day. Try not to think about me too much.'

Aiden chuckled and with a wave, he walked out, leaving me staring after him.

I went back to the sofa. I was so lost in this haze of Aiden; writing was the only way to make sense of it. I'd left my characters after their kiss in the rain but now I had spent the night with Aiden (oh my God, I'd spent the night with Aiden!), my characters needed to catch up with us.

Before I could open my laptop, my phone vibrated with a message. When I saw Aiden's name appear on the screen, I grabbed it eagerly.

I'm already thinking about you. My car still smells like your perfume.

Smiling, I sent one back referring to his Mini by her name.

I hope Molly isn't too upset.

She's sulking, took a minute to start but I assured her she's still my number one girl.

I put my phone down, wondering what I needed to do to become Aiden's number one girl; that position sounded more appealing than I wanted to admit.

I opened up my laptop and picked up where I'd left Lily and

Adam over their picnic on the beach. I'd started a new chapter the next day, planting them at work together in the café, unsure how to be with one another now they had kissed.

I looked up from my laptop and thought back to me and Aiden last night. I couldn't stop smiling. I had been accused of being a hopeless romantic more than once. I'd self-confessed to being one too. Before last night though, I'd worried that I'd never have anything close to what you found in stories, nothing close to an epic romance movie or the kind of thing people waxed lyrically about in poems or sang love songs about.

But what if I had just been waiting for Aiden?

I didn't think I'd ever be able to tell him that so I went back to writing. I could write down how he had made me feel. Immortalise it in my book. So, even if it didn't last in real life, it would last on the page.

When it's time to close the café, Lily admits she doesn't want to go home so Adam invites her to come to his place. It starts to rain as they walk there so Adam takes her hand and they break into a run, laughing as they make their way to his beach house close by.

Inside, they shake off the rain and Adam finds a blanket to wrap around Lily. Rubbing her arm, he looks down at her and when she smiles, he can't resist kissing her again.

Lily kisses him back eagerly. She has never felt this alive before. This confident. This sure of someone. Sparks fly around the room as she lifts her arms up and Adams peels off her wet shirt, then his own. The room is lit only by the moonlight. The only sound they can hear is the beating of the rain and their hearts.

'I need you to touch me. Please,' Lily says, the ache inside her building.

'So polite,' Adam says with a smile. But he gives her exactly what she wants. He would give her everything. She only has to ask.

When I finished their sex scene, ending it with them curled up on the blanket on the floor looking out at the sea, holding one another like they never wanted to let go, I realised a tear had rolled down my cheek. Surprised, I brushed it away and closed the laptop. I felt like I could breathe again. I'd been writing for an hour, my fingertips dancing over the keys, desperate to get the words – and all my feelings about my night with Aiden – out onto the page.

I'd kept my feelings so tightly bottled up for years that I had no idea what I should let out. If anything.

My phone lit up with a message and I pounced on it, hoping it was Aiden again. But it was Stevie.

Aiden just came into the library to ask me something… It sounded suspiciously like the two of you are going on a date later. Are you holding out on me?!!!

What did he come to ask you?

I sent back, instantly curious.

My lips are sealed!!!!! But you never gave me the details from the night you met him at the pub. You are really leaving me hanging. Not what a best friend does *stern face*

I chuckled at her message. She was right though. I had been keeping Aiden to myself. Because I was still finding it hard to believe it was all real. I needed to tell her though. If I said it all out loud, maybe I would believe it was actually happening.

I wrote back to Stevie to see if she wanted to meet on her lunch break and discuss and, of course, she replied with a very enthusiastic yes including lots of exclamation points.

I smiled and jumped up to get ready.

31

I sat in the coffee shop around the corner from the university at a table by the window waiting for Stevie to arrive. This was a café that I knew staff at the university rarely used. I didn't want anyone to overhear our conversation.

'I ordered us cheese toasties,' I said when Stevie came in, pushing a coffee across the table in her direction.

'Oh, this is serious,' she said, taking off her jacket and sitting down opposite me. Cheese toasties were our comfort lunch if we were having a bad day.

'You could say I'm in emotional turmoil or that we like to exaggerate,' I replied. I already felt better to be talking to Stevie about it all though.

'Start from the beginning,' she requested, picking up her coffee. 'And finish with how Aiden is taking you out tonight. And speak quickly, we only have an hour.'

So, I did. I leaned over and told her about going to see him at the pub after my disappointing date with Jasper, how Aiden and I had flirted and eventually kissed, and how we had finally talked about the night we met and realised we had got it wrong. Her eyes widened when I got to the part where we slept together.

'You don't mess around, do you, Liv?'

'I *have* known him ten years. Why, do you think we moved too quickly?'

'Hell, no. I'd have jumped his bones too after all that!'

I laughed. Stevie always made me feel better.

'This is so crazy though. I mean, me and Aiden!'

'I don't think it's crazy at all. When you told me about him, I could tell you'd been dying to talk to someone about him for years. I don't think you ever stopped fancying him even though you couldn't admit it even to yourself. And I think he feels exactly the same way.'

'We haven't talked about what this all means though. I'm so worried about Dan. What will he think? Or maybe Aiden thinks this is just for fun, while Dan is away. Maybe he doesn't want him to find out?'

Our toasties arrived and we tucked in eagerly.

Stevie thought over what I had just said and when she'd swallowed her first bite, she responded.

'Listen, I've been single for as long as you have, so take any advice from me with a pinch of salt, but all these questions – you're going to have to ask Aiden them at some point.'

'Ugh, I know.' I grimaced. 'I'm scared though. This all feels so much bigger than anything else I've had before, you know? This isn't a random hook up, it's Aiden. It's scary.'

'I bet he's just as nervous.'

'He never seems scared about anything.'

'Everyone gets scared. He might hide it better, that's all,' she pointed out. Leaning back in the chair, she sighed. 'You really are my inspiration right now. Not only are you writing a novel and going after your dream, but you've also snagged the man you've been in love with for years!'

I choked on my toastie and had to take a gulp of coffee before I could speak. 'No one said anything about love!'

Stevie raised an eyebrow. 'Well, I'm still kind of jealous. You're writing a love story then it starts happening for real!'

I smiled. 'It's crazy. I started using Aiden as my inspiration almost subconsciously but once you pointed it out, I couldn't unsee it. It made me realise that maybe I'd always wondered if he could be my own love intertest. God, I sound so cringe.'

'It's so cute. Will you tell him he inspired your book?'

I looked at her in horror. 'No way. We are still in such new territory, I don't want to scare him off.'

'But surely—'

'No way,' I cut her off firmly. 'Okay, I think we need to change the subject.' I pointed at her. 'If I'm making you feel so inspired, why not do something about it?'

Stevie tutted at the subject change. 'I told you, I'm over dating right now.'

I shook my head. 'Not dating. Publishing! You should go after your dream job. You'd be brilliant at it.'

'When I tried before, I didn't even get any interviews. I applied for some editorial assistant positions and got nowhere.'

'Hmm, maybe you should consider another role?'

Stevie thought about that. 'You know what? When I did an event at the library with that sci-fi author, her literary agent did say something about me being really good at events compared to other libraries they'd been to,' she said slowly.

'Ooh, that's great,' I said eagerly. 'So, maybe you could think about marketing or publicity? I wonder if the agent knows anyone looking. You could ask her?'

'Is that the done thing?'

'You don't know until you ask; the worst she can say is no, right? Ask her if you could have a coffee and a chat about publishing.'

Stevie smiled. 'That's actually a great idea. I'm going to email her. You're right, Liv, life's too short not to try and do what I want to do. Look at what happened to Dan.'

'That was so scary,' I agreed. 'It does make you think.'

I wondered if I could take the same advice and use it to not be scared of what was happening with Aiden. Why was it that you could want something but be scared of it all at once? It was like I was equally worried about things not working out with Aiden as I was of things working out.

'We only have a couple more days until Dan comes home. He won't stay longer; Mum is annoying him with her hovering and TikTok banning.'

'So, talk to Aiden and figure it out together. Now...' She leaned forward. 'Does this mean we get a sex scene in your book?'

'I may have written one yes,' I said. 'There's no way this book can ever see the light of day though.'

'All writing is good practice, whatever you decide to do with it. But I think you should finish the book. I need a happy ever after.'

I sighed. 'God, me too.'

* * *

Stevie refused to give anything away about what Aiden had asked her so I got ready for our first official date without any clue as to where we'd be going or what we were doing. When I asked, Aiden just told me to wear whatever I wanted. And when I told him that was incredibly unhelpful, he amended it to smart casual.

I changed five times.

I hated not knowing where I was going but I was excited to go out with Aiden. It was strange. We had been out, spent time together, so many times through the years. Now it was different. New. Unfamiliar. And I had a lot of butterflies churning around in my stomach.

Finally, I settled on wide leg trousers, a blouse, heels and my boucle blazer, topping the outfit off with a bag I'd found at a charity shop that was a dupe of a Chanel classic flap, a bag I could only dream of owning. When I was somewhat satisfied with my outfit, I left my room and found Aiden waiting for me in the kitchen.

I smiled to see he'd changed from work. He wore black trousers and a dark shirt and held out a red rose for me as I walked over to him.

I breathed in the pretty scent of the rose.

'This is a bit romantic.'

'I know who I'm dealing with.' He kissed my cheek. 'Better not mess up your lipstick just yet. You look gorgeous.'

'You look very handsome,' I replied.

'This is new,' Aiden said. 'Compliments instead of arguments.' He checked his phone. 'Our taxi is here, come on.'

'I'm nervous, not knowing where we're going or what we're doing,' I said as we walked out of the flat. It was a clear night and the stars above the tall buildings were twinkling as if they were in on our secret date and giving us their blessing.

'You can't be nervous with me,' Aiden said cheerfully.

I looked across at him as we climbed into the taxi. He was smiling and looked relaxed, as if this was something we did every night. As we drove away, he picked up my hand from between us and held it.

'This okay?' he asked, rubbing his thumb over the back of my palm.

I wondered how many times I'd wished to be able to touch him. And now here we were, holding hands. All I could do was nod for fear of blurting out a request to never stop touching me. We drove first to a restaurant to eat. I recognised it from TikTok. Dan had talked about going. It was an Italian with beautiful flowers hanging from the ceiling and a wall filled floor to ceiling with bottles of oils and wine. We had a table right in the middle and the atmosphere was lively but intimate, with candles on the table and the chairs pushed close together.

'Delicious,' I said when I took a bite of my truffle pasta. 'Did Dan tell you about this place?'

'I remembered you mentioned it the other night,' Aiden replied, before taking a sip of wine. 'It's really good, isn't it? The company isn't bad either.'

I tapped him with my foot under the table and he grinned.

'You know, this is only the second time we've been out just the two of us.'

'When was the first?' I asked in surprise, not remembering doing anything close to this before with him.

'Last Christmas at your mum's. Theo and Dan got stuck in traffic from London – I'd arrived before them and you were already there. Your mum told us to go to the restaurant she'd booked and keep the table while she waited for them. But then they were so late she cooked something at home.'

I nodded. 'Oh, yeah. That cosy pub. You stayed two nights with us then went to Zara's family home. We got a bit drunk on wine.' I waved my glass. 'It's happening again.'

'You said something that night that made me think,' Aiden said, topping up our glasses again. 'You said you'd never met anyone special enough to want to spend Christmas with. It made me realise that I wasn't looking forward to spending Christmas with Zara and her family. I would rather have stayed with you and yours.'

We held each other's gaze. 'I'd rather you'd stayed too. Not that it was the same; you were there as Dan's best friend.'

Aiden reached across the table to squeeze my hand. 'Whenever I was with you guys, I was always there for you as much as Dan.'

'I used to tell myself I wasn't looking forward to you being there,' I admitted. 'But it was always more fun.'

'Always,' Aiden agreed. We smiled at one another. It was like we were rewriting our history. In the best way. He checked his watch. 'We need to get the bill or else we'll be late.'

'Late for what?'

Aiden paid for our meal and ushered me out into another taxi, which took us to Waterstones in Piccadilly. My eyes lit up. 'We're going book shopping?'

Aiden took my hand. 'Better than that. Come on.'

Intrigued, I let him pull me through the doors and lead us upstairs to the fiction floor. There were lots of people milling around and Aiden weaved us through to the back where chairs were laid out and in front of them were two women. I recognised one of them immediately.

I stopped short. 'Is that...?' I stared at her in shock.

Aiden smiled. 'Felicity Fowler. She's doing a talk and signing tonight. I checked with Stevie that I hadn't got it wrong and she's one of your favourite authors...'

I didn't let Aiden finish. I reached up and kissed him.

'This is the best first date I've ever had,' I told him.

His eyes lit up.

And I wished this night never had to end.

32

Once Felicity had read an extract from her latest book, the crowd formed a queue to get our copies signed.

'You go,' Aiden encouraged. 'Tell her about your book.'

'I can't,' I squeaked.

'You won't get this opportunity again,' he said.

I took a breath. 'Okay.' Aiden squeezed my hand and I got up and joined the queue to meet Felicity. I glanced back at Aiden in his seat. He gave me a little wave and my stomach flipped as I smiled back. I couldn't quite believe he'd organised this for me. He knew how much I dreamed of being an author and doing events like this myself one day, and it was sweet he'd thought of bringing us here.

As I reached Felicity, I held out my book. 'I love your books,' I said like a real fangirl.

'Thank you. Who shall I make it out to?'

'Oh, Liv, please. Can I ask you something?'

Felicity smiled as she signed my book. 'Go ahead.'

'Did you always know this was what you wanted to do?'

Felicity handed me the book back. 'Always. And it was hard, lots of rejections along the way, but writing my first novel was the best thing I've ever done.'

'I'm trying to write my own romance.'

'Oh, amazing, good luck with it. If it's what you really want, don't give up, okay?'

'I won't,' I promised, awed by her. 'Thank you!'

I took my signed book happily back to Aiden. 'She told me not to give up writing,' I said as he stood up.

'Well, of course you shouldn't. I think it's amazing you're writing a book, I just wish you'd tell me what it's about,' he said, placing his hand on the small of my back as we left the room.

'Maybe this date will give me inspiration,' I said, glancing at him to see what he thought about that. I longed to tell him he'd inspired my book more than he knew but I was still feeling kind of shy about it. I had no idea how Aiden felt about me, or us, yet.

'What would you rate it out of ten so far?' he asked.

'Hmm. Nine. There's always room for improvement.'

'I take that as a challenge,' Aiden replied.

We left the bookshop and went to a nearby jazz bar where a band was playing.

Aiden raised his cocktail glass as we found a free table. 'What shall we toast to?'

'Our first date,' I said.

We clinked and took a sip, watching each other. I wanted to add how much I hoped we'd have many more dates but we still had the looming deadline of my brother returning home to discuss.

Aiden looked like he was going to say something but I didn't want the magic of the evening to end so I spoke first.

'How are you finding the new job? I feel like I haven't asked you.'

He smiled. 'I love it here. I think I definitely made the right move.'

'You are good at making moves,' I agreed, pulling my cocktail closer to me so I could take a sip.

Aiden leaned in to speak over the band. 'You said you couldn't imagine me in a lecture theatre before. Are you admitting I'm a good teacher now?'

Our banter had continued as it always had but now we didn't have to hide the flirty edge to it. Which I was obviously thoroughly enjoying.

I kept my face confused though. 'I have no idea what you mean. You haven't taught me anything.'

'Sounds like another challenge,' Aiden replied. 'Want to dance?'

'Huh?' I asked, my mind clearly more focused on the direction of the bedroom than his was.

'Dance with me.' He nodded to the back of the bar. I turned to see a small dance floor by the band, and a few couples were swaying to the music.

'You don't dance,' I said in surprise.

'You've never been with me when there's been an opportunity. Come on.'

He held out his hand and I took it, feeling like I couldn't stop myself from doing whatever he suggested. As a self-confessed hopeless romantic, the idea of the man I liked asking me to dance had me swooning a little bit. We walked over and joined the dancefloor. Aiden put his arm around my waist and spun me in a circle as I reached up to grip his shoulders. He smiled down at me as we moved to the music. And I wished I could take a picture of us right at that moment so I could look at it forever.

'You've been holding out on me,' I said as he spun me around again.

'What would you have said if I'd asked you to dance before this?' He put his hand on my back and dipped me down to the floor. 'Is this a ten yet?'

I reached up and brushed my lips against his. He pulled me up gently and held me close.

'I think I need to see more of your teaching skills first.'

Aiden chuckled. 'So demanding.'

He kissed me then and I eagerly kissed him back, turning the kiss into something that was not quite publicly decent.

'Can we go home now?' I asked when we reluctantly pulled apart.

'I think we'd better.'

We hurried out of the bar and into a taxi. As we drove, I looked across at Aiden's face lit up by the lampposts, thinking I'd never had such a romantic evening before. I felt happier than I thought possible.

When we got back home, I put down my signed book and sat on the sofa.

'My feet are killing me in these heels. They are not dancing shoes.' I reached down to undo the strap.

'But you had fun?' Aiden asked, watching me as he took off his jacket.

'That's better,' I said, kicking off my shoes and sinking my feet into the rug. 'It was the best first date I've ever had. Although I'm still waiting for you to teach me something,' I added, arching an eyebrow.

'Hmm.' He looked at me. 'I need to think of something then.'

He smiled as I stared at him. He really was so attractive. Definitely the kind of man that fictional romances were written about. I mean, I had done just that. I was hooked. Completely hooked.

Then I ruined the moment and yawned.

Aiden chuckled. 'Tired?'

'No,' I lied. 'A little bit,' I admitted.

'Come on, let's go to bed.'

'Without doing anything?' I asked, disappointed, but I really was tired.

'We have plenty of time,' Aiden replied, giving me a soft kiss. 'Want a piggyback again?'

I smiled. 'Nope. I want full-on eighteenth-century romance vibes.'

Aiden's mouth twitched although he tried to keep a straight face. 'Could you be any more high maintenance?'

'I thought you were a gentleman?'

'Is this a Mr Darcy fantasy again?' But with a heavy sigh, he scooped me up off my feet. 'Happy now?'

'I do enjoy your muscles,' I said, reaching up to squeeze his arm.

This time, he couldn't stop the laugh. 'I like you like this. Saying exactly what you think, what you want. Come on then, princess,' Aiden said, carrying me into my bedroom.

33

My alarm went off at seven in the morning. I groaned as I opened my eyes but I smiled when I realised Aiden had stayed with me last night and was still in bed with me. I hit the snooze button, snuggled back into Aiden's arms and instantly went back to sleep.

'Olivia!' He rubbed my arm and when I opened my eyes, he moved his arm out from under me. 'We slept for another hour. We need to get to work.'

I groggily moved over to my side of the bed. 'What do you mean?'

'I have a lecture in forty-five minutes and you need to open up the library.'

I sat bolt upright. 'Oh, shit.'

'Exactly. You go to the bathroom first, I'll make us coffee.'

I jumped out of bed and stared at Aiden next to me. 'We're both in our underwear.'

'You were too tired to wait for us to get into PJs,' Aiden reminded me. 'I distinctly remember you pleading with me to "hurry up and snuggle".'

'I don't remember any of that,' I said, trying not to giggle. 'Oh. I know how we can save time – we can have a shower together.'

Aiden groaned. 'How will that save time, exactly?'

'No funny business, just showering together.'

'Funny business?' He laughed. 'Are you eighty?'

'Please?' I asked, eager to get some naked time with him after falling asleep last night.

Aiden ruffled my hair fondly. 'Come on, then, no funny business.'

We rushed into the bathroom and Aiden turned the shower on, steaming up the room. We stripped and climbed in. I reached up to kiss Aiden as he wrapped his arms around me.

Then he pulled back. 'This is torture,' he said. He looked at my body as the water rained down on us. 'I do like the view though.'

'Stop looking at me like that or we'll never make it to work,' I said, grabbing the shower gel. This had not been a good idea of mine. I wanted to run my hands over Aiden's bare chest. I pouted. 'We didn't think this through.'

Aiden chuckled. 'Let's just get clean and get out of here.'

'The words every woman wants to hear,' I replied with a laugh. But we got through it and got out of the shower quickly, Aiden leaving for his room to get dressed, which was a good thing as my body was feeling grumpy at being in such close proximity to his without any touching. It was so strange how you could go so long without touching someone but once you did, you craved it like it was a gateway drug.

I got ready at top speed, and Aiden did too. Somehow only half an hour later, we rushed out to his car, fully dressed although still slightly flustered by our late wake-up call and joint chaste shower.

'I slept so well,' I said as Aiden started the engine. 'But I'm not feeling very satisfied.'

Aiden snorted. 'You keep surprising me.' He glanced at me. 'I'm horny as hell. Seeing you naked this morning... and that dress.' He looked down at my bare thigh peeking out of my midi polka dot dress. It was a bit summery for the changing season but I'd thrown a blazer and a pair of boots on with it to help.

'What about me? You're wearing my favourite shirt.' It was crisp and white and my fingers itched to unbutton it. 'It's your Mr Darcy shirt.'

'Stop undressing me with your eyes or we won't make it to work. Let's distract ourselves.' He turned on the radio. We smiled as a Taylor Swift song came on and started to sing along. As usual, we tried to compete with who could sing the loudest. We arrived at the university in much better spirits.

Aiden parked and checked the time. 'We'll just make it.'

'Thanks for getting us up. And for last night,' I said as I climbed out of the car.

'Last night was so much fun. I'll come and find you when it's time to go home?' He came around to my side and leaned in. 'Please say I can see you naked again later?'

I squeezed my thighs together. 'Stop or I won't be able to concentrate today.'

'Good. I want you thinking about me all day.' His voice was so husky, I wanted to groan.

'You're being really unfair. Do I at least get a kiss to tide me over?'

Aiden brushed his lips with mine. Just once and so gently, I whimpered.

'I need to leave you wanting more,' he said with a wink.

'Such a tease,' I complained.

'I will tease you a lot more later, I promise.'

I couldn't believe how turned on I was right now. We were outside our workplace, for God's sake. Somehow Aiden talking to me was just as hot as him touching me. Maybe our banter really had been foreplay all along.

I leaned in to whisper to him. 'I'm wearing new underwear by the way.'

Aiden groaned this time. 'And I'm the tease?'

I pulled back and smiled. 'Have a good day, Professor Rivers.'

'Stay out of trouble, Olivia Jones.'

* * *

Stevie wasn't working with me in the library that day – she'd had to go to an admin meeting – which meant I had even more time to be distracted by thoughts of Aiden. The day passed slowly and quietly and my mind wandered a lot. I thought that Aiden was likely to want to talk about things soon.

Dan was due back this weekend, after all, and it was Thursday now. We couldn't keep putting it off but I had no idea what he'd want to do.

Finally, closing time drew near so I told the students still in the library to pack up and I made sure everything looked tidy.

Then Aiden showed up and waited behind my desk for me while I locked the library doors. I instantly felt better for seeing him. Sometimes it felt like what was happening between us was in my imagination, like my novel had come to life just for me, so seeing him in the flesh made me feel better. This wasn't just my fantasy, this was really happening. And the smile on his face told me that he was just as happy to see me again too.

'I just need to put these two books away as they never leave the library; they're in the old book section that hardly anyone goes in or needs a book from,' I explained, picking up the two heavy leather-bound books that a student had been using that day.

'I need to see this mysterious section,' he said, following me. It was tucked away right at the back of the library. The lights were dimmer there and you had to walk around a big stack and a corner so you couldn't see it from the main section.

'Wow.' Aiden whistled as he looked at the shelves of antique books.

'Some are quite rare I think but it's hardly used, which is a shame,' I said, reaching up on my tiptoes to shelve the two books. 'We have to keep an eye on it for that reason,' I added, giving Aiden a significant look over my shoulder.

Aiden's eyes lifted from blatantly looking at my bum to my eyes. 'What do you mean?'

I put my feet back down and straightened my polka dot dress.

'It's well out of prying eyes,' I said suggestively.

'People might steal the books?'

'No! Well, maybe, but I don't think they're worth much. No, it's known through the university as a place where you can have some private time, if you know what I mean.'

'Why are you blushing?'

'Shut up!'

'It's cute.'

I touched my cheeks and shook my head. 'Fine. This is where students have been known to carry out amorous activities.'

'Hmm.' Aiden looked around. 'I can see the appeal. Have you ever thought about it?'

'No!' I cried, but he raised an unbelieving eyebrow. 'Fine, yes, I have.'

'Who with?'

'Nope. Not saying.' I bit my lip to keep from smiling because it was pretty obvious who had crossed my mind. I was sure Aiden could read the lust on my face as I looked across at him.

He smiled. 'If it helps, I've fantasised about you before,' he said, stepping closer and lowering his voice. 'Tell me what happened in your fantasy.'

I was definitely blushing now. 'I don't think I have the dirty talk gene.'

'You did when we slept together. I seem to remember you asking me to fuck you please.'

'That was a one-off. Unless you want to teach me?'

'Well, I am a very good teacher, Olivia, I keep telling you that.'

'Hmm, the jury is still out on that.' We stared at one another. He was giving me that challenging look again and his lips were curved up in that smirk of his that was always half sexy, half irritating. I wanted to wrong-foot him. I leaned back against the bookshelf and took his hand, drawing him to me. I pulled him close and looked up at him. 'Okay. I have thought about you and me in here,' I confessed. 'Today, I imagined us like this.'

I lifted his hand and he propped it against the shelf beside my head, then I drew his other hand around to the small of my back. Aiden's eyes darkened as he looked at me. 'Then I pictured you having me up against this very shelf,' I admitted, my voice barely above a whisper. 'Until I screamed your name, breaking the rules of being quiet in here.'

Aiden's breath hitched and he leaned in closer. 'Maybe I'm too good a teacher,' he said gruffly. 'We shouldn't have started this conversation. It's now all I can think about.'

'What's stopping us?' I asked, tilting my body towards his like he was a magnet drawing me closer.

'I'm shocked, Olivia,' he said softly. His lips almost touched mine. 'What would the books say?' he teased me.

I smiled. 'I think they'd look the other way.' I lifted my face and brushed my lips against his. Aiden murmured contently and then his lips were on mine, hungrily devouring my mouth with his. I wrapped my arms around his neck and his hand slid up my back, pulling me closer. His other hand came down to cup my face. I curved my body against his as we kissed frantically and I let out a whimper when I felt how equally turned on he was.

Aiden drew back breathlessly. 'You're trouble, Olivia Jones,' he said huskily, looking at me in wonder.

'You don't want to?' I asked, this time challenging him.

'I think you can tell I want to,' he replied. Then he brushed his fingertips across my cheeks. 'Are you sure?'

I dropped my hands from him and smiled at the flash of disappointment on his face. I started to unbutton my dress. It had buttons all down it and I worked quickly, keeping my eyes on his. Aiden watched as the dress fell open, exposing my new red lace underwear set. 'What do you think?' I asked, raising an eyebrow.

'I was imagining this new set a lot today,' Aiden said, gazing down at me. 'I think you're incredibly sexy but you already know that.'

My whole body warmed at the way he looked at me. I was suddenly desperate for his hands to be on me again. 'We need to hurry, the security guard will be starting soon.'

Aiden chuckled. 'You really can talk me into anything.'

I pulled him back to me, kissing him as I pressed against the bookshelves. Aiden stepped in between my legs, his hand cupping my breast as he moved his lips down my cleavage and along the edge of the lace. He pulled one side of my new bra down and his lips covered my nipple.

Gasping, I put my hands on his waist and pulled him even closer. 'Too slow,' I complained. Not only was I conscious we could be disturbed any minute, my fantasy was consuming me.

Aiden looked up. 'What do you want, Olivia?' he asked, purring my name.

I got the feeling he was waiting for me to get cold feet but he underestimated how much I wanted this. I reached for his belt. 'I want you to have me up against this shelf right now. Hard and fast,' I breathed, yanking the belt off and pulling at his zipper.

'God, you're amazing,' he replied, his eyes turning dark with want. 'Here,' he said as I fumbled, unzipping his trousers and pulling them down with his pants all in one go. 'Fast enough now?'

'Yes,' I breathed, pulling my knickers down and kicking them off.

Aiden grunted in appreciation and he took out a condom from his wallet.

'Hurry,' I gasped as Aiden slid on the condom, the ache between my legs driving me crazy.

Aiden propped one hand on the shelf beside me. I leaned back against the books, not bothered by how hard they were pressing into my back. All I could think about was being with Aiden. He watched me as he reached down with his free hand and slid two fingers inside me.

'Mmm,' I said happily. I'd been craving his touch all day.

'You're ready for me,' he said, leaning down to brush his lips against mine. 'I'm so hard for you,' he added.

'Aiden, please,' I begged. I pulled at his arm and he removed his fingers. 'I told you hard and fast,' I said, not even caring now about talking to him like this. He definitely brought out a side in me I didn't even know was there.

Aiden kept his eyes on me as he reached down to lift up one of my legs, wrapping it around him. 'Say it again,' he requested.

'Hard and fast,' I gasped. 'Please.'

Aiden chuckled. 'Always so polite,' he said as he thrust inside me in one movement and I pressed back against the shelf so hard, one of the books next to me wobbled and almost fell.

'Too much?' he gasped.

I shook my head. 'Perfect. I don't care if they all fall off.'

Aiden grinned and he pressed into me again. I cried out in pleasure. There was something so incredibly naughty about being so loud in the library and I really let loose. Aiden thrust into me again and again, the shelf wobbling with our movements as I urged him on. I heard a few thuds around us but I just didn't care. Aiden kept one arm on my leg and the other one gripping the shelf. I clung to his waist for balance.

Aiden leaned in and kissed me. 'You feel so good.'

'So do you,' I replied. 'I'm close,' I added as the pleasure built.

'Me too,' Aiden gasped as he thrust into me faster and harder and I lost all control of my moans. Crying out his name over and over, an orgasm shattered through me.

'Oh my God,' I said, my whole body throbbing in the most delicious way.

'Olivia,' Aiden breathed into my ear as he collapsed onto me with a guttural groan. After a couple of shaky breaths, his eyes met mine. 'That was incredible.'

'It was,' I said. My knees trembled, so I gripped the shelf behind me to stop myself falling.

Aiden raised an eyebrow when he noticed several books on the floor. 'We definitely deserve a lifetime ban for this.'

'I can't believe we just did that,' I said in wonder, biting my lip.

'Are you ready to admit I'm a good teacher now?' Aiden asked.

'I think I might have to,' I said, still breathless.

Aiden lifted himself off me. His hair was a tousled mess, his cheeks were pink, his eyes black and he was panting. God only knew what I looked like. He handed me my knickers as he sorted himself out. Once I had buttoned up my dress, I hurriedly picked up the books that had fallen off the shelf and once they were back in their rightful places, I glanced at Aiden pulling his trousers up.

When our eyes met, I started laughing. Aiden shook his head but joined in as he finished getting dressed. I felt like I had never been more alive.

When I contained my giggles, I gave him a long, slow kiss. 'We'd better get out of here,' I whispered.

'I think you're right.' He grabbed my hand and we walked out of the library together, stealing glances and smiling because neither of us could quite believe we had just done that. It had been the best sex of my life.

I really wanted it to have been the best sex for him too but I knew he had more experience and had had much longer relationships than me. I hadn't been with someone for more than a couple of months but Aiden had had two long-term relationships.

I suddenly could see myself falling hard and fast for Aiden, but that was terrifying. I'd never felt this way before and it scared me. I wished there was a handbook for this kind of thing. Right now, it felt like driving in the dark without any headlights on. I hoped Aiden would guide the way but I had the feeling that he was waiting for me to do it instead.

34

We picked up some food in the small M&S on the way home – I offered to cook and Aiden promised to not complain about eating a meat-free meal. As we walked into the flat together, I was hit by a feeling. Maybe like the opposite of déjà-vu? As though I was getting a peek at our future. Coming home from work together, cooking a meal, talking about our day then going to bed together. It was a very different fantasy to the one we'd just played out back in the library but I could get on board with it.

Theo called me as Aiden unpacked the shopping.

'Hi, Theo,' I said.

'Hey,' Aiden called out in the background. I turned to glare at him but he just shrugged.

'What are you guys up to?' Theo asked, a little bit nervously. Maybe he was checking we hadn't turned the flat into a battleground without Dan around.

'Just making dinner. Well, I'm cooking, and Aiden is pouting at there being no meat involved,' I said, poking out my tongue when he glared at me.

Theo chuckled. 'Well, I'm glad everything is okay. I just spoke to

Dan and I'm going to pick him up on Saturday morning. He's desperate to come home but I think it's done him good to relax and have your mum looking after him.'

'I think so too,' I agreed. 'I'm glad you're going to get him.'

I really hoped their time apart might have done them both good and things would get back on track. I didn't want to be in the honeymoon stage of something if my brother was heartbroken over Theo. I wanted us all to be happy.

Then I frowned. I had no idea if Dan or Theo would be happy about me and Aiden. What if they thought it was a complete mistake and talked us out of it?

'Shall we have a bit of a welcome home lunch for him?' Theo was asking me, pulling me back to the conversation.

'Sounds good. I'll get some things in. Let us know when you're on the way back.'

'I will. Say hi to Aiden from me. I'm glad you're spending time together.'

'We're just having dinner,' I protested, but he'd already hung up.

Aiden raised an eyebrow. 'Just dinner, huh?'

'I didn't know what to say,' I said. 'He's going to get Dan Saturday morning and wants us to have lunch together so...' I trailed off. We both knew that we needed to make some decisions about us before then. We looked at one another. It was like neither of us wanted to say the wrong thing.

I broke the silence with a joke because the tension was worrying me.

'Can you imagine if they walked in to just find us kissing?'

'They would be shocked,' Aiden said. He gave me a small smile. '...that you ever gave me the time of the day.'

'Well, you're not boyfriend material, we have discussed this a lot,' I said. I could see a flicker of hurt cross his face so I went over to him and gave him a kiss. 'Aiden...' I began but he shook his head and rubbed my arms.

'It's okay, let's just enjoy our evening and we can talk tomorrow. I get you need time. I do, really.' He gave me a quick kiss. 'What can I chop to help?'

He moved away to grab a vegetable knife. I wasn't sure what to say. I needed time? I supposed I had indicated I didn't want to talk about what we were going to do until Dan came home but we didn't have long now. I swallowed and passed him the peppers.

I wanted to know what Aiden wanted to do but it felt like he'd closed the conversation. I shouldn't have brought up the boyfriend material thing. I'd only said it back then to cover my embarrassment and pretend that I didn't like him. And it had become a habit. And maybe now it was a way to help my heart hide its true feelings. But how could I get him to understand that?

The irony was that I *did* think he was boyfriend material. But was that what Aiden wanted? Could I picture us together as a couple with Dan and Theo, hanging out with Stevie and our colleagues from uni, with our parents?

'Smells good,' Aiden said, his voice drifting into my thoughts.

'Oh, did you see that new film has gone up on Netflix?' I asked, desperately wanting to get things between us back on track. 'We could watch it after dinner?'

He agreed and began to pour us two glasses of wine while I finished making the fajitas. I loaded the spiced vegetables onto two plates with wraps, grated cheese, guacamole and sour cream and we sat down to eat.

We made casual conversation – Aiden started to tell me a story about a discussion he'd had in one of his film classes – and I managed to relax eventually, moving past the awkwardness of the moment between us before.

After the meal, Aiden picked up our plates. I watched him go to the sink and took a breath. I had to say something.

'Aiden...'

He hummed as he washed up our plates.

'Shall we talk about everything tomorrow?' I asked nervously. I supposed I was putting it off until the last moment, wanting this time with him to be without any complications. But I'd have to find out what he was thinking soon. And tell him what I wanted. Which was scary as hell.

He looked over his shoulder and smiled. 'Sure.'

His phone beeped on the counter in front of me. My eyes automatically went to it.

My stomach dropped. A message from Zara.

I turned away quickly before he could see me looking and went into the living room, but my mind was racing. Why was he still in contact with his ex?

* * *

Friday arrived like one of those days you dreaded and just wanted to get over with, like exam days, driving tests, dentist appointments and job interviews.

Aiden had to be in work early as he had a day of student one-to-one meetings in his office. So, the flat was empty when it was time for me to go to the library and it felt strange not going to work with him now.

I walked through the park and the September breeze blew some of my cobwebs away. The trees were beginning to show signs that autumn was on the way. A season of change and new beginnings. I hoped it would bring only good ones my way. Everything with Aiden felt so precarious right now. And I had no idea what to do about it.

I got to the library early so I sat behind the desk and waited to open up. To pass the time, I inserted the USB stick with my book on it into the library computer. I hadn't written for a while as everything with Aiden had taken over. The last part I'd written was the first time Lily and Adam had had sex, which was very much wrapped up in my real-life situation with Aiden. I had been so happy when I'd written that scene after sleeping with Aiden, but now I felt uncertain.

All I could think about was his message from Zara that I'd been too chicken to ask him about, and that Dan was coming home tomorrow. I also started to think about that night when I was seventeen. Aiden hadn't wanted to kiss me for fear of upsetting Dan. We were adults now but their friendship was even stronger. They were more like brothers. Aiden would never want to jeopardise that, and neither would I. What if us getting together did that? I could never forgive myself.

I supposed it came down to whether we thought this was the real thing or not. Whether we could be an actual couple. I'd never had a long-term relationship, another cross against me, I knew. I'd been waiting for a romance that was as special as the ones I read about. Was this thing with Aiden finally it?

I found myself pouring some of my thoughts into the book. I supposed it had been the story of me and Aiden right from the start, and I couldn't stop now. Writing allowed me to unpick what had been happening between us.

Lily wakes up before Adam. Their night together was incredible but she is nervous now. Adam warned her they needed to take things slow but then they had ended up like this. What if he regretted it when he woke up? She wishes she knew what he was thinking, that she could climb inside his mind and walk around in there. She knows she could ask. She wants to ask but also doesn't want to in case he says something she doesn't want to hear. She is scared of being hurt. It feels like he could hurt her more than any other man she's ever met. Because her heart already belongs to him.

I stared at the page. God, was that how I felt about Aiden? I couldn't bear to see myself, in the disguise of Lily, so vulnerable, so I quickly deleted the new words and scrolled back to the sex scene. That was safer.

I knew I couldn't wait any longer to talk to Aiden. I logged onto the university intranet and opened up a new message, typing in 'p' and scrolling until 'Professor Rivers' appeared. It was a clunky system but I knew Aiden was more likely to check his work email than his phone during his student one-to-ones. As I started to write a message asking him if we could meet for lunch, my phone rang on the desk beside me.

It was Stevie. 'Should my supervisor be calling me at work?' I asked her with a smile.

'You're not on the clock just yet,' she said. 'Liv, I'm walking to the Tube and I'm so nervous for this meeting!' Stevie was on her way to meet the literary agent she'd told me about for a coffee so she could pick her brains about getting a job in publishing.

'Don't be nervous,' I said, thinking I was a fine one to talk. 'It's just an informal chat. She's agreed to help, so think of it as the start of your journey to getting your dream job.'

'I knew you'd have a good pep talk for me,' Stevie said. 'Usually I'd take my mind off my nerves by reading but I stupidly left my Kindle at home so now I have a Tube journey with only my thoughts to accompany me.'

'Never a good thing,' I agreed. I liked to have a book for all journeys. I looked at my book on the computer screen and remembered how much Stevie had wanted to keep reading it. 'I suppose I could email you the latest chapters of mine to read on your phone,' I said doubtfully, as I wasn't sure whether I wanted anyone to read the sex scene.

'Ooh, yes, please! I was enjoying it so much.'

'I could do with your advice,' I admitted. 'I feel stuck. It was all fine using Aiden as inspiration when it was about enemies to lovers but now things have happened in real life, I'm not sure if I should carry on this story or if I do, what should happen next.' I didn't add that it was because I had no idea what was going to happen between me and Aiden now.

'I think this is just good practice. Even if you decide not to try to publish it, you should finish it so you know you can write a whole novel. I'll tell you what I think. And don't worry, I know Aiden is only the inspiration, it's not like you've written exactly what happened between the two of you.'

I was relieved we were on the phone as I blushed because I knew how closely that sex scene resembled mine with Aiden. But Stevie didn't need to know that. 'Exactly,' I said with a nervous laugh. 'And I do need to know if I can write spice, I suppose.'

'Hey, you know how much spice I've read, I'll tell it to you straight. Okay, I'm getting to the station so email it to my work account while I have good internet!'

'Okay, okay. Good luck!' We hung up and I quickly opened up another message on the intranet, scrolling through the endless names of students and staff to find 'Phillips, Stevie.'

My phone vibrated with a message.

Hey Liv, so excited to come home tomorrow. Shall we have a pizza night? Theo said he'd come, with you and Aiden? Can you ask him for me? xx

I stared at Dan's message and swallowed hard. I didn't know how I was supposed to navigate my brother coming home with me and Aiden. Then I remembered Stevie needed my book before she got on the Tube so quickly, I tapped the mouse on the open message on the computer and began typing.

> First of all, good luck with the meeting, can't wait to hear about it when you get back. Maybe put in a word for me and my books, haha! The manuscript finishes at the sexy bit, which is embarrassing to share but if I am going to publish a book eventually, I'll need to get over that. Definitely don't picture us when you read it. Ignore the fact Adam is Aiden and I'm Lily please! And I will need your advice about more than the book when I see you. I need to talk to Aiden later. About us. And I have no idea what to say to him. See you soon x

As I attached my book to the email, there was a knock on the library double doors. Startled, I looked up and saw it was five minutes past opening time and there was a lecturer outside, waving at me.

'Crap,' I muttered, and sent the email with my book to Stevie and the one to Aiden asking him to meet me for lunch, then I pulled out the USB stick with my book on it, and jumped up to open the doors and let the professor in.

I had to point him in the right direction of the book he wanted then a couple of students came in and I helped them find the text-books they needed. When I returned to my desk, I had another message on my phone.

> We can meet for lunch but where is your book? I'm getting on the Tube now... xxx

I stared at Stevie's message. Huh. That was weird. I had sent my book to her.

I opened up the intranet again and went to the sent messages.

And then my heart leapt into my throat.

'What? No...' I double checked and put my hands over my mouth. I'd sent the emails the wrong way around. Clearly, Dan's message interrupting me had meant I'd clicked on the wrong email and invited Stevie to lunch and sent my book to Aiden! Both their emails started with 'P'; I hadn't been paying enough attention in my haste to send them.

'Why can't you unsend emails on this rubbish system?' I muttered, panic setting in that Aiden might see my book. I decided the only thing I could do was ring him and persuade him not to open my email.

I grabbed my phone and rang him but there was no answer. So then I picked up the library phone and made an internal call to his office.

'Yes?' Aiden answered gruffly.

'It's me. Listen, I accidentally sent you the wrong email and—'

'I know,' he interjected coldly. 'I was confused as to why you sent me a message wishing me luck but then you were talking about me and you, and you'd sent a link so I opened it...'

My heart rate spiked as my hopes of stopping him from seeing the book were dashed. 'You opened it already?'

35

'That was meant for Stevie, not you,' I said after an awkward silence on the phone.

'So I gathered.'

Aiden sounded... angry? I wasn't sure why.

'This is so embarrassing,' I said, forcing out a laugh. I wondered if he could hear my heart beating down the phone.

'Embarrassing for you? This is humiliating for me.'

'What? What do you mean?' I shook my head, confused.

'You've written about us! I didn't know what it was until I started reading, and I realised it was your book and then I got to the sex scene.'

This couldn't get any worse. 'You read the sex scene?' I cried into the phone. 'Oh, God.'

'What the hell, Olivia? It's pretty much exactly like the first time we had sex,' he hissed. 'You included things I said, things you said, things we... did. No wonder you'd never tell me what you were writing, you wanted to hide the fact you were writing about us!'

'No, hang on,' I said quickly. 'It wasn't like that. I wanted to write a novel but was struggling. Then you came to the university for your job interview and I just started picturing you as the character. I felt mortified admitting that to him but now he'd read some of it had to explain. 'I didn't plan to write about us! I used you as inspiration. I didn't even really realise until Stevie pointed it out. And I'e used myself as inspiration for the leading lady. I guess it wa wishful thinking.'

'You didn't realise? The man is called Adam and the woman i called Lily! I don't understand why you'd write something so close to the truth,' Aiden said, his voice raised.

'I suppose it was helping me to make sense of everything! One minute I was writing about you and thinking that maybe I did fanc you, then you were flirting and we were flirting and then we wer kissing... Writing about it helped me believe it was real.'

'Was it real?' he asked quietly.

'Of course it was! This book, once I knew it was about us I knev no one would ever read it and—'

'Except Stevie. And some agent you asked her to put in a goo word with,' Aiden interjected.

'I was only joking. I would never do that without asking you.'

'So, you do want to publish our story?'

'I didn't say that,' I cried. This was not going well at all.

'Is that what you wanted to talk to me about? Get my permis sion to use what happened with us in your book? And let me guess they live happily ever after but we don't,' Aiden said, his ton turning bitter.

'No, that's not why I wanted to talk,' I said. 'I was worried abou what happens tomorrow when Dan comes home, how we're goin to handle it. If what's going on is just going to stop or—'

'If you want it to stop then it stops,' Aiden cut in again. 'If yo want to pretend none of it happened then fine.'

'Of course not. How can you think that?'

Now I was hurt.

'I don't know what to think! I find out you're writing this book and using exactly what happened when we slept together in it. It's confusing. They are us. Adam and Lily. I just don't understand why you didn't tell me about it.'

'I was embarrassed,' I whispered. My head was swimming. I had planned to tell Aiden one day about the book, when we were officially together and we could laugh about it. But instead, I'd messed up and sent it to him before we'd talked about what we wanted. And he was taking it completely the wrong way.

'Embarrassed that you like me? Has this all just been a game to you? Was it all fake so you could write your book?'

'Fake?'

'Did you try to kiss me so you could write about it? Make sure you got, what, the positioning right? I was just there to practise on?'

'Aiden, come on...' I was getting frustrated now. I didn't know why he wasn't listening to me or understanding what I was saying.

'You kept putting off talking about us, so I thought you were just scared like I was. But now it feels like this was all a fantasy you could write about. That's why you never wanted to talk about it being real. God, us in the library... You wanted to do *that* just for your book?' He sounded aghast.

'No! I wouldn't write about that. I haven't told anyone about what we did here, I swear.'

'Because you don't want anyone to know about us.'

'Stevie knows,' I protested.

'Only because she's been reading your book – not because you wanted to tell her about a new relationship.'

'Have you told anyone about us?' I countered then, tired of getting all the blame. I may have wanted to put off talking about us because I was scared, but Aiden had let me. 'Ten years ago, you were worried about what Dan would say and you're still worried now.'

Aiden sighed heavily. 'I thought we were going to work that out together. I was hoping we would anyway.'

'We still can.'

There was a short silence. 'Look, I have to go, I need to get ready for my next student.'

'We can't leave it like this,' I pleaded with him.

'Let's just talk when we're home later,' he said. Then he muttered so quietly I wasn't sure I heard him correctly, 'I thought we had something special.' Then he hung up.

'We do,' I whispered, but I was too late.

I sighed. That couldn't have gone any worse. I'd been so scared to tell Aiden how much I liked him, hiding the fact he'd inspired my book and putting off talking to him, that I'd pushed him away. He didn't believe I liked him.

He couldn't have been more wrong.

36

The next hour passed like I was walking through fog. I had no idea what was going on around me as students came into the library. My mind kept replaying the phone call with Aiden over and over. I'd royally fucked it all up.

I had been too much of a coward to ask Aiden how he felt about me in case I didn't like his answer. We hadn't talked about what sleeping together meant and now Aiden was questioning why I'd been with him. He didn't know I liked him more than I'd ever liked anyone.

Stevie arrived then. She took one look at my face and said she'd get us both a coffee. She came back with two cups and ushered me into our small back room, which was more of a storage cupboard than an office.

'What's wrong?' She held out the iced coffee. 'You look like you need this.'

'I do. Thank you.' I gulped it down and then shuddered at the coldness. Stevie watched me with concerned eyes.

I felt guilt wash over me then because I was so focused on my problems I hadn't asked about her day. She had important things going on too. I swallowed my panic about Aiden and focused on my friend.

'How was meeting up with the agent?' She was about to argue but I cut in. 'Please, I want to know. And I need a minute before I can talk about my stuff.' I gestured for her to go ahead.

'If you're sure.' Her face broke out into a smile. 'It was so good to talk to someone who knows about the industry. We talked about how I organised her author event and she really thinks that I would be good in publicity. She actually knows a publishing company with a vacancy so she told me to apply and said she'd give me a reference. How kind is that?'

I smiled. 'That's great. Are you going to apply?'

'Yes. I'm so nervous but even if I don't get it, I'm so glad I'm taking a step towards what I actually want, you know?'

'Absolutely. It's so exciting. And you would be great at that job. I'm going to cross everything for you.'

'Thanks, Liv. Okay, no more stalling. What's happened?'

I took a breath and told her that I'd emailed my book to Aiden by accident, and the disastrous phone call that followed. By the time I'd finished, my eyes were filled with tears. 'It was horrible. We've always bickered, sure, but this was different. This was an argument that I have no idea how to fix.'

'I'm so sorry, Liv. Come here.' She held out her hands and I let her pull me into her arms.

'He misunderstood me using him as inspiration for my book. He thinks I slept with him as research for it or something.' I sniffed into her chest.

'God, the dangers of technology or what! I feel terrible. I shouldn't have told you to email it to me.'

I leaned back. 'It's not your fault. I was so stupid sending it to him. I should have been more careful. No, I should have bloody told Aiden about my book to begin with! I was embarrassed hough. I didn't want him to know that I saw him as this romantic hero. I don't know, I got so wrapped up in the fantasy of me and him that when it started happening for real, I was terrified of messing it up. I suppose I didn't believe he could actually really want to be with me. And now he thinks it's the other way around and I don't want him.'

'But you can talk to him, right? Tell him that you made a mistake and that you do like him?'

I nodded. 'I've been waiting for my own love interest for so long that I didn't believe I had finally found someone like the heroes in the romance books we love so much.'

'Oh, Liv. Tell him that. There's no way he can still be angry with you after you tell him that.'

I looked at her hopefully. 'Really? I don't know though. We've not been straight with one another since we met ten years ago. We both pretended we didn't fancy each other that night. I don't know if we're capable of being honest about our feelings. That's how we're in this mess.'

'Listen, it will be scary to tell Aiden how you feel, especially because of your past. But what's the alternative? Losing him.'

I really didn't want to lose him. 'Maybe he doesn't feel the same way though. He hasn't said anything to me about what he wants to happen next. And he still talks to his ex.'

'You have to ask him, Liv.'

'I know I need to be honest,' I said, nodding. 'But it's hard.'

'You can do it. I meant it when I said you'd inspired me to try for my dream job. You started writing a novel and you kissed the man you've liked for a long time. You just need to keep being brave and tell Aiden how you really feel.'

'What if he won't listen though?'

'Then you find a way to get through to him. If this is what you want.'

'I thought it was. But I'm scared. This is Aiden. Us being together would change everything in my life, you know?'

Stevie nodded. 'And it would change everything for him too. That's why he got so angry, so upset about your book, thinking it meant you didn't like him. If he didn't feel anything for you, he would have shrugged it off, right?'

I looked at her and my heart lifted just a little bit.

'I really hope so.'

* * *

At lunch time, I walked to Aiden's office. I knew he'd said we'd talk at home but this felt too urgent to wait. I was hoping if we saw one another then I could make him understand about the book. Talking on the phone was never the same as speaking in person.

Turning into the corridor where his office was, I saw his door was open and someone was already inside. I stopped a few feet away and waited for them to leave, not wanting to interrupt a student meeting.

But it was someone familiar who walked out two minutes later.

'Thanks, Aiden,' Zara said.

I watched as Aiden followed her but I couldn't hear what he said. She smiled and reached for him, giving him a hug before walking away. Then before Aiden went back into his office, he turned and looked down the corridor, finally seeing me standing there.

'Olivia,' he said, and for a moment his eyes lit up, but then he saw my stunned face. 'I can explain,' he said, hastily coming towards me.

'You just blamed me for everything going wrong with us but here you are, spending time with your ex! She's been calling you and you went out for a drink with her, but I didn't say anything.

assumed it was for closure or something. How am I supposed to feel about this?'

'Olivia, I can explain,' Aiden said as I backed up. 'It's not like that.'

Tears pricked behind my eyes. 'Why are you spending time with her then? Is this payback for me writing my book or something?'

There was a short silence as we looked at one another.

'I thought I could trust you,' Aiden said. 'I thought you trusted me. I was humiliated when Zara cheated on me. It really hurt and I thought I'd never trust anyone again. Now I'm wondering if I was right not to. And it sounds like you don't trust me either. It doesn't bode well for us, does it?'

'My book is nothing like you still seeing your ex.' I spun around before I could start crying. I didn't want him to see me cry.

Aiden called my name but I hurried down the corridor and out of the double doors before he could stop me.

Outside, I rushed smack bang into a body.

'Oh, sorry,' I said, brushing away a tear that had rolled down my cheek.

'Liv, are you okay?'

I looked up into Jasper's eyes and shook my head.

'Not really, but I have to go back to the library.'

'Take a minute first if you're upset. Want a cup of tea?'

Oh God, the tears came a bit faster at him being so nice to me.

'No, I don't want to bother you,' I said, feeling super guilty that after everything he was still trying to help me.

'We're friends, you're not a bother. You're also a member of staff and I don't want anyone working when they're upset. Come on.'

He led me gently but firmly around the corner and to his office where he told me to sit down while he made me a cup of tea.

'Here.' He passed me a mug then sat down on the other side of his desk with his. 'You don't need to tell me anything but if I can help then just say.'

I wiped my tears away and sipped the tea. 'Thank you, I don't deserve that.'

'Whyever not?'

'Because of...' I gestured weakly between us.

'Ah. Look, I wasn't lying when I agreed that we were better off as friends. I like you, Liv. But I don't think we're compatible. I promise I'm not broken hearted.'

He smiled and I let out a weak chuckle. Jasper watched as I took a sip of my tea. He looked thoughtful. 'I might be overstepping here, but is this about Aiden?'

My eyes widened. 'Why would you say that?'

'I won't pretend to be a romantic expert but since I met him, he has talked about you a lot. I told you when he came for his interview that he said you loving it here was a big motivation for him agreeing to come, and since then, he's told me how much you being in London has helped him settle in. At the film festival, I could see how he looked at you and I realised he wasn't really keen on letting us be alone together that day.'

'He was annoying, you mean,' I said wryly.

'I asked him, you know, after our second date didn't go very well and you came to see me, if there was something between you two. And he apologised for how he'd been acting, said he had felt jealous seeing us two together and he really wanted to ask you out but it was complicated.'

'You could say that,' I said with a sigh.

'And it was clear your mind and heart were elsewhere when we went to dinner so I assumed you wanted to be out with Aiden instead.'

'I'm sorry. I swear I didn't realise how much I liked Aiden until we went out.' It was so strange to tell someone I liked Aiden after all my years of being pissed off with him. I just wished it felt good and not sad after our argument. 'I'm just not so sure he feels the same way.'

'I can't believe that.'

'We've known each other a long time, and I think that maybe we are just too used to acting like enemies, you know?'

'But there's a fine line between love and hate, don't they say?'

'Maybe. Maybe not.' I didn't know any more. 'I'd better get back now. Thank you, Jasper. You're a great guy, you know?'

Jasper smiled. 'Are you sure you're okay to go back to work?'

'Yes, don't worry about me. We'll sort it out,' I said, although I wasn't 100 per cent sure about that.

'I think you will,' Jasper agreed. 'Let me walk you back to the library. I need to bring back a couple of books and talk to Stevie. I'm leaving early for a date.'

I smiled.

'She's a lucky lady,' I said, and I really meant it. He blushed and I thought how much easier it would have been if we had been into each other.

The way Aiden made me feel was far from easy, but he had my heart and I couldn't deny it.

37

Finally, it was home time. Stevie wished me good luck and told me to phone her if I needed to talk, and I set off for the flat. It was a chilly evening and as I hurried through the streets of Islington I wished I'd worn a thicker jacket. I tried to practise what I would say to Aiden when I saw him.

All I could I think about was him saying we didn't trust each other. It wasn't that I didn't trust him. I knew deep down he'd never string both me and Zara, or anyone else, along, but I supposed I didn't trust his feelings for me yet.

This had all happened so quickly, I hadn't had time to catch my breath. And we'd had the pressure of Dan returning home on our minds plus the misunderstanding about the book I was writing. It felt like things were unravelling before they'd had a chance to even begin. I really didn't want that to happen.

I rushed up the steps and through the door, letting out a breath of relief when I heard Aiden was already home.

'Hi,' I said, walking in to find him making a cup of tea.

'Hi. Do you want one?'

'Uh, sure,' I said, putting my bag down onto the counter and leaning against it. 'How was your day?'

'It was okay, you?'

I stared at his back.

'This feels weird and formal,' I blurted out. I longed to wrap my arms around him but I didn't feel like I could.

Aiden turned around. 'It does. Here.' He handed me a cup and we looked at one another. 'I feel like I did this all wrong.'

'What do you mean?'

'I should have asked you out – taken things slowly.' He smiled a little bit and my breath caught. He really was gorgeous when he smiled. Why had I tried for so long to ignore that? 'I should have wooed you.'

'Wooed?'

Despite the situation, I smiled.

'I know how much you like Mr Darcy,' he said, smiling back, but then he shook his head. 'You know what I mean. But that night when you came to the pub, I don't know, it all moved so fast...'

'Because we know each other so well,' I said. 'I wanted it to move fast.'

'I'm not sure you did...' He held a hand up when I opened my mouth to interrupt so I waited. 'You're a romantic, Liv. That's what you want – romance. And maybe you were right all along: I'm not boyfriend material for you. You want the fairy tale. Maybe that's why you wrote about our story. You wished it had been more like the ones in books.'

I shook my head. 'That's not it. Can't you see that I made you my love interest? Before we even kissed. Because—'

'You wish I could be,' Aiden broke in. 'But I'm not. Maybe there's a reason we didn't get together these past ten years.' He put his cup of tea down. 'You really thought I was seeing Zara again?'

'No, not really, but I was unsure of us, and seeing her today... do trust you in that way. I guess I didn't trust *us* yet. That this wa real.'

'Zara's father is really ill. I don't think he's going to make it. She far away from her family and struggling and I've known her for long time. She needed someone to talk to. But we are finished. Sh cheated and she knew it wasn't right. It was never right. It hurt a lo that she did that. But she wasn't the one.'

I couldn't stop the whisper in my heart: *I* wanted to be the on for him.

'I'm sorry for her. I'm sorry I jumped to the wrong conclusion. do trust you.'

'But you don't think this is real,' Aiden said. 'Look, I think should stay somewhere else for a bit...'

'Wait, what?' I said, my head spinning. 'You're leaving?'

'I think it's for the best.'

'Best for who?' I stepped towards him. I had to make him se that he was more than good enough. That I'd created him as th love interest in my book because he was the love interest in my life Wasn't that obvious? 'Aiden, listen...'

I opened my mouth to speak, to tell him clearly that I did lik hm. Even if he still walked out, I had to tell him. But before I could we heard the flat door open behind us. We both turned around i surprise to see Dan on crutches, Theo beside him carrying his bag.

'Surprise!' Dan cried, stopping by the kitchen with a big grin o his face.

I stepped back from Aiden automatically. I felt his eyes on me.

'Oh my God,' I said, trying to sound as excited as my brothe clearly was.

Dan looked from me to Aiden then back to me. 'Everythin, okay?' he asked slowly, as if realising something was up.

'Of course!' I cried brightly before rushing over to give him a hug, which wasn't easy with him on crutches. 'How are you? How was the journey? How come you came back tonight? We thought you were arriving tomorrow,' I gabbled. 'You look loads better,' I finished, smiling at him.

'I feel a lot better. Mum has some kind of meditation evening planned so I begged Theo to rescue me. I've had enough meditation and green tea to last me until Christmas. She's been great but I wanted to come home.'

'I'm glad you're here,' I said sincerely. 'We missed you.'

I turned back to look at Aiden, wondering what he was thinking. Then I greeted Theo who put Dan's bags down and gave me a kiss on the cheek.

'It's good to see you.' Aiden came over and he and Dan did that manly one-armed hug thing and then he shook Theo's hand. It felt weird to think it had been less than a week since Dan left us here alone. So much had changed since then but they had no idea.

Aiden jangled his keys. 'I was just off out actually. I'm staying with my friend for the weekend – they need help with something. So, can we catch up tomorrow?'

Dan looked surprised. 'Oh, okay, sure.'

'Great. Glad you're feeling better. I'll call you.' And with that, he walked past us all towards the door.

'Oh, I forgot to...' I said before dashing after Aiden without finishing my sentence. 'Aiden, you can't just go,' I said, touching his arm before he reached the door.

'As soon as Dan came in, you stepped away from me,' he hissed. 'I know you, like you said. You tell your brother everything. If you don't want to tell him about this then maybe you're right, maybe it isn't real.' He yanked the door open and finally met my eyes. 'See you, Olivia.'

My heart sank into my stomach as I watched him walk out and close the door.

'Everything okay?' Dan called out.

'Fine,' I lied, trying to hold back tears. Aiden had gone and it was all my fault.

38

Theo had to go soon after Aiden left as he was preparing for a meeting with a gallery that he was hoping might put on a small show of his pieces, which was exciting. I managed to act somewhat normal with them both and once I was alone with Dan and he was comfy in the living room, I made us macaroni cheese, which we ate on trays on the sofa.

'I love Mum but there is only so much green juice and salad a man can take, am I right?'

I pushed my pasta around my plate, my appetite nowhere in sight. 'Hmm,' I agreed, but my mind was wherever Aiden was. What friend was he staying with? Was he thinking about me?

'Earth to Liv,' Dan said, turning to look across at me.

'Oh, sorry,' I replied. 'What were you saying?'

'I've been thinking a lot this week. I had a lot of time on my hands. And the accident was a bit of a wake-up call to be honest.'

'The police still haven't traced the motorbike rider?'

'No, I'm not sure they ever will. But yeah, I was lucky, it could have been so much worse. And spending time with Mum away from here, from you guys, I realised just how much I love my life. And we talked too – about Dad.'

I looked across at him. 'You did?' Mum rarely liked to talk about Dad. And we hadn't heard from him in years. He was almost a mythical creature from our childhood.

'I told her how I felt worried I might end up like him, that I was scared of making such a big commitment to Theo. And she said I'm not like our father. But I needed to believe that for myself. And she was right, I've always worried that I'd run like he did. But the accident, it showed me that I've found the person I want to be with. That night was so scary but having you all with me made it fine and I'm so lucky to have so much love in my life. Why should I let fear stop me from showing that to the people I love? Theo has shown me by proposing but I've made him worry I don't feel the same because I'm scared. Why have I done that to him?'

'It's not your fault you were scared,' I said, wondering if I was telling Dan or myself or both.

'I still am but it doesn't have to stop me from committing to the man I love. Feel the fear and do it anyway. So, I've decided... I'm going to propose to Theo.'

I put my plate down and turned to him. 'What?'

He grinned. 'Yeah. I'm going to propose. Surprise him. Show him he's the one. He always has been. I was just too nervous to say yes. But I'm not now. The thought of losing him is so much worse than committing to him. And fearing that I'll leave him, hurt him, is crazy when I'm hurting him now, you know?'

'Oh, Dan.' I reached out and wrapped my arms around him. 'You guys belong together.' I couldn't stop a tear rolling out. 'This is so exciting. Can I help you plan it?'

'I need you to. And you need to film it!'

I laughed onto his shoulder. 'Of course I will.' I pulled away and wiped my face.

'Why are you crying?'

'Just happy for you guys.'

Dan looked at me closely. 'Are you sure that's all it is?'

'I suppose it makes me think about my own love life,' I said, admitting half of the truth.

'You'll find someone, Liv. You just need to put yourself out there. What happened with the guy at work? Jasper?'

I thought about what Aiden had said – that if I really did like him, I'd tell Dan. I'd been as scared about my feelings for him as Dan had been about Theo but my brother had been brave. Now it was my turn. I couldn't let fear of what would happen let me lose Aiden.

I sniffed and took a breath. 'Dan, I need to tell you something.'

Dan's eyes widened. 'Are you pregnant?'

'What? No.' I took his hand in mine.

'Something kind of happened this week.'

Dan grinned. 'You met someone?'

'No. Yes. Kind of.' I squirmed on the sofa, not sure what his reaction was going to be at all. But if I ever had a chance of fixing things with Aiden, I had to come clean. 'This might be a shock.'

'Liv, you're freaking me out now.'

'Sorry. It's just I'm nervous about what you'll think, what you'll say, and also I've fucked it all up. And I need your help.'

'You're babbling.'

I nodded. 'Yes. Yes, I am. Okay, I'm just going to pull the plaster off and say it.'

'And I thought I was the melodramatic one.' I gave him a look. 'Sorry, sorry, please, go on.'

'Okay, while you were away, something kind of mad happened but also not mad at all. But you might think it's mad. Maybe it is. I don't know any more. But, Dan, I... I slept with Aiden.'

There was a long silence. Dan's eyes bulged but his mouth stayed shut.

'Dan? Did you hear what I said?'

He nodded slowly.

'And what do you think? You're killing me here!'

'You slept with Aiden?' he repeated, his voice high pitched.

'Yes,' I said, exhaling with relief at finally having told him.

'I don't know what to say,' he said slowly. 'Shit, Liv. That's kind of huge.'

'Are you mad?' I asked nervously.

'Mad?'

'Because he's your best friend. Did he break your guy code? Did I muck things up between you? Because I would never ever look at him again if that was the case.'

'Hang on,' Dan said. 'When you say you slept with him... Was it a one-night thing?'

I shook my head. I wasn't about to tell my brother we'd already done it more than once, and certainly not about the library encounter – that one I'd take to my grave, and smile about it while I was in there. But it was more than just sex.

'Dan, I really like him. I think I'm falling for him.'

He leaned back against the sofa and I copied him. There was another long silence. Dan's eyes were still wide. It looked as if I'd blown his mind. I didn't blame him. This whole thing had turned my world upside down. The old me would have said something now to fill the silence, take back the words I'd just said, worried my brother wouldn't like the idea at all, worried Aiden didn't feel the same way, but I didn't want to go back to the old me, the one that ten years ago thought Aiden had rejected me and that he'd never be mine. I wanted to believe that he could.

Finally, Dan whistled. 'Wow. Okay. You and Aiden. I need to get my head around this. But I'm not mad.'

'No?'

'If you really like him... that's good?' He said it like a question.

'I think it is,' I said.

'Oh, crap, I just realised. I owe Theo £50.'

'Huh?' I swivelled to look at him.

'Soon after me and Theo got together,' Dan explained, turning his head to face me too, 'we'd all gone out for my birthday. And he asked me if you and Aiden were exes. I laughed and said no way but he was adamant there was, I don't know, chemistry between you two and that I was too close to you both to see it. He bet me £50 you'd kiss one day.'

'Wow.'

'This is the first time, isn't it? I haven't just been blind for ten years?'

'It's the first time we properly kissed but...' I then told Dan the story of the night we met. 'I thought he didn't want me and he thought the same. But I guess we always did. And being around him all the time, it got harder and harder to ignore this pull. And when you left us alone...'

'Well, shit. I don't know whether to say "you're welcome" or "I'm sorry". But hang on, why did he just leave? You had a fight? There was tension when I walked in, I knew I didn't imagine it!'

'I messed it up, I think. And I don't know what to do. Basically, the book I've been writing, I kind of based it all on Aiden and me.'

I told him about how Aiden had become my inspiration for my love interest and as I felt more and more for him in real life, I poured that onto the page. I even told him how I wrote about the first time we had sex and accidentally sent it to Aiden, which was mortifying. But there was no point in not being completely honest at this point. If I had any hope of showing Aiden how I felt, I had to tell my brother everything.

'Wow, Liv. So, he thinks you used what was happening for your book and that means it wasn't real?'

'I guess. Honestly, I think I've told him so many times through the years he's not the man for me, he thinks that's how I feel. It all happened so quickly. It was thrilling but terrifying. I had in the back of mind that he'd rejected me when we were younger, that he couldn't really want me now; maybe he thought the exact same thing?'

Dan sighed. 'I feel like banging your heads together. For how much you two can talk, you haven't been saying the right things.'

'I know, I know. But what do you think? I mean, about the two of us?' I asked, knowing that Dan's opinion held a lot of weight, not just for me but for Aiden too. If he hated us as an idea, how could it ever work?

'I love you, Liv. And I love Aiden. If the two of you can be happy together, why would I ever stand in the way of that? It'll take some getting used to, I'm not going to lie, but Theo was right – you do have chemistry.'

'I think we do,' I said, smiling. Then I bit my lip. 'But even if you're on board with us, it doesn't mean Aiden is. Maybe I've ruined it. Maybe he doesn't really care about me?'

'Come here.' Dan gave me a squeeze. 'Listen, I've known Aiden for ten years. He puts on a front sometimes. He likes everyone to think he's super confident. It's like when I said be nice to him when he started that new job. He was scared shitless but he would never have said that to anyone else.'

I nodded. 'I can see that. When he asked whether we should tell you, I did keep putting it off,' I admitted. 'I was so nervous about the whole thing. It all felt so new and I didn't want anything to ruin it.'

'You need to tell Aiden how you feel. Because maybe he has got it confused. I've heard you tell him he's the last man you'd ever kiss. So, when you did kiss, maybe he wasn't sure it was real?'

'I was too good at pretending to hate him,' I agreed. 'He never actually told me that he wants us to be together though,' I said, fear bubbling up under my skin again.

'Did you ask him?'

I shook my head. 'No and I didn't let him ask me either.'

I thought about how it felt when we were in bed and he'd looked down at me and smiled, and how it felt like it was just the two of us in the whole world. That was real. I hadn't imagined that moment. I hadn't imagined how warm his touch was or how urgent his kisses were, like he didn't want to ever let go. Or that special smirk he saved just for me. Or the delicious way he said my name with that accent. Or how he'd read *Pride and Prejudice* just because of how much I loved it. The way he'd always looked after me and I'd ignored it or got annoyed at him for it. The way he'd always looked at me like I was the only one in the room and I'd pretended he wasn't that for me too.

'I tried so hard all this time not to like him.'

'Yep. So, you need to tell him that you do. And ask him if he feels the same.'

'I'm going to need to get so drunk.'

'Liv!'

I laughed. 'I'm joking, I'm joking. But how? How do I do it?' I thought about how people did it in love stories. It was all about grand gestures in those. But in real life, did anyone actually make a grand gesture? Then again, I'd waited for someone as special as a character in a romance novel so if I believed I had found him, shouldn't I practise what I preached? 'I think I might have an idea. It's cheesy as hell though.'

'I like cheesy,' Dan said.

I turned to look at him. 'I'm going to write the rest of my book.'

Dan frowned. 'Is that a good idea? When the book kind of broke you up?'

'Only because I hadn't written the whole story. I need to finish it, get the characters together like they were always going to be and give them a happy ending. Maybe then Aiden will see that we should have one too.'

'Maybe,' Dan said, though he sounded doubtful.

'It's my grand gesture,' I told him. 'You know, to show someone you love them. You're going to propose to Theo, I'm going to write the rest of my book and give it to Aiden to read so he knows how I feel about him.'

'You maybe should tell him as well.'

'I will. And I know what else I need to do.'

'What's that?'

'Make him see that I've been hiding how I feel for a long time.' I stood up. 'I'm going to start now. Unless you need me?'

'I just need you to be happy. But, Liv, don't think I missed what you just said.'

I looked at him, confused. 'What did I say?'

'That a grand gesture is to show someone that you *love* them.'

'Oh.'

Yep, I had said the word love.

Cheeks flaming, I turned and rushed to my room so I wouldn't have to respond to that. If I hadn't admitted that to Aiden, I wasn't going to tell my brother. But maybe I could say it to myself. See how it sounded?

'I love Aiden,' I whispered as I went into my room.

Oh help.

It sounded really good.

39

With my hair in a bun, comfy PJs on, soft music playing and a scented candle burning, I sat on my bed ready to continue writing my book. First though, I picked up my phone.

I scrolled to Aiden's number, my heart picking up with each name I passed. Dan had been right about the things I'd said to him over the years, the way I'd acted, how perhaps I'd played my part so well Aiden couldn't believe that I liked him now. I really hoped he would give me a second chance. I needed to show him how I really felt. Like Jasper said, there really was only a fine line between love and hate. I needed to make Aiden see that.

I doubted Aiden would answer if I tried to call him so instead, I recorded a voice note.

'Hi, uh, Aiden, it's me. I'm sorry. I hate that we fought today. That you left. I think the problem is we've been fighting for so long, it's our default position. It's what we know how to do. That's easier for us. But I don't want to fight with you any more. I want to fight *for you*. For this. For us.

'I was thinking about how we have fought so many times these past ten years but maybe we were saying completely different

things in reality. Like when I was drunk and went on that hour'
rant about *Pride and Prejudice*. You told me to shut up but then you
went and bought the book and read it. And that made m
remember a time when I wanted to watch a film that you loved.'

I took a breath and continued.

'I told you we'd never spoken on the phone before. But we got i
wrong. I remembered. I phoned you once.'

I climbed off the bed and began to pace as I continued the story
really hoping that Aiden would actually listen to it.

'It was when I was at university. Christmas was a few week
away and I was feeling homesick and wishing that the holiday
were closer so I could go home and be with Dan, and... you.
couldn't sleep so I went out on campus and saw they had
midnight showing of a horror film you'd told me was really good a
the university cinema.

'So, I went in to see it. I was the only person in the screening
Afterwards, as the film ended, I phoned you. You picked up in a ba
I think you were drunk as you didn't seem surprised that I wa
calling you. You took the phone outside and I told you I'd been t
see that film and you were impressed I'd seen it by myself as it wa
so scary.

'You said it would have been more fun to have seen it togethe
so I promised to get it on DVD when it came out and we'd watch i
We never spoke about that phone call. Maybe you forgot about it a
you'd been drinking. But I didn't. For Christmas the following yea
I came home with the DVD and we all watched it on Boxing Day. I
always reminds me of how watching something you loved, I don
know, made me feel like I was at home even though I was far away.'

I paused to remember.

'And by the way, I still have that film in my DVD collectior
Because it reminds me of that night.'

I stopped recording my voice note and sighed. I hadn't though about that night in a long time. But Aiden had helped me even though he hadn't known it and I hadn't fully realised why at the time. Aiden had somehow always been there for me even when he wasn't there. He had always been special to me even though I had never admitted it to myself. I could see it now. Admit it now. I just hoped that by doing that, Aiden would realise this was something special.

I walked back to my bed, opened my laptop and started to write. Picking up my book after Lily and Adam slept together, I rewrote the part I had deleted about Lily wondering if Adam would think it was a mistake. I hoped that if I worked things out for my characters, they might also work out for me and Aiden.

* * *

'It's so exciting,' I said to Stevie on Saturday night. 'I really hope you get an interview.' Stevie had applied for the publicity vacancy the agent had told her about. I'd invited her over to have pizza and wine with me, Dan and Theo. I was trying really hard not to keep thinking about how much better it would have been if Aiden was here too.

'I have googled "good interview tips" about a million times already,' she admitted.

'We can run through dummy questions whenever we're quiet in the library to help.'

'As long as Jasper doesn't catch us. Although he comes in far less now that he knows you prefer Aiden,' Stevie said with a laugh.

'Poor Jasper,' Dan said.

'No, we didn't get on, he agreed,' I protested. 'We just weren't compatible. And he's seeing someone else so he's fine. It's me you need to worry about.'

'I don't think you need to worry once you've finished your book,'

Stevie said with a dreamy look on her face. 'It's so romantic. Writing a book about someone! I wish I could find someone to do that for me.'

'But you love romance novels like me. Aiden might not feel the same way,' I said, biting my lip.

'Who doesn't love a grand gesture?' Dan said, giving me a wink when Theo couldn't see him. 'Plus, Aiden is a romcom fan,' Dan added.

'So, how do you feel about the idea of your best friend and your sister?' Stevie asked as she munched on pizza.

'Honestly, if I had seen them kissing at that party ten years ago, I might have whacked Aiden, but now... The way Liv smiles when we say his name...' They all looked at me then and, of course, my face turned bright pink. 'They talk about each other so much, and considering the number of times I've had to play peacemaker or referee over the years, this will be a breeze.'

'I don't talk about him that much,' I protested.

Dan snorted, and the other two laughed. 'You're always trying to bring him into the conversation and I've seen the way you both try to stop yourselves from smiling when you're arguing. I think I should have seen this coming.'

'I told you so,' Theo sing-songed. 'And now I'm fifty quid the richer for it. I'm going to buy a new pair of earrings with my winnings.'

'I'm glad you all find this so amusing,' I said with an eye roll. 'But you won't be laughing if Aiden doesn't come around and leaves me broken hearted.'

They all shut up at that.

'Tell us about the rest of your book then,' Stevie said. 'We can help make sure he won't be able to resist it.'

'The last bit I've written is Lily being unsure how to feel after they slept together as she was nervous that Adam would think it was all a mistake. So, I have her being a coward and not asking him but making an excuse and leaving his place,' I said sheepishly, thinking about how much of a coward I'd been. 'So, they need to argue about that when they see each other at work, both of them not admitting how much they like each other... Then one of them makes a grand gesture, and they tell each other they are in love. Then they kiss and live happily ever after.'

'Dreamy,' Stevie agreed. 'What's the gesture?'

'I need to think about that. They're in Cornwall so something romantic at sunset? On the beach?'

'Something to do with films?' Theo suggested.

I turned to him, my eyes lighting up. 'That's a great idea. That will speak to Aiden.'

'What about a film you've seen together?' Dan suggested. 'Or something that means something to you both?'

I thought for a moment. 'Oh, I know! An enemies-to-lovers film. It's perfect – *You've Got Mail*.'

'Never seen it,' Theo said.

'It's a classic!' Stevie told him.

'Aiden admitted it was one of his comfort films and we both mocked him for it,' Dan said, nodding at me. 'So, he made us watch it together at Christmas at our house. And we both loved it too.'

My phone beeped then with a voice note.

I disappeared into the bedroom to listen to it, my heart racing.

When I heard Aiden's voice, I felt relief. He was still speaking to me.

'I was drunk but now I remember that phone call,' Aiden said softly. 'I loved it when you enjoyed something I suggested, even though I could see it pained you to tell me.' He chuckled. 'Remember one Christmas, I was cold and grabbed a hoodie? I assumed it was Dan's because it had a dagger on the front. But when you saw me in it, you informed me it was merch from Felicity

Fowler's latest book, *Stabbed By Love* or something. You were so annoyed. I, of course, kept it on and took it home with me.'

Aiden paused then continued. 'It backfired though. It was so soft and warm, I wore it all the time and I didn't want to wash it because it smelled of your perfume. I still have it now.'

I smiled when his voice note finished. I did remember that hoodie. I was so pissed that he'd taken it. I picked up the phone and recorded another message.

'That's pretty sentimental of you,' I said. 'I'm starting to realise you pay more attention to my clothes than I ever thought.'

'If you're trying to make me think about your nightdress, that's a low blow, Olivia,' Aiden fired back straight away.

I laughed and sent him another message instantly. 'What about you? You love showing off those goddamn muscles. Remember the time you persuaded Dan to come to the gym with you over a Christmas break? Both of you challenged me to keep up with your workout so, of course, I had to save face and come along. But I fell off the treadmill. Face planted right on the floor.' I laughed at the image of myself that day. 'I was so embarrassed as you helped me up. I blamed my laces being untied. It was a complete lie. I'd been watching you lifting weights in the mirror and that's why I slid off it. You had distracted me. I told myself it was because you were being all vain with your muscles, acting like a peacock, but those muscles were delicious. They still are.'

When I re-joined the others, Stevie was talking about how much she wanted the publishing job. 'I feel like my whole book-worm life has been leading up to this and I'm scared stiff.'

'They'd be mad not to want you,' I told her.

'It's scary to try something new, isn't it? But you're right, this is what I've always wanted. I'm not sure why I've waited so long.'

'I know what you mean,' Dan said softly, looking at Theo who was pouring us all some more wine.

After we'd finished lunch, Dan and Theo went to the pub and Stevie headed home so I settled down to write more of my book. I wrote until the light started to dim and then Aiden responded to my voice note. It was crazy how my heart lifted when the notification appeared.

Aiden laughed softly at the start. 'I am sorry for distracting you in the gym. But let me tell you, it was worse for me. You wore that yoga outfit you have, it's tight and it's pink, and it's imprinted in my brain. Let alone when you're actually doing yoga like the other day in the flat. It's very hard to keep your thoughts pure when the most gorgeous woman in your life is wearing next to nothing and doing sexy poses. Are they taking the piss with Downward Dog or what?'

I snorted and then recorded him another message. 'You have a filthy mind. You are banned from watching me do yoga forever. But I do like it when I distract you, I can't deny it. At least I'm only distracting in the daytime. *You* sneak into my dreams. There's a reason I like that white shirt of yours and I get embarrassed anytime you mention Mr Darcy. I had a dream about that lake scene but instead of Colin Firth, it was you coming out of the lake. And let's just say, Jane Austen would turn in her grave over what happened next!'

He answered a few minutes later.

'I get why you're so obsessed with that scene now. When you left the film festival and I followed you outside and it started raining... I thought I'd never seen anyone look more perfect and how I didn't kiss you that day, I have no idea. I was jealous as hell you came to that with Jasper. I told you I knew you didn't like him but that was just wishful thinking. I was scared you would like him. So I acted like a twat. It's haunted me ever since. Trying to come between you. That argument. Your face in the rain. Your blouse wet through. I should have kissed you.'

I recorded a reply straight away.

'When I walked in and saw you'd chosen my film theme, I couldn't help but hope you'd picked it because I'd chosen it. And you were so annoying with me and Jasper but what annoyed me the most was that I was preferring arguing with you to talking to him. And I think I got so angry because I didn't want to be there with Jasper. And outside in the rain... I wanted you to kiss me that day. I didn't want to admit it to myself but I wanted you to.

'Aiden, when you finally did kiss me, it was the best kiss I've ever had.

'And if we're talking about jealousy, when I saw Zara phoning you, when you went out with her and when I saw her outside your office, I was so jealous I could barely see straight. I was so scared you'd go back to her. That you wanted her, and not me. I still am.'

My confession poured out. I felt like I could be so much more honest with him like this. Not face to face but speaking our thoughts through our phones. I wanted to be with him but I wanted to tell him everything first. If we only got one second chance, it had to be just right. I hoped if I admitted how jealous Zara made me, he might understand how much I wanted to be with him. That I was worried I couldn't compete with what they had had together.

Miscommunication had been our raison d'être. But it was time to change that.

As I got ready for bed, Aiden replied to my message.

'I'm sorry you thought that,' Aiden said softly into the phone. 'And I'm sorry about the way things were left with us, for walking out like I did. I love talking to you. I always have, always will. Even if all you want to do is tell me off. I...' He thought for a moment. 'I don't know what else to say right now but I wish you were here.'

I replayed his message five times as I climbed into bed. I missed him so badly, I didn't think I'd ever be able to sleep. As I started to get drowsy finally, I recorded one more message for him.

'I wish you were here too.'

40

I had two days off from the library and I spent every minute in a writing fever. I didn't even bother to shower or get dressed, I just wrote like a fiend, desperate to finish my book.

'Honey, I'm home,' Dan said late on Tuesday evening. He came and sat beside me on the sofa, propping his cast up on the coffee table. 'This thing is driving me mad. So, how's the grand gesture coming?'

'I think it might be ready,' I said, rubbing my eyes, which were sore after staring at the laptop screen all day. 'Do you think he'll read it if I ask him to?'

'I think he'd always do whatever you asked him to.'

I turned to him and smiled. 'And what about you? Have you thought about the proposal?'

'I have. I thought I could do it where we had our first date. We went out for a meal but then we went for a walk and we watched the sunset on the South Bank. Plus, Theo painted it and that gallery who are interested in his work are looking at that piece. They might show it. He's really excited. It would be perfect. And I want everyone we love to be there with us. Theo proposed when we were on our own but I think he'd love everyone to see it.'

'It sounds perfect to me,' I said. 'When were you thinking?'

'I'm waiting for him to have the meeting at the gallery because if they say yes, I can suggest a celebration night out, right?'

'That would be perfect,' I agreed.

'I'll get everyone on a group chat about it,' Dan said, pulling out his phone.

I curled up on the sofa as Dan typed out a message, smiling to see him so happy. He was inspiring me. If he could do it, finally make the commitment, then maybe I could too. Maybe Aiden and I didn't have to let the past hold us back any more. Maybe it was possible to have a real life happy ever after.

I thought about how long I had dreamed of a romance in my life like the ones in books and movies. I had focused so much on the fantasy of it all, I'd missed what was happening right in front of me. Aiden was the love interest of my dreams – he always had been – but now, finally, the timing was right. We were both here in London, single and ready for a relationship. I was still scared it might not work out and I'd lose Aiden from my life, but deep down, I didn't think I ever would. We'd been through too much and we had this bond that we had both tried to ignore, but it was special. I thought about how it had felt when he'd kissed me and touched me, and how he'd brought out this side of me I didn't know existed. I'd had sex in a library, for God's sake! I had never had sex outside of a bedroom with the lights off before.

But aside from the very delicious physical side of being with Aiden, I knew he could make me happy because he always had done. Even when we were arguing, I'd never had more fun with someone. And when Dan had his accident, I knew everything would be okay because I'd had Aiden there with me. Surely we could get through anything if we had each other.

'Do you want me to talk to Aiden?' Dan said, clearly noticing I was lost in my thoughts.

'I never want to cause any issues with your friendship.'

I knew whatever happened with me and Aiden, I'd never forgive myself if it hurt what he had with my brother.

'I know,' Dan said, then held up his phone to me. 'Look, Aiden's asked to have lunch with me tomorrow.'

'Oh,' I said, my heart rate instantly picking up.

'I'm guessing he wants to talk to me about you guys. Do you want me to say anything about you?'

'I finished the book,' I said. 'I'll give it to him at work. Then you don't need to say anything.'

'Okay. But I can tell him he'll be losing out on something amazing if he walks away from you, right?'

I smiled. 'Yes, you can. I feel the same way about him though.'

'Aiden is great. And so are you. You both just need to take that leap. And I know I can't really push you together. It's like me and Theo – it only works if you both have your feet in.' Dan frowned. 'Did that make any sense?'

'Somehow it did. Now, I think I need a shower.'

'I didn't like to say...'

I picked up a cushion and threw it in his direction.

After a long shower, I pulled on a cosy dressing gown and combed through my damp hair. Then I put my book on a USB stick.

I had titled it *First Impressions* – it was reportedly the original title for *Pride and Prejudice*, which I knew I'd told Aiden when I'd waxed lyrical about my love for the book that time. And the title worked for my characters and for us.

I loved giving my characters a happy ending.

Lily admits she has been scared Adam regrets sleeping with her and Adam is gutted that she thought he would think for one second it was a mistake. Lily had changed everything for him that summer, so he decides he needs to show her what she means to him with a grand gesture.

Adam remembers when they talked about her favourite movie of all time and he knows just what to do. He invites Lily to meet him on the beach. The day is slowly drawing to a close and the beach has quietened down from the day. She spots him and walks over.

'Hello,' Adam says, his eyes lighting up when he sees her. He has placed two deckchairs on the sand with a projector on a table. Ahead is a screen on wheels. It's huge. She stares at it, eyes wide.

'What is this?'

'I hired it for us,' Adam says as the sun sets behind the screen. 'I need you to know how much you mean to me. I never want to forget this summer. I want to be with you for all the summers to come if you'll have me.'

Lily watches the sun dip towards the horizon, the sky turning beautiful colours, and at Adam's hopeful face.

'What film are we watching?' she asks, smiling as she makes him wait for her answer.

Adam smirks. He knows what she's doing. 'Your favourite – You've Got Mail. *You said it's about two enemies who become lovers, right?'*

Lily breaks into a smile. 'Just like us. Come here.' She pulls him to her and they share their sweetest kiss yet.

'You are who I've been waiting for, you know that, right?'

'It was worth the wait,' Lily declares as the film starts up behind them, and the stars in the sky above them start to shine.

I really hoped this would show Aiden that this book was about our love story. He wasn't research or an experiment or a test; he was my love interest and always had been. I knew he'd appreciate the film references, and I really hoped we would get our own happy ending scene.

All I needed now was to work up the courage to actually give the book to him.

* * *

Over breakfast the following morning, Dan told me he wanted to come with me when I gave my book to Aiden, but what with his leg and the fact that I was a grown woman (if we ignored all the evidence to the contrary!), I told him to stay at home and he grudgingly agreed that it was for the best. Then I spent ages trying to pick an outfit. What was the right outfit for an 'I'm sorry, please forgive me, I really want to be with you' conversation?

'We need the big guns,' I said as I flicked through my wardrobe with a critical eye. I cast my mind back, trying to think of a time when I'd noticed Aiden double take on an outfit. I paused at my pencil skirt. He did always seem to notice my curves when I was in his. I slipped it on with a pair of heels then added a fitted jumper which did wonders for my boobs, and a blazer. Then I added the clear glasses he'd laughed at me for wearing when he'd first come into the library. I pinned my hair up half and half and added hoop earrings. Then I finished off the outfit with red lipstick of course and spritzed the perfume I'd been wearing when we'd slept together for the first time, because scent memory was not something to be sniffed at (pun intended!).

I knew deep down it didn't matter what I wore, that it was more important that Aiden read my book and realised that I did believe his was real, that my feelings for him were real, but I hoped this would give me a boost in confidence and if it reminded him that he was attracted to me, so much the better.

'You've got this,' Dan said encouragingly. 'Are you sure I can't give him a clip round the ear when we meet for lunch?'

'Because violence is the answer?' I smiled. 'I told you, this can't come between you two. I'll give him my book and then it's up to him whether he gives me a second chance.'

I pulled at my top. I was nervous as hell.

Dan could see it. 'If he doesn't then he's not worth your heart. love him but I stand by that.' He gave me a big hug. 'Remember yo said we deserve our happy endings?'

I nodded. 'We do. And yours is coming. Plus, Stevie jus messaged and she's landed an interview for the job she applied fo They need someone quickly so are interviewing this week and nex and have squeezed her in for Friday as the agent put in a goo word.'

'That's great news!'

'I'm so excited for her. I'm also hoping it means there is goo energy all around.' I crossed my fingers. 'Okay, I can't delay an longer.' I picked up my handbag and checked the USB stick wa still safely inside. 'I am confident. I am worthy of love. I am—'

'What are you doing?' Dan butted in, amused.

'Remember Mum told us to do affirmations? It helps you fake i until you make it. Gives you positive energy. I'm trying to manifest good outcome.'

'I think you're meant to do it alone in front of the mirror,' h said. 'Is that why you often talk to yourself?'

'Maybe.' I grinned. It was a habit from growing up with m mother. Saying things out loud helped me make sense of them.

'Get out of here, loser,' Dan said, laughing.

I stuck a finger up at him, ruining my grown-up woman vib then strode out of the flat with a hair toss – I needed to channe sassy energy today.

As I walked to the university, I noticed the trees were turnin even more beautiful colours now. I loved it when London becam shades of orange and gold and red, leaves crunching under foot an the evenings drawing in for cosy nights at home. I hoped Aide might be around to enjoy those cosy nights with me.

As the university appeared in my eyeline, nerves settled into m body. My outfit wasn't giving me much confidence now the momen to actually speak to Aiden was here. I had never made any kind of romantic gesture in my life. I'd never found anyone that I wanted to make one for.

Now, I finally had.

I went through the gate towards the car park, a soft breeze blowing in my hair as I looked for his familiar Mini. Molly was parked under a tree and my heart lurched as I saw I'd timed it perfectly: Aiden was just getting out of the car.

I hurried over and waited for him to climb out.

'Hi,' I said.

It felt like it had been much longer ago than Friday that I'd seen him last. I'd got used to having him around every day and I didn't like not seeing his smirk over breakfast any more. He had a line of stubble on his chin and I could see, like me, he hadn't slept well. But he was wearing my favourite white shirt tucked into grey trousers and a black jacket slung over it. His hair was tousled from the breezy day and when his green eyes focused on me, a smile appeared on his face which made me feel slightly braver.

'Where have you been staying?' I asked, feeling shy in front of him for the first time in ten years. I was so familiar with Aiden. I had looked into his face so many times but right now, I had no idea what he was thinking.

My heart sped up as he took in my outfit, his eyes roaming over me then resting on my face with an urgency, as if he wanted to memorise what he was seeing.

'At a hotel,' he said.

Immediately, I was annoyed. I wanted to stay in a hotel with him. To be in a big hotel bed with him. Crisp white sheets just like that damn shirt of his.

Aiden must have read something in my expression because he said, 'Yeah, it's a big bed for one.'

I shook my head to clear the thought of him in a hotel bed. Why was he always so distracting? 'Here.' I produced the USB stick from my bag. 'So, you know how in books and movies there's often a big grand romantic gesture at the end? This is me attempting one. For you. For us. I wrote the rest of my book. Please will you read it?'

Aiden took the USB and looked at me. 'A grand romantic gesture? Isn't it usually the guy that does that?'

His eyes twinkled with amusement and I hoped that meant all was not lost.

'That's very old-fashioned of you,' I replied. 'It should be done by the person who has fucked up or won't commit or hasn't said how they really feel... This time, it was me.'

'Olivia...'

'No. I missed it. All the signs. All the times you tried to show me, tell me, how you felt and what you wanted... I missed it because I was too scared of you telling me it had all been a mistake. You think that I don't believe this is real. But I'm terrified because I think that maybe it could be real. And I've never had that before.'

'Nor have I,' he said softly. He stepped closer and I breathed in his aftershave. I hadn't realised how much that scent reminded me of home. How Aiden reminded me of home. That Aiden *was* home to me. 'I'll read it. I'd read anything you wanted me to. I read *Pride and Prejudice*, didn't I?'

'And you're wearing your Mr Darcy shirt,' I said, smiling up at him.

'Hmm.' Aiden leaned in close to my ear. 'And you're wearing an inappropriate outfit for work as usual.'

He stepped back as I chuckled. This was us. And I desperately wanted it to continue like this.

'I'm a slow reader,' he warned me as he pocketed the USB stick and locked his car. 'I'm also late for my first lecture, not a good look for the head of department.'

I nodded. I understood, even if I really didn't want him to go.

Even though I ached for him to kiss me. To touch me. To hold me. And basically, never let me go.

We looked at one another and I nodded again.

'Sure. Of course. Have a good day.'

With a wave, Aiden strode off and I watched him go, exhaling with relief. So, it had gone as well as it could. He said he'd read it. He'd even noticed the tightness of my skirt. All I could do now was wait for him to hopefully realise that if he did have feelings for me, they were very much reciprocated. And then maybe we could try again. If not, I would have to accept it and try to find a way to forget him.

But if the past ten years were anything to go by, that was likely to be impossible.

41

On Friday night, I met Stevie in a bar and slid into the booth by the window she was occupying. It was a dimly lit place but I was relieved to see she was smiling.

'So, how did it go?' I asked in lieu of a greeting. She'd had her interview at the publisher's today so we'd planned a debrief over a glass of wine. 'You look fabulous by the way.'

We'd picked out her outfit last night over FaceTime but in the flesh, she looked even better in her blue suit that made her eyes an even brighter blue and suited her blonde hair.

She grinned. 'Why thank you. Coming from you, that's a compliment. I've never been into fashion as much as since we met.' She slipped off her jacket as I tapped the table impatiently. 'I think it went well. The interview was with the woman who would be my manager and she was lovely. We chatted about books and we had really similar tastes and she seemed to think my experience in the library would be perfect. She said she used to work in a bookshop herself.'

A waiter came over and we ordered a bottle of wine to share.

'Ooh, that sounds promising,' I said. 'People love to hire people who remind them of themselves.' I clapped my hands together.

'That's... true actually,' Stevie said, clearly thinking about what 'd said. 'She did give off a mentor vibe, which would be amazing. She has more interviews next week but said she'd tell me her decision by next Friday so that's going to be a very long and stressful wait.'

'I'm keeping everything crossed,' I said. 'I can see you working here, although I will miss you in the library so much.'

'You won't be there much longer anyway. You'll be a bestselling author before you know it and will forget all about me.'

'Never.'

'Pinkie swear?'

We reached over the table to twist our little fingers together. Then our wine arrived.

I lifted my glass. 'To you getting the job.'

Stevie smiled. 'Thank you. To us both getting what we deserve.' We clinked to that toast. We both took a sip. The wine was lovely and cold.

'And I'll be waiting right along with you for my answer from Aiden,' I said. I was desperate to know if he'd started reading my book or not.

'Well, he's a fool if he lets you go.'

'Aw, well, thank you. I don't know though. Ten years of pretending to hate someone is a very long time. Maybe we pretended too well.'

'I saw the way you two looked at one another; that was definitely not hate. I've never lusted after someone that much. Well, not for a very long time.' She sighed wistfully. 'Am I being selfish in hoping you get your happy ending so I will have hope I'll get one too?'

'There's more than one happy ending in life. You're going after your dream job; not many people actually do that.'

Stevie nodded. 'You're right. I'm really excited. How's Dan dealing with the idea of you two? He doesn't want to kill Aiden does he?'

'That probably would have been the case if we'd kissed when we were teenagers but I think now, especially with everything that happened with his accident and realising he wants to commit to Theo, he just wants us to be happy. Life's too short not to be with the person you want. I'm not sure how he'd feel about Aiden staying over in my room though.' I grinned but then my face fell. 'That's if he ever wants to again.'

'He hasn't had the book long; give him time to read and process. Also, do I get to read the ending? Pretty please?'

I smiled. Stevie always managed to cheer me up. 'Yes, you can read it. I'll email it over to you. And this time, I'll make sure I send it to you.'

'Too soon to laugh about that?'

I tried to look stern but we both giggled.

'Maybe one day I'll work on a publicity plan for one of your novels,' Stevie said.

'Can you imagine?'

We let that fantasy sink in for a moment.

I lifted my glass again. 'To going after your dreams.'

'Amen to that,' Stevie said, clinking her glass against mine again. 'Are we going to need a second bottle? Just to deal with the stress?'

I laughed as she waved to the waiter.

*　*　*

On Monday, Theo arrived in a whirlwind of excitement. 'They said yes!' Theo said as he walked in to the flat.

I had scrambled at the knock on the door to hide the ring Dan and I had picked out earlier for him. I hurried back into the kitchen. 'What's going on?' I asked, panting a little bit from running into my room.

'I met with the gallery,' Theo said excitedly. 'They are going to show two of my London pieces in their exhibition next month.'

'Oh, thank God,' Dan said, looking over Theo's shoulder at me; that meant our idea for drinks and the surprise proposal could now happen as we'd hoped. 'I mean, yay! That is amazing, I am so proud of you!' He pulled Theo into a hug and gave me a thumbs up behind his back.

'That's so exciting,' I agreed. 'I knew they would say yes. I love those paintings so much.'

'Thank you,' Theo said, smiling from ear to ear. 'I've been grafting for so long, I didn't think I'd actually ever get into an exhibition. Ooh, I need to ring my parents!'

'We have to celebrate,' I said as he reached for his phone. 'Let's do something on Friday.'

Dan had made us practise this conversation over and over again beforehand, as if it was one of his TikTok skits.

'Ooh, I have the best idea,' Dan said before Theo could get a word in. 'Let's go to the spot where you painted them. We could have drinks by the bench to toast to the success of the pictures.'

'Ooh, I love it,' I said, so hysterically Dan gave me a 'calm down' gesture with his hand. 'What do you think, Theo?' I asked, ignoring him.

Theo smiled. 'That sounds fun. As long as it doesn't rain, then we'll have to go the pub. Shall we ask Aiden, Liv? Or keep it to us three?'

Theo had no idea Dan had all their friends plus my mum and Theo's parents and brother on standby. 'Of course invite Aiden,' I said, knowing Dan would need Aiden at the proposal. Theo went to the loo and Dan jumped straight on his phone to tell everyone in his group chat that the proposal was on for Friday.

The sound of Aiden's name had made me nervous. I hadn't seen him since I'd given him the book. I'd looked around for him each day I worked at the university but I had the distinct sense he was avoiding me. I had no idea if Aiden had read my book yet or not, and the suspense was pretty much killing me now.

I'd left him another voice note but he hadn't responded to it, which had sent me into a bit of a panic. I'd even broken my rule of not involving Dan by asking how his lunch with Aiden had gone. He'd seen through my casual question and reminded me that I'd told him to stay out of it, so staying out of it he was. I cursed my past self but had to accept this. Either way, I supposed I'd get to see Aiden on Friday even if the news was bad.

'Oh, Liv, can you please give me a hand tomorrow after work?' Dan asked then.

'Uh, sure?' I said, wondering if this was something to do with the proposal but Theo came back in, so I couldn't ask.

'I just need to film a video for a brand and with my leg, I'm not sure I can manage it alone. Are you okay to come straight home from uni please?'

'No problem,' I said. At least it would be another thing to help take my mind off Aiden.

Dan saw me biting my lip. 'Try not to stress.'

'It's just Aiden hasn't said anything since I gave him the USB stick on Wednesday. It's Monday. It's been five days! Has he read my book? If not, why not? If he has, what does he think? And why is he not getting in touch?'

'He's a fool if he doesn't leap into your arms,' Theo said firmly.

Dan nodded. 'Exactly. It will all work out and if it doesn't then it wasn't meant to be. That's what you'd tell me.'

'How annoying of me.' But I smiled. He was right.

My phone rang then and I leapt on it, my chest sagging when I saw it wasn't Aiden.

'It's Mum. I'd better take it, it's her second call today.'

I'd missed several calls from her over the past few days, not sure whether I should tell her about me and Aiden. Grimacing at Dan and Theo, I walked into the living room and answered. 'Oh, hi.'

'Oh, hi? You're avoiding your mother! And don't say you're not. Dan says you're a little bit down. What's wrong?'

I threw a glare over my shoulder but Dan pretended he couldn't see me.

'I'm fine,' I insisted.

'Do you need to do some meditation with me? Affirmations? We could FaceTime a yoga session?'

'All of the above?' I admitted.

'Or do you just need some advice?'

I walked into my bedroom and sank onto my bed. 'It's a man.' I sighed out the words.

'Naturally,' she replied. 'Is it Aiden?'

'Dan told you?' I asked, surprised.

'No. Just that you weren't having a great week. But I saw the two of you when I came down after Dan was hit by that reckless motorbike rider.' She spat out those words, clearly not feeling very Zen when it came to that person, which I thoroughly understood, then returned to her usual calm tone. 'The way he looked after you and the way you looked at him.'

'Oh. You never said.'

'You know that I love Aiden like he's my own son. I was never sure if your determined dislike of him was real or not. When I saw how you were now that he was living with you guys, I thought he must have grown on you.'

'You could say that. But I think I messed it all up.'

'I doubt that. He's liked you for a long time.'

I was sometimes thrown by my mother's intuition. I hoped one day I might be as wise. It was doubtful though.

'You knew he liked me too?'

'Every time you walk into the room, he smiles. I thought it was just a crush when you were both younger but he really thinks the world of you, Liv. Whatever happens between you two, you won't lose him.'

'I think the world of him too,' I said, feeling a whole lot better about things. I then lowered my voice to a whisper. 'First, helping Dan see he should propose to Theo, now helping me and Aiden. You matchmaker.'

'Sometimes my children need a helping hand.'

'What about you?' I asked. 'Do you need anything from us?'

'Just to be happy. That's all I ever want. Ooh, I must go, I'm having lunch at a new vegan restaurant. I'll see you Friday for the proposal. I'm getting a blow dry for it.'

I laughed. 'Treat yourself.'

I hung up and told myself I needed to be more like my mum.

42

'Why don't you go and find Aiden, or just go home,' Stevie said to me the following day when I looked at the library doors for the hundredth time. I had got to the university early and had hung around in the car park until I was late for work. There was no sign of Molly anywhere. I went to Aiden's office at lunchtime but it was locked. I messaged him to see if he was there but I had no reply. Now the afternoon had continued with silence from him and no glimpse of him in the building. Was he avoiding me? Off sick? I was driving myself mad with scenarios.

'I can't leave you,' I insisted, not bothering to pretend I wasn't looking for him.

'You're not much good to me like this,' Stevie pointed out.

'Anyway, I can't go and look for him. I promised Dan I'd come straight home tonight to help him film something for work.'

Stevie looked at the time. 'There's only an hour left of your shift; why don't you head home early? The sooner your video with Dan is done, the sooner you can track Aiden down. I really don't mind.'

'Are you trying to get rid of me?'

She smiled. 'Yes! Let Dan deal with you. Aiden has fried your brain.'

'I'm sorry. I just thought he would have said something about my book by now.'

'Speaking of, I finished it last night and I loved it. I really loved it. I think you could get a literary agent for it, Liv, I really do. It's such a lovely story. I was rooting for Adam and Lily the whole time.' She nudged me. 'And I'm rooting for you and Aiden, you know that right?'

'I do, thank you. I don't think Aiden would ever want me to do anything with the book and if he doesn't forgive me, I'll want to delete the whole thing for causing so much trouble anyway.'

'I hope you don't do that,' she said, shaking her head.

I watched as she then went to check her email, something she'd been doing nearly as often as I'd been staring at the door.

'Nothing yet?' I asked, knowing she was also on tenterhooks about her interview.

'No. I know she said I wouldn't hear until tomorrow. I was just hoping I suppose...'

'She has to finish the interviews,' I said. 'But it sounds like it went brilliantly. I really think you have a chance.'

Stevie looked at the time. 'Seriously, go now, Liv. I'll be fine to close up. And I'll see you at the proposal tomorrow, yeah?'

I gave her a hug. 'Thanks, Stevie. Did I tell you today how you're the best?'

'Nope, and you should tell me every day.' She beamed. 'You are too, Liv. Go on, and try not to worry, okay?' I grabbed my things and headed off to a cheerful wave from Stevie. I felt bad leaving early – definitely needed to make it up to her.

When I reached the flat, I let myself in and called out for Dan. I slipped my shoes off, hung up my jacket and wandered through to the living area but there was no sign of him.

'Are you in the bathroom?' I called out louder, hoping he hadn't got stuck with his crutches, but he didn't respond. 'Weird,' I muttered, pulling out my phone to ring him. He'd kept on reminding me to come straight home from work but he wasn't even here. I was confused.

Before I could ring him, something caught my attention in my peripheral vision.

There was a bright pink Post-it note stuck on the TV.

Curious, I walked closer and saw that it said in big Sharpie letters: *Press play.*

'Hmm.' I picked it up then looked around again. 'Dan?'

Nothing.

'Okay then,' I said to myself, wondering what my brother was up to. But I grabbed the remote, perched on the arm of the sofa and hit the play button.

BBC's *Pride and Prejudice* popped up on the screen. I straightened up. It was the start of the lake scene. I frowned, confused. Why was this on here? I hadn't watched it since I'd had that dream about Aiden.

I watched as Colin Firth playing Mr Darcy started stripping off, enjoying the moment as he leapt into the lake. Then suddenly the image cut from the outdoor lake to an indoor swimming pool. Startled, I watched as a figure in the pool swam to the edge and started to climb out.

He looked familiar.

I got up off the sofa to step closer to the TV, my eyes widening when I recognised Aiden.

'What the hell?' I murmured as Aiden got out of the water. He was wearing a white shirt and black trousers just like Colin Firth on the TV show, all soaking wet and clinging to him. He pushed back his equally wet hair as he looked into the camera, smouldering at it.

My mouth opened. This was exactly like my dream.

'Are you sure about this?' Aiden asked then, breaking his smoulder to look uncertainly at whoever was behind the camera.

'Oh, yes,' I answered, clapping my hands twice at the delicious image of Aiden on the screen. Then it all went black, with white graphics appearing in its place.

My attempt at a grand romantic gesture

I read the words and then the video finished.

I grabbed my phone and dialled Aiden's number. I could hear it ringing in the flat and my heart soared. He was here? He'd made this for me? I put my phone down and looked around hopefully. I walked towards my bedroom.

'Aiden?' I called out.

The bathroom door opened and he stepped out.

'Oh,' I said, smiling at the sight of him. Then I did a double take. Because he looked completely different to normal.

I took him in from head to toe. He was wearing a Regency-style black tail coat with cream trousers, a white shirt and neck scarf. On his feet were black riding boots.

And as I lifted my eyes, I saw he had a black top hat on, which he took off before bowing in greeting.

'Oh my God,' I said as I stared at Aiden's outfit, realisation sinking in. 'You're Mr Darcy.'

43

'At your service,' Aiden said, putting the hat back on. I wasn't sure whether to laugh or cry or pounce on him, and Aiden seemed to realise that. 'Olivia is lost for words. This is a first,' he said, chuckling.

'I'm dreaming, right?' I said, finally able to speak.

'I'm afraid not. I don't how I let Dan and Stevie talk me into this,' he said, grinning at my dazed expression. He moved to step forward.

'No. Stay there. Let me drink this in,' I said, holding a hand up.

He dutifully stopped while I gave him another appreciative head-to-toe once over.

'You're ogling me again,' he said finally.

'I'm not going to apologise. You're dressed as Mr Darcy!' I let out a laugh. 'How is this happening right now?'

'I'm trying to do a romantic gesture like you did,' he said with a sheepish look. 'Too much?'

'No, it's perfect. Wow,' I said. 'Okay, come here please.'

Aiden came out of the bathroom and we walked into my room. 'I came up with the idea of hijacking the lake scene and persuaded

Dan to help me film it. Then he told Stevie who said the theatre department had the perfect outfit for it. They, however, refused to let me wear this costume in the water so here I am now.' Aiden shook his head at himself. 'I look ridiculous, right?'

'No, you look like Mr Darcy. I can't believe it.' I grabbed my phone. 'One photo, please? So, I can never forget this.'

No one had ever done anything like this for me before and even though I knew it was half a joke, it really was a fantasy come to life. Aiden posed, the hat back on.

'This really is my dream come true,' I said, throwing my phone down and reaching up to take his hat off and put it on my head. 'It suits you.'

'Yeah?' Aiden gave me my special smirk and then reached out to brush my hair back from my face. 'Underneath the madness of this outfit, the truth is that I want to give you all the romance you deserve. I want to be the man of your dreams,' he said, his voice husky as he looked down at me. 'Just like Mr Darcy,' he added, his eyes twinkling.

'You're better because you're real,' I replied. I looked again at him dressed up. He was hot. There was no other word for it. The outfit fitted him perfectly and, tall and handsome, he wore it better than Colin Firth – and I never thought I would say that about anyone.

I met his eyes. I was ready to swoon. But I wanted to be sure we were finally on the same page.

'So, you're here, dressed as Mr Darcy, to what... woo me?'

Aiden grinned. 'I will woo you every day for the rest of your life if that will make you happy.'

I wanted to jump into his arms but I held back. 'You read my book?'

'I did and I loved it. I realised I was completely wrong. I'm sorry I thought you were only with me so you could write it.'

'It's my fault. I never told you how I felt.'

'It was my fault too. You were worried it wasn't real. I was too much of a coward. I should have told you how I felt before I even kissed you.'

I reached up and wrapped my arms around his neck, the top hat tumbling down to the floor.

'I'm falling in love with you,' I told him, all fear gone now he was back in my arms.

'It's always been you,' he replied, simply.

'Say again about the wooing thing.'

'I will woo you every day for the rest of your life if that will make you happy.'

'Yes, please,' I said, pressing myself against him. He picked me up and I hooked my legs around his waist. 'Can you kiss me now?'

'Always so demanding,' he replied. His hands pressed on my back, he brought his mouth down on mine. Heat rose up under my skin as soon as our lips met. Aiden murmured, as if he felt it too, and kissed me back frantically. My hands moved to his hair as his tongue caressed mine. I lost myself in his kiss, my heart soaring. He was here. He was really here. And kissing him felt as good as it had done before. Like his lips had been made for mine. And mine had been made for his.

I squirmed and, ignoring his protest, climbed off him and went over to my bed.

'Will you take your outfit off for me? Slowly,' I said, sitting on the edge of the bed and looking up at him.

'You are insatiable.'

I clapped a hand over my mouth. 'Too much? I can't help myself with you,' I said behind my hand.

'I'm not complaining that the woman of my dreams is demanding I take my clothes off,' he replied, grinning.

'It's the outfit,' I said. 'I need to really take it in. So I can remember this moment when I'm old and lonely.'

'Why won't you be with me when you're old?'

I stared at him. 'Saying things like that is only making me more lusty. Please will you take it off for me?'

'What do I get in return?' he asked, reaching for the jacket.

'I'll think about that,' I replied. 'Rip it off.'

'I'm not a piece of meat, Olivia,' he scolded, but his eyes were as dark and hungry as mine, and his smile was wide. 'But seriously, can't rip it, the university drama department will kill me.'

'Okay,' I said, thoroughly enjoying myself.

'I knew dressing like this was a mistake,' he said as he slipped off the jacket.

'You love it,' I replied, watching as he unbuttoned the shirt and shrugged it off, then stepped out of the boots. He stood there in the trousers, his chest bare. 'I'm a big fan,' I said.

'I think you should join in now,' Aiden said huskily, beckoning me with a finger.

'Okay,' I said, standing up. 'Mine is easier.'

I held my arms up and Aiden slipped off my knit dress in one go.

Aiden took in my new underwear set. I'd bought it with the set I'd shown him in the library. I hadn't had a chance to wear it with him and it had been making me sad so I'd put it on today. It was silky and black and gave me curves in all the right places. Now, I thanked the underwear gods because Aiden was looking at me like he'd never seen anything sexier.

'Is this death by silk? Because I'll happily accept my fate,' he said, drinking me in.

I laughed. 'Take your trousers off and I'll join you.'

He did as I asked and came over to finally touch me. He reached for my chin, gently tilting my face to meet his.

'I missed you,' he said, and he kissed me gently, like I was a piece of precious china that might break in his hands.

'I missed you too,' I said, pulling him back to me and kissing him harder. 'I think we've done enough talking.'

'I like talking to you,' he protested, slipping his hands around to my back, dipping his lips to my chest.

'I like talking to you too,' I said as he undid my bra. I sighed as he slipped my nipple into his mouth. I laid my hands onto his chest, enjoying the muscles I'd been without for a few days.

He lifted his head. 'I really missed you,' he said. Then he pulled me down onto the bed with him. Leaning over me, he smiled. 'Really missed you.'

He kissed me again then moved down. He kissed my chest, my breasts, my stomach, then he moved to my thighs, dropping soft kisses there. I gasped as his lips then moved towards the spot that craved him most.

I arched my back as his tongue found me. Heat shot through my body as he tasted me. I wanted Aiden to touch me everywhere and I wanted to touch him everywhere.

Sensing my need, Aiden slipped his hand between my legs.

He caressed me with both his mouth and his hand, and I let out a moan. I had never responded to anyone like this. Every nerve of my body was tingling.

'I really missed you too,' I gasped. 'Aiden, that feels so good.'

I only lasted a second longer.

My legs trembled as Aiden lifted off me. I looked at him in wonder, as pleasure rolled through my body like a wave. 'I want you naked too.'

Reaching for him, I pulled at his boxers, slipping them off, enjoying how hard this was making him. 'Does this feel good?' I asked as I wrapped my fingers around him.

He groaned as I stroked him. 'You can't even imagine.'

'Aiden, I need you inside me,' I begged him.

'You have no idea what you are doing to me,' he said, pulling away from me to reach for his wallet to pull out a condom. 'It's not like this with anyone else.'

I nodded as my legs writhed on the bed, desperate for him to come back to me.

'It isn't.'

Aiden knelt beside me and with hooded eyes watching me, he slid the condom on. Then he leaned back over me, settling in between my thighs. He kissed me and hooked one arm under my leg.

'You are perfect,' he said as he slid slowly into me.

I gasped as he lifted my leg a little higher and entered even deeper.

'Olivia,' Aiden moaned as he started moving inside me.

'Faster,' I begged as I clung to his back and he thrust into me again and again. 'Oh, God.'

'This is too good,' Aiden gasped.

He propped himself up higher and moved faster. My head fell back against the pillow.

'I love you,' he said then.

I lifted my head. I was sure I looked wild and I didn't care one little bit.

'Show me,' I urged him.

Aiden moved faster and, if it was even possible, deeper inside me. His body was as hot as mine, sweat slicking our skin as he thrust into me like we'd been apart for months, not just a week.

'Okay, I believe you,' I moaned as we moved together.

'Are you close? Because I am,' he said, his lips on my neck.

'I love you,' I cried as delicious pleasure rocked through me.

Aiden pulled me to him and kissed me, crying my name into my mouth as we came apart together.

'Fuck,' I said then. There was no other word for it, as my body throbbed beneath him.

Aiden let go of my leg and with one last kiss, rolled off me.

'You're right. Fuck,' he agreed.

We slumped against one another on the bed, both panting. My heart was pounding inside my chest. My leg ached but it was the best ache of my life. Bliss washed over me and I looked at Aiden's smile and knew he felt the same.

'My back hurts,' Aiden said once our breathing had calmed down a bit. 'It was completely worth it though.'

'We're going to pay for that tomorrow,' I agreed with a laugh.

I was pulled away from the moment by the sound of my phone vibrating on the bedside table. I glanced over at it and laughed. 'It's from Stevie asking me to rate seeing you dressed as Mr Darcy out of ten.'

'Tell her it was an eleven.'

I laughed. 'Why did we wait ten years to do this?'

'Right now, I have no idea.' He pulled me in for a long kiss. 'So, do you still hate me?' he asked, his lips curving into a smile.

I nodded. 'Oh, yes, it's definitely hate,' I replied with a laugh.

Aiden was looking at me like I was everything he could ever want. I wasn't sure I'd be able to stop smiling. He kissed me again and I felt like I was exactly where I was supposed to be.

I pulled back. 'I think you should put the top hat on for round two,' I suggested.

Aiden shook his head. 'I've unleashed a monster.' But he put the hat on and pulled me onto his lap, making me giggle.

44

As the night drew on, we stayed in bed. We ordered Deliveroo and sat up side by side to eat, watching the lights of London twinkling outside my window.

'I could get used to this,' I declared as I pushed my plate away. We'd built up an appetite but I was now stuffed.

'Eating in bed or us like this?' Aiden asked as he gathered the food up off the bed and moved it onto my desk out of the way.

'Both,' I replied.

'We can make it happen a lot,' Aiden promised as he climbed back into bed. He was in a T-shirt and pants now, the Mr Darcy uniform careful folded on the chair to return to the theatre department. He wrapped an arm around my shoulders and I snuggled into his chest. He felt warm and secure, like I'd always been meant to fit into the nook of his arm like this.

'So, how did you end up recreating the *Pride and Prejudice* lake scene?' I asked, tilting my face to look at his profile. He really was so handsome. I felt like if she could see us now, seventeen-year-old me wouldn't have been able to believe her luck.

Aiden smiled down at me, reaching out with the hand not round me to run his fingertips through my hair.

'I was just so amazed by your book. Telling our story like that. Giving us a happy ending. I knew I'd misunderstood your intentions behind writing it. To be honest, I knew it as soon as I walked out, but I suppose after ten years of never believing we'd get together, it was hard to trust this was real. I shouldn't have blamed you for not being sure. It was my fault.'

I shook my head. 'I was scared to tell you how I felt. After telling Dan he should commit to Theo, I failed to take my own advice.'

'We got there in the end,' he said, giving me a kiss. 'I had lunch with Dan and I told him I was head over heels for you. I told him I felt really bad I hadn't told him first before asking you out, but it happened really quickly and I suppose deep down, I didn't want to in case he told me to back the hell off.'

I smiled. 'I didn't want to tell him for that reason either.'

'He did admit he wouldn't have been quite as happy for us if we'd got together all those years ago. We're older and wiser now and he knows that our friendship is for keeps and that I'd never hurt you. Although he still warned me he'd kill me if I did.'

I grinned. 'Good. So will I.'

'I think I have to worry more about you hurting me,' he replied. 'You look so beautiful right now.' I smiled and he touched my lips. 'I love making you smile. I always have.'

'Me too.' I kissed him. 'I wrote a whole book about wanting to be with you, after all.'

'It's a beautiful book. You will definitely be published one day. You're so talented, Olivia.'

'Thank you. I'm not sure about your film making skills though.'

'Nor me. I told Dan to stick to making his own TikTok videos; he's not director material.' He laughed. 'Five times he made me get out of the swimming pool. I'll probably catch a cold.' He took my

hand in his. 'I am sorry I didn't tell you why I'd been talking t
Zara. I never wanted you to think I might get back together with
her.'

'I think it's sweet of you to be there for her.'

'Well, her dad was good to me. She knows about you though.
About us. I told her before I'd even told you.'

'What did she say?'

'She wasn't surprised at all. I don't think anyone is really. I told
my parents and they were like "of course".'

'I like that you've been talking about us,' I said, smiling.
reached up and touched his cheek. 'My mum said she knew you'd
liked me since we were teenagers. Funny how no one told us
though.'

'They are all going to be very smug.'

'Not as smug as us.'

'Not as smug as us,' he agreed.

'You were the last person I thought I'd fall for, but also it's so
obvious that you're the one I should be with. Does that make
sense?'

Aiden grinned. 'Only to me. Dearest, loveliest Olivia,' he said,
his delicious accent coupled with that line sending shivers down
my spine.

'God. Don't quote *Pride and Prejudice* at me. I will never get over
you otherwise,' I said, nudging his shoulder with my hand.

'You won't need to, because I don't plan on ever letting you go.'

'Good, because I don't plan on letting you go either.'

* * *

Reluctantly, we had to leave bed in the morning. Aiden had taken
the day off work so we were able to have a slow breakfast together.
Then Dan messaged to say he was on his way home and said, t

quote him, to make sure 'he didn't see anything he didn't want to see'.

'I think I'd better find my own flat now,' Aiden said next to me on the sofa. My legs were draped over his lap as I curled up with my coffee beside him. His arm rested on my legs easily as if we always sat like this together. I thought neither of us wanted to stop touching now we'd told each other how we felt. We had ten years to make up for, after all.

'You want to move out?' I pouted.

Aiden squeezed my legs. 'No, but I think I should. If we'd just met, we wouldn't be living together, would we?'

'No, but we spent a long time living together not being together,' I argued. 'We should make the most it now we are.'

'I think Dan would prefer me out of his spare room so he can use it for work again, and besides, I want to date you,' Aiden said. 'I don't want to screw this up. Again. And when I move in with you properly, I want it to be the two of us in our own place.'

I knew he was talking sense.

'What kind of place will we have?' I asked. Now that I didn't need to fantasise about us getting together, or Aiden being Mr Darcy (I had lived that and would never forget it!), I needed something else to daydream about.

'I think we will want to move slightly out of the city, have a garden, have all our friends over, but without a spare room so they have to go home again and we can be alone.'

I laughed. 'I think it sounds perfect. I hope I'm a writer in this fantasy, with my own space for a desk.'

'Of course,' Aiden said. 'And I need a cinema room.'

'We'd have to move far out of London to have space for that,' I said, shaking my head. I reached out and took his hand in mine. His skin warmed me more than the hot coffee. 'Am I allowed to do this later when we're around all the people we know?'

'You can do anything you like,' he replied with a happy smile. 'Although maybe keep it PG.'

I leaned over. 'I'm making no promises,' I whispered into his ear then kissed him just below it, enjoying the way his breath hitched.

'I'd better not wear a white shirt and you'd better wear trousers,' he said. 'Just in case.'

The front door behind us opened.

'Can you both put one another down please and help me because I'm freaking out!' Dan called out as he walked in.

45

The sun was setting over the South Bank. Behind us, the River Thames sparkled under the orange sky. It felt like we'd been here for hours. Dan was paranoid someone would claim this bench so we had basically been camped out on it, taking it in turns to bring supplies.

'He'll be here soon,' Dan said after checking the time. Theo was coming straight from the gallery where he was hanging his paintings. He was expecting just Dan, me and Aiden with a can of beer to toast his success. But there was a large group of us here now. Theo's parents and friends, our mum, Stevie, and Theo's painting teacher, who was still his mentor. Dan had put pots of flowers around the bench and draped fairy lights over it. We'd put up a makeshift table, laden with drinks and bowls of crisps. We weren't 100 per cent sure this was allowed in the middle of London but hoped any passing police officers would turn a blind eye as it was for a proposal. A few people were milling about wondering what we were doing here.

'Everything looks great,' I reassured him. 'The sun is setting and it's so romantic.'

He patted his pocket for the hundredth time to check the ring box was still there.

'I feel sick,' he admitted.

Aiden slung an arm over his shoulders. 'We're right here with you. It's going to be great.'

'I hope he says yes. What if he doesn't?' Dan hissed, looking around at our friends and family in sudden panic.

'He loves you, don't worry,' I said.

I turned as Stevie's phone rang. She made a 'back in a minute' gesture and walked over to the river to answer it.

I smoothed down my blue silky dress. I had ignored Aiden's suggestion and worn my new dress and paired it with boots to make it more casual. My hair was loose and I'd added a trilby hat to complete the look. I looked at Aiden who was bringing over cups of Prosecco to us. He was wearing trousers and a dark shirt, and after I'd told him I loved how he smelt, he'd put extra aftershave on.

He wrapped an arm around my waist.

'You look so lovely,' he murmured into my hair.

I turned to whisper in his ear. 'I'm wearing the underwear I wore in the library.'

His hands gripped me tighter. 'That's unfair. Now all I'll be thinking about is taking that dress off you.'

'I'll make sure we're the last ones to leave tonight,' I teased him.

'I'm used to you torturing me. I've endured ten years of it,' he replied. Then he spun me around to face him. 'And it's been the best ten years of my life. I love you, Olivia.'

I sucked in a breath as my heart swelled with happiness.

'I love you too,' I replied.

Aiden pulled me in for a long, lingering kiss. Every part of me reacted to his touch. I couldn't wait until we were alone again later.

Someone cleared their throat and we drew apart.

'I would say sorry for interrupting, but I'm not,' Stevie said,

ppearing between us. Her eyes were dancing. 'That was the
ublishing company. I got the job!'

'Stevie!' I cried, letting go of Aiden to grab her and pull her into
hug. We both started jumping up and down. 'You did it!'

'I can't believe it,' she said.

'I can. You were meant to do this!'

'I never would have had the guts to do it if you hadn't pushed
ne, Liv, so thank you.'

'You would have done but I'm glad you did it now,' I said, smil-
ng. 'You have your dream job!'

'Oh my God,' she said as it sunk in. Then she stepped back and
ave me a significant look. 'And now all we need is for you to get
ours, right?'

Aiden nodded. 'Exactly,' he said, smiling at me.

I looked at them both grinning at me and narrowed my eyes.

'Why are you both looking at me like that?' I asked suspi-
iously.

'We decided that there was no way that *First Impressions* should
tay hidden on your computer,' Aiden said, his eyes twinkling with
nischief. 'Stevie got into your email and we submitted the book to a
ew literary agents.'

Stevie held her hands up. 'Don't kill me but I knew you'd protest
o much and it's such a good book!'

'It wasn't a shock to find out that your password was "IheartMr-
)arcy",' Aiden added.

I stared at them both. 'Hang on, you've sent my book out to
gents?' I squeaked.

'Yes. Well, the first three chapters, and you've already had a
ouple asking to read the whole book,' Stevie said. She looked at
ne nervously. 'Are you mad at us?'

'Always,' I replied, but a grin spread across my face. 'I will be
hanging all my passwords, but thank you. And I can't believe an

agent might want to represent me. And you have a job in publishing. What a night.'

Stevie grinned. 'I know, right?' She held out her cup. 'I need more Prosecco to celebrate. I'll be back.' And with that, she dashed off.

'I'm sorry we did it without asking you,' Aiden said, turning to me. 'But I wasn't sure you'd agree to sending in our story.'

'You really would be happy for people to read it?'

'Now that we've got our own happy ever after, yes,' he replied. 'I want your dream to come true.'

Dan came back then. 'He's here, oh my God!'

'Don't be nervous,' I said as we all turned to see Theo walking along the South Bank. He waved and smiled but then his eyes widened when he saw how big this celebration was.

Dan hobbled forward on his crutches to greet him.

'I feel nervous now,' I admitted to Aiden.

'I'm not sure I'd be brave enough for a public proposal but I guess Theo *has* already asked him.'

'I agree. I'd rather it was done in private.' I took a sip of my drink as we locked eyes. 'Then I'd be ringing everyone I knew.'

Aiden grinned. 'Noted.'

We watched as Dan took Theo's hand and drew him up to the bench. We all formed a circle around them. The fairy lights twinkled around us as the sky turned indigo. I quickly pulled out my phone to record everything as Dan had requested.

Dan held Theo's hand and we all fell quiet. Theo looked very confused.

'So, I guess these drinks are a bit bigger than you were expecting,' Dan said.

'They are.' Theo looked around, taking everyone in. 'What's going on?'

Dan cleared his throat. 'I wanted everyone we love to be here tonight. First of all, to celebrate you and your paintings, and the fact you're going to be in the gallery!' We all clapped. Dan looked at us. 'I think you all know that we met when I became Theo's best customer and he felt obliged to take me out for dinner to say thank you.' We all laughed and Theo smiled adoringly at him. 'The rest, as they say, is history. I always knew he'd be a huge success.'

He took one of Theo's hands in his while he rested the other on a crutch.

'Theo, you are the kindest, most generous and loyal person I've ever met. You are the love of my life. My best friend, my partner and my family. You are the man I want to spend the rest of my life with.'

Dan took a breath. 'I wish I could get on one knee but...' He gestured to his leg. Theo looked confused but then Dan pulled out the ring from his pocket.

'Theo, you asked me to marry you and now I want to give you my answer. It's a yes. And I want to ask you the same question back. Will you marry me?'

He opened the ring box.

'Really?' Theo asked.

'I wasn't ready to say yes when you asked me but the last week or so has shown me that life is short; we should make every minute count as much as we can. And I want to spend my life with you. If you'll still have me?'

Theo reached into his pocket and pulled out the ring he had bought for Dan.

'Yes!'

They swapped rings, while we all erupted into cheers. I stopped filming and rushed over to hug them, which prompted hugs from everyone. We were all so excited for them.

'Did you get it all on video?' Dan asked.

'Yes. I'll send it over,' I said. 'Congratulations, you two.'

I beamed as Dan and Theo kissed again, their happiness radiating out from them to include us all in it.

After I'd congratulated them again, I moved back over to Aiden.

'That was so romantic,' I said. 'I could get used to all these grand gestures.'

Aiden chuckled. 'You're a hopeless romantic.'

'I'm hopelessly in love with you,' I replied.

'Good. Because I only ever want to make grand romantic gestures for you.' He reached out and tucked a strand of my hair behind my ear. 'I'm going to make you so happy.'

'You already have,' I replied, and I pulled him down for a kiss. Then I whispered into his ear. 'Maybe I'll dress up as someone you like as your reward.'

'Oh, I'm going to hold you to that. This is forever,' he whispered back, and I had a strong feeling he was right.

'Should I say "I told you so"?' my mum said then. She'd come over with drinks for the three of us. She was beaming. 'You look so cute together.'

I leaned into Aiden who wrapped an arm around me.

'I agree,' I said happily, taking my drink from her.

'It's all Olivia,' Aiden said, looking down at me fondly.

'Oh no, I think I'm going to cry again,' Mum said and began to pull out another tissue from her bag.

Someone switched on speakers at that point and the mood turned even more festive as we celebrated and danced with our family and friends in the middle of the city that had brought us all together.

EPILOGUE

I looked around the bookshop, hardly able to believe what was happening. It had been eighteen months since Dan and Theo had got engaged and here we all were at another gathering. One that I hadn't even dared to dream of. I walked over to the table that was stacked high with books. I picked one up and ran my fingertips over the cover. There was a man and woman on it, and I had to laugh at how much they resembled their real-life counterparts.

I opened up the first page and saw the dedication.

For my own love interest

'I really should be getting a share of the profits,' an Irish accent purred into my ear.

I turned around to smile at Aiden. He looked gorgeous tonight in his dark jeans and the infamous white shirt, and I still thought he was the most handsome man I'd ever met.

'I think you get enough rewards from me,' I purred back and gave him a quick kiss.

My publicist called me over then – it was time to do my reading. I took a breath and smoothed down my pleated skirt.

'Wish me luck.'

'Knock them dead, Olivia,' he said, giving my hand a reassuring squeeze.

I walked over to my where my publicist was and stepped up to the stand where a microphone and my book were ready at the section I'd be reading from.

I looked out at the room. I could see Dan and Theo, fresh from their honeymoon in Italy; Stevie, who was the happiest I'd ever seen her; my agent, my editor and the whole publishing team that had worked on my book; colleagues from the university where Aiden still worked and where I'd just left to write full-time, including Jasper with his pregnant girlfriend; and my mum, who was beaming with pride and holding hands with her new boyfriend, a yoga teacher. They were perfect together.

Smiling, I gestured to the book in front of me.

'I wrote *First Impressions* as I was falling in love myself, and all the feelings that my main character Lily experiences, I was going through with her.' My eyes met Aiden's. He winked at me. 'You have no idea when you meet someone what they will end up meaning to you. This book is about that journey and I'm so happy that people will get to read it and hopefully enjoy it. I never thought you actually got a happy ending in real life, that's why I loved reading romantic stories and watching romantic films, but you know what – it's good that we don't. Because life is not about the ending, it's about being happy as much as you can be while you're in the middle of it. I can't wait to share Lily and Adam's story with the world. Thank you for being the first people to hear it. And celebrating the release with me tonight. If there's someone special in your life, make sure you tell them you love them.'

I looked at all the people who I loved in turn. It had definitely been worth the journey to get to this point. I stopped at Aiden. My love interest.

'This is all your fault,' I said to him, making everyone laugh.

Then I started reading aloud from my debut novel.

ACKNOWLEDGEMENTS

A huge thank you to my agent Hannah Ferguson for believing in this book from the beginning and being the best cheerleader for my books. I can't quite get my head around the fact I signed with you ten years ago! Thank you for being in my corner always.

I'm so excited to have joined the Boldwood family and I want to thank the whole team for being so enthusiastic about this book, and for all your hard work. Special thanks to my editor Emily Yau for giving me such fabulous editorial input and advice, and for loving these characters as much as me. *The Love Interest* is the book it is today because of you!

Thank you so much to George Lester, Anna Bell and Kiley Dunbar who read a very early sample of this book and gave me great feedback – you're always so supportive! And a huge thank you to everyone at Hardman and Swainson who look after me and my books so well.

To everyone reading this – I am always bowled over by your wonderful support for my books, and I really hope you enjoy *The Love Interest*! Thank you for picking up copies of my books, shouting about them on social media, sending sweet messages to me and making this all possible. Love you guys! Xx

PLAYLIST FOR THE LOVE INTEREST

Fictional – Khloe Rose
Library Card – J. Maya
Love It When You Hate Me – Avril Lavigne feat. blackbear
Late Night Talking – Harry Styles
Written by a Woman – Mae Muller
John Hughes Movie – Maisie Peters
Daydreaming – Harry Styles
The Way I Loved You – Taylor Swift
We Can't Stop – Miley Cyrus
I Should've Kissed You – Lucas Davies
Nervous (In a Good Way) – Mae Muller
Dirty Thoughts – Chloe Adams
Dress – Taylor Swift
Lights On – H.E.R.
So Annoying – Mae Muller
Love Is Embarrassing – Olivia Rodrigo
Late Night Thoughts – shy martin
You Feel Like Home – Keeley Elise

Comfortable – H.E.R.
Kiss Me Like the World Is Ending – Avril Lavigne
My Brother's Best Friend – Hannah Trager

ABOUT THE AUTHOR

Victoria Walters is the author of both cosy crime and romantic novels, including the bestselling Glendale Hall series. She has been chosen for WHSmith Fresh Talent, shortlisted for two RNA novels and was picked as an Amazon Rising Star.

Sign up to Victoria Walter's mailing list for news, competitions and updates on future books.

Visit Victoria's website: www.victoria-writes.com

Follow Victoria on social media:

instagram.com/vickyjwalters

facebook.com/VictoriaWaltersAuthor

x.com/Vicky_Walters

bookbub.com/authors/victoria-walters

youtube.com/@vickyjwalters

 LOVE NOTES

LOVE IN EVERY CHAPTER

WHERE ALL YOUR ROMANCE
DREAMS COME TRUE!

THE HOME OF BESTSELLING
ROMANCE AND WOMEN'S
FICTION

 WARNING:
MAY CONTAIN SPICE

SIGN UP TO OUR
NEWSLETTER

https://bit.ly/Lovenotesnews

Boldwⲟⲟd

Boldwood Books is an award-winning fiction publishing company seeking out the best stories from around the world.

Find out more at www.boldwoodbooks.com

Join our reader community for brilliant books, competitions and offers!

Follow us
@BoldwoodBooks
@TheBoldBookClub

Sign up to our weekly deals newsletter

https://bit.ly/BoldwoodBNewsletter

Printed in Great Britain
by Amazon

41671185R00185